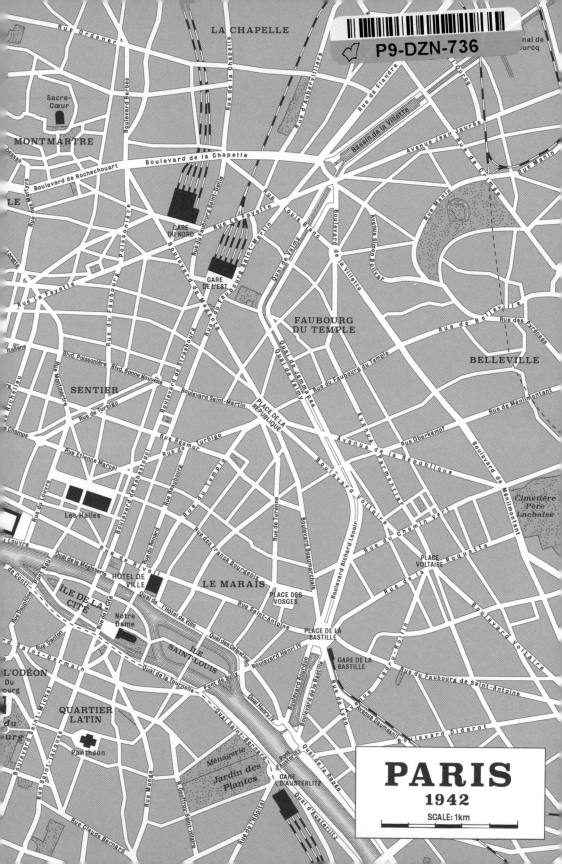

PARIS
1942

SCALE: 1km

Praise for *Three Hours in Paris*

A National Bestseller
A *Wall Street* Journal Best Mystery of the Year
A *Washington Post* Best Thriller and Mystery Book of the Year
A *Seattle Times* Best Crime Novel of the Year

"Breathtaking! I found it hard to breathe from the first page . . . This thriller takes Cara Black to a whole new level."
—Rhys Bowen, *New York Times* bestselling author of
***The Tuscan Child, In Farleigh Field* and the Royal Spyness series**

"Black keeps you guessing—and biting your nails—up to the very last page."
—Susan Elia MacNeal, author of
the *New York Times*–bestselling Maggie Hope series

"An unbreakable American heroine pitted against a charismatic German detective: pure gold in a wartime thriller. This hair-raising cat-and-mouse race across Nazi-occupied Paris left me breathless."
—Elizabeth Wein, award–winning author of *Code Name Verity*

"As the author of 19 murder mysteries set in Paris, Black knows the city's hidden squares and winding alleys. The wartime city and its grim undercurrent of fear are evocatively portrayed . . . *Three Hours in Paris* is reminiscent of Alan Furst at his best." **—*Financial Times***

"An evocative depiction of wartime Paris and a lead you can't help rooting for . . . If you're seeking old-fashioned escapism, this has it in spades."
—*The Times* (UK)

"[*Three Hours in Paris*] is both a stunning and brilliant work of imagination, and a tour de force of rigorous research . . . Fraught with tension and suspense." **—*Bonjour Paris***

"This stand-alone, with its resourceful, all-American heroine and breathless pace, allows [Black] to flex a different muscle, aided by her deep knowledge of and affinity for all things French . . . A superior thriller with much to offer fans of World War II spy fiction drawn to intriguing what-if scenarios." **—Air Mail**

"Brilliantly building on the novel's premise, Black constructs a surprise-filled plot, fueled by breathless pacing, Alan Furst-like atmosphere, and a textured look at Resistance fighters in Paris . . . Black stretches her wings here, soaring to new heights." **—*Booklist*, Starred Review**

NIGHT FLIGHT
TO PARIS

NIGHT FLIGHT TO PARIS

CARA BLACK

SOHO
CRIME

To those lost to history who lived this story.

Published in the United States by

Soho Press, Inc.
227 W 17th Street
New York, NY 10011

Names: Black, Cara, 1951- author.
Title: Night flight to Paris / Cara Black.
Description: New York : Soho Crime, [2023]
Identifiers: LCCN 2022039040

ISBN 978-1-64129-355-6
eISBN 978-1-64129-356-3

Subjects: LCGFT: Novels.
Classification: LCC PS3552.L297 N54 2023 | DDC 813/.54—dc23/eng/20220831
LC record available at https://lccn.loc.gov/2022039040

Interior map © Mike Hall
Interior design by Janine Agro, Soho Press, Inc.

Printed in the United States of America

10 9 8 7 6 5 4 3 2 1

*"You must be careful. Watch out for your princes here.
They are not all what they seem or real."*
—**Cecily Mackworth, Marquise de Chabannes La Palice, in conversation**

*"A spy should be like the devil;
no one can trust him, not even himself."*
—**Joseph Stalin**

*"In wartime, truth is so precious that she should always
be attended by a bodyguard of lies."*
—**Winston Churchill**

Part I

Scottish Highlands

⸺

Kate Rees slid into the Georgian mansion's salon and found herself staring into the shining eyes of a dead duck on a platter. An enormous oil painting.

Goosebumps crawled up her neck.

Kate's fingers roamed behind the painting's rococo gilt frame to find the rifle pieces taped to it. She slit the tape with the penknife she'd strapped to her ankle. Seconds later she'd assembled the rifle's shank and bolt head and attached the telescopic sight.

Adrenaline coursed through her. Her pulse thudded in her ears.

Outside the window, a curl of mist drifted in the dimness, blanketing the mansion's back garden. Night birds peeped and dewed grass gleamed in shafts of diffuse moonlight. She undid the window's latch and pushed. It wouldn't budge.

The sash was jammed. Painted shut.

Of all times.

Kate tried the second window, the third. All the same story. Her breath quickened. A sinking feeling bottomed out her chest.

Could this get any worse?

She had to get a window open. Somehow.

Bit by bit, the fourth window yielded to her knife. Paint flaked the sill. Grunting, she shoved aside the sash, lifting it the three inches she needed for a viable shot.

She poked the rifle tip out of the window and hoped the window's bubbled, distorted glass wouldn't throw off her aim. Aimed. Ticking off the variables—second nature to her—she factored in the evening breeze from the west and the clouded orb of the moon casting gray shafts of light.

Her eyes scanned the garden.

What if she got this wrong? Miscalculated?

Then her gaze caught and fastened on her target. She adjusted. Aligned the scope to reflect a half centimeter left. Prepared to double tap the target's temple.

Focused. Took a breath. Then another. Let everything in the world become this moment. Only this dark night, this dense black-green shrubbery, this hazy figure at the far end of the garden, barely visible against the copse of yews.

She inhaled. Squeezed the trigger on the exhale.

Thupt. A sharp crack.

She realigned and squeezed the trigger again. *Double tap to be sure*, Pa always said. And so she always did.

Now to escape.

By the time she'd skittered over the mansion's slippery roof tiles, torn her sleeve monkeying down the rust-flaked water pipe and legged it over the wet grass, her lungs were heaving.

She bent down. Turned the figure over. A dozen flashlight beams blinded her.

Wilkes clicked a stopwatch. "You're fifty seconds late, Madame X."

Absurd code name.

"Better luck next time," he added.

Better luck next time? She kicked the dummy, lifelike in a Gestapo uniform. Two head shots to the temple. It was perfection.

"Try not painting over the window sashes and I'd be here in a minute," Kate said.

"Field conditions vary; factors change," Wilkes said. "It can go pear shaped in seconds. Snipers need to adapt. Remember: any mission's a gamble."

He had that right.

Wilkes, a broad-chested former police sergeant from Shanghai and a specialist in bare-hand killing, held a clipboard and turned toward the huddled students. "You always face the unknown, as this exercise with Madame X illustrates. Learn to handle a worst-case scenario. The unexpected."

Three of them clustered around the dummy, with its painted leer and childish outlines of a Hitler mustache. The bullet holes in the temple leaked wood chips instead of blood. Kate heard a snigger.

"This lesson wasn't designed for Madame X to show off," Wilkes said. "You're seeing what can happen in the field, learning how to cope, manage, and think on your feet. Now, return to the classroom, dissect this operation and discover what else she could have done. Find the mistake she made."

Kate, the sniper instructor, hadn't made a mistake. But that was the point of the "lesson."

"Whoever gets it right goes next," Wilkes said.

The students had been up all night, as had she. An odd mix, these: a young woman with the peach and cream complexion typical of Brits, mournful and with bad English teeth; a wiry beanpole of a man with a deadened gaze and four fingers on his left hand; and the last, a freckled Irish potato farmer with a quick grin and an even quicker tongue. Raw, untrained, all of them. None would last a minute on a clandestine mission in occupied Europe.

But she'd been the same two years ago, hadn't she? Worse, even.

Tired, she headed to her lean-to cottage adjoining the caretaker's lodge. It was perfect for her with its lime-washed walls and gnarled beams supporting a part-sod roof. It reminded her of the house in *Little House on the Prairie*, her favorite book. Chopping wood for her fireplace made her feel at home. It was like the forest cabins on the trail her pa camped in.

The caretakers, a young Scottish couple, lived at the lodge and took care of the manor house: supplies, transportation, camouflage duty. You name it. Robert was a gamekeeper and general fixer at the manor. Alana, his wife, was a nurse who treated the injured and ill.

Kate came to the facility following a disastrous mission, the fiasco in Copenhagen. She'd broken two bones in her arm. After she'd been stuck in the hospital for several months, her twisted arm still hadn't healed and she couldn't teach. Was useless.

It took the surgeon's re-breaking her arm and convalescence in the cottage under Alana's expert care—aided by her wild herb poultices—for Kate to heal like new. Alana, a highland farmer's daughter, bubbled with a wicked sense of humor and could mimic Wilkes to a T. Kate found she and Alana had much in common. After Alana's third miscarriage, she and Robert had given up on having children. Kate felt it a shame that this decent, hardworking couple couldn't have a child when they seemed so well-suited to parenthood—although Kate knew better than most that "suited" didn't always equal "able."

BEFORE SHE COULD ENTER HER door, Wilkes had appeared. "A word, please?"

Not now. She didn't feel like a lecture or an analysis of the training exercise. "Can it wait?" she said.

"They said *now*." He handed her an envelope and a Webley pistol. Not her favorite piece—too clunky.

"What's this for?" she asked, taking it from his outstretched hand.

"You should never be unarmed. The car's waiting in front."

SHE GOT IN THE BACK of a military vehicle painted in brown and green camo. On the seat sat a man's wool overcoat and her worn, faded khaki regulation carryall. Surprised, she unbuckled the bag to find that all of her belongings had been packed. There wasn't much.

Inside was a baby photo of Lisbeth, Kate's gorgeous daughter, taken Christmas 1938.

Less than a year later, Lisbeth and Dafydd, Kate's husband, had gone up in smoke in the German attack on Orkney. All she had of them was this photo and a severed heart.

Not now, she told herself, biting back her tears.

The driver—a man dressed in fatigues—started the engine. The car swept down the gravel driveway and the highland mansion receded behind the trees. This training center for clandestine operatives—this spy school—faded in the heather and mist.

Kate felt a bittersweet pang. In between training and missions, she'd grown fond of the manor house—the frescoed ceiling, faded floral wallpaper, and the view of the foggy mountains, which never ceased to remind her of childhood in Oregon. Her rustic cottage and her friendship with Alana were the closest she'd come to planting roots since losing Lisbeth and Dafydd.

In a side pocket of her bag was her diary, which

she'd hidden behind the carved woodwork of her room. The Brits had gone through all her personal things. No privacy at all. A red-hot feeling of violation bubbled within her.

They'd kept a bead on her since the Denmark assignment, she knew. It seemed to be getting worse; her movements were relentlessly assessed.

She was a rifle/sniper instructor, goddammit. First and foremost. The rest wasn't their business.

"Where are you taking me?" Kate asked.

The driver turned around. "All I know's the address they told me. Nothing else."

Off to another training camp? Somewhere to be useful, to contribute? That's what counted. It was about getting back at the Germans who killed her husband and daughter. Her job was to take out the enemy.

Wasn't it?

She crossed her fingers.

"By the way, miss, these came for you at the last minute."

"It's missus," Kate said.

The driver ignored her. He handed her an envelope, turned back, and closed the smudged glass window between the driver and rear. Conversation over.

The first letter—censored—was dated three months earlier. Kate's heart jumped upon seeing the US stamp and Oregon postmark. Finally. A letter from home.

From Jed, her middle brother—she had five of them. Jed was the sassy one who swam like a fish and teased her day and night. She tore open the envelope.

Dear Kate,
I joined up—the air force. All of us did. I don't know where they're sending me. None of us do. Ranch got sold after Pa passed in July. We buried him next to Ma in

Medford. I'm sorry for the bad news. Before the fever took him, he asked me to write and say he never stopped missing you.

> *Your brother,*
> *Jed*

An aching opened deep inside of Kate. Like a punch in the gut. Pa had been their rock. He'd fed and clothed them as best as he could. They went hungry sometimes, sure, but he kept them together throughout the Depression, and they'd loved one another fiercely. Pa was the one who had believed in her. Who'd taught her how to shoot, to survive, to rely on herself. *Katie, when you fall down, the only one who gets you up is yourself.*

Her eyes welled. The trees and hedges blurred.

An overwhelming sense of aloneness knocked the breath out of Kate. Home was gone. Her brothers were dispersed. She was, ultimately, an orphan. She'd never had the chance to say a proper goodbye to Pa. Or to Lisbeth, or to the man she fell in love with one balmy Paris afternoon in '37. The war had taken them all away from her.

Her tears spilled on the letter, smearing the ink. Only then did she see Jed's scrawled PS in the corner:

I'm sorry I called you chicken when you were little. Should have said chick.

She grinned despite her grief. Wiped her nose. Good old Jed.

Where were her brothers now?

The car downshifted. She'd better open the other envelope Wilkes had given her.

Only one line:

Destination and mission upon arrival at London office.

Typical. It revealed nothing.

THE LONG TRAIN RIDE TO London, interrupted by military traffic and power outages, took the afternoon and night. They passed bombed-out cities and stopped for troops countless times. Passengers stood jammed in the corridors—all the seats were taken. Kate felt lucky to have the large wool overcoat and the floor space she'd found in the freight car, camping out by crated rabbits who nibbled in their cages all night.

A car waited at King's Cross station and dropped her at an anonymous London building, one more clandestine intelligence facility lodged in plain sight. She paced inside the drab office, irritated by innumerable cups of weak tea, the waiting and the incessant clacking of the receptionist's typewriter.

Back and forth Kate walked until a FANY, First Aid Nursing Yeomanry, came by and pinned up the latest War Office list of the wounded, dead and missing in action. Kate went to it immediately. She always read the War Office lists, feeling like she was watching a car accident. Couldn't stop herself, no matter the agony it evoked. Each of these men on the list was someone's son, brother, uncle, father, cousin, friend or husband. She skimmed through the list, her heart sinking at the black-and-white proof of loss, until her eyes snagged on a name.

Philippe Leroy.

On the Free French list of those injured in North Africa.

The air left her lungs.

Philippe.

Steady, girl, she told herself, reaching for the wall. *Injured isn't dead.*

Another voice said, *Yet.*

Kate sensed the air shift, the elements change.

"He'll see you now," the FANY called from the interior office.

"Say I'm delayed. My train's late." Kate grabbed her cap from the office bench.

"What do you mean?" the FANY said. "You can't disobey orders—"

But Kate was already slamming the door on her way out.

IN GUY'S HOSPITAL KATE SEARCHED for the airmen injured in North Africa. Philippe's Free French division, she discovered, was in the north wing.

Her anxiety mounted as she passed beds filled with hardly recognizable figures. Bloody bandages, enamel bed pans, stacks of dressings and laundered white sheets—the whole place was mayhem. The cries and moans ate at her.

Strong. She'd have to be strong for Philippe. No matter how badly injured he was, she'd have to insist that he would recover.

She'd plaster on a smile for her sometime-lover's sake. Steel herself for the worst.

She wished she'd changed from her training attire of oil-smudged overalls. Had time to run a comb through her hair, find some lipstick.

A nurse with a clipboard nodded. "He's over there in thirty-eight."

Curtains surrounded the bed. She tried to prepare herself. But how?

"Can you tell me his injuries?" she asked the nurse.

"Don't you know?"

She sighed. She wouldn't be asking if she knew. "I just got the message to come here."

"Patient suffered several fractures, exhibits severe dehydration. But he's stable."

Stable. *That's good. Think positive.*

The nurse pointed to a waiting room. "His family is here, so you'll need to wait."

Kate's shoulders tightened. "His family?"

The nurse responded icily. "Yes, miss, his wife and child are with him now."

When the nurse left, Kate skirted the beds and reached the curtains. Heard voices speaking French. A woman coughing.

Or was it crying?

She peered through the slit between the curtains. Philippe was sitting up, an intravenous drip in his arm, part of his chest smothered in a cast, bandages on his neck. His face, bronzed by the desert sun, looked thinner. She couldn't see his eyes because of the woman leaning over, kissing him and cradling his head. Beside her stood a little girl—four or perhaps five—with shiny blonde curls.

Kate caught herself before she cried out.

She stared at the small, lovely family, speechless. A petite Frenchwoman with a braid down her back and a little girl with tiny, fluttering hands. And here she'd thought her brief stolen weekends with Philippe meant . . .

What?

Face it, he'd made no promises. And neither had she.

Chalk it up to a wartime fling. *LALAL,* as her pal Edna called it: *Lasts As Long As Leave.* Affairs provided heat and connection with another human, until, like the blitzkrieg, they burned out. Turned to ash.

She and Philippe had been thrown together in Paris two years ago, she a recent widow who still loved her husband, Philippe a handsome flirt who'd saved her life. Then she'd saved his. Since then, they'd met up whenever she got leave from Scotland. It had never been serious, she reminded herself. Yet he could have told her that this other part of him existed. It would have made her think twice.

Never trust a Frenchman.

Then came the inevitable:

Why did he get to be the one whose family survived while hers had been killed?

She turned toward the exit, her gaze straight ahead.

BACK AT THE OFFICE, THE FANY put an envelope in her hand. "There's a car waiting for you."

"Now? But I thought the meeting would be here."

"Orders. The muckety mucks said hurry." She gave Kate a level look. "You owe me, Yank."

Kate pulled out a pack of Craven A cigarettes—disgusting, non-filtered things—and slid it across her desk. "You covered for me, right?"

"Delayed train," she said. Winked and took Kate's offering.

In the car, Kate was handed a Thermos, a paper bag with sandwiches and a folder marked ELB38.

"Where are we going?" she asked the driver, a non-com by the looks of his civilian clothes.

"You'll get instructions upon arrival. Otherwise, no conversation, miss. Orders."

It was missus, but she let it go. It was like her rose gold wedding band was invisible.

All hush-hush. Always. Her stomach twisted. The secrecy, the not knowing. She thought of the Copenhagen mission.

From the Thermos she poured out a stream of the steaming, caramel-colored mixture. Sipped. Semi-sweet and milky, but so strong it could bend nails. Tea was the English's answer to everything.

She glanced at the sandwiches. She had no appetite. First her pa. Now Philippe.

They drove past a warren of rubble-strewn streets in the bombed-out East End, through the rot of debris and charred wood permeating the streets. Curiously, a mailbox still stood intact, its cap painted with the yellowish-green gas-detecting paint. The odor of dry heat and the decay of decomposing bodies pervaded. She felt death in her bones.

There weren't even enough ambulances these days, yet here she was in a car with a driver. It felt wrong.

Feeling guilty, she slid down in her seat, trying not to look.

The car stopped to let fire wardens and old men with shovels pass. Gas masks, issued by the government to every-one, hanging from their belts. She knew they were here to clear the rubble and comb for bodies. A small boy sat on a pile of scorched bricks looking curiously content even with his sooty face and torn short pants. He held a woman's liz-ard handbag.

Kate eyed him. Was he waiting for his mother? She glanced side to side. There wasn't a woman to be seen.

"Hold on a minute." She took the bag of sandwiches and jumped out of the car. "Would you like a sandwich, young man? I've got so many extra."

He had puffy black eyes and sunken cheeks. A child-size gas mask hung from a loop on his belt. "I'm not supposed to take things from strangers."

"You're right, of course. But this is extra from the government. It's meant for people who've missed their breakfast."

"Really, miss?"

She nodded. "It's quite all right. See? The stamp means it's from—"

His eyes widened. "That's the royal symbol!"

Observant boy. His hair and body, caked with plaster dust, gave him the appearance of a little ghost. He looked no more than eight.

"I'm sure his majesty would want you to have it," Kate said.

"May I take one for me mum?"

"Of course." Kate peered around again. "Where is she?"

"She told me to wait here. She's coming back after she checks our flat."

His fingers tightened on the dusty lizard handbag. Fashionable. Or had been, once.

"How long have you been here?" she asked softly.

He thought. "Must be yesterday morning."

Her throat caught. How could passersby and rescue workers ignore him sitting here?

"Doesn't she need her purse?" Kate said.

"I'm to wait here. That's what me mum said."

The high-pitched horn bleeps startled her. Traffic had started to move; her driver called to her from the window. She had to do something. But what?

"What's your name and where did . . . *do* you live?"

"Billy Easton. Twenty Folgate Street in Spitalfields."

She committed it to memory.

"Billy, it's time you let a policeman take you to where you can find your mother. Okay?"

He just smiled. "Thank you, ma'am, but me mum will come back. But if the king wants me to eat his sandwiches I will."

She smiled at him, tousled his hair, then ran back into the waiting car. Her last image through the back window was of Billy Easton eating a sandwich, his mother's handbag on his little lap.

"DO YOU HAVE A RADIO transmitter in this car?"

"Why?" asked the driver.

"That boy needs help."

"Like so many, miss."

But if one child could be helped, she had to persist. "Can you contact the rescue crews and alert them? He's Billy Easton from twenty Folgate Street in Spitalfields."

"Afraid this car's not radio equipped," he said. "And we have to hurry."

She felt helpless at all the devastation, the orphaned children and utter senselessness of it all.

"But we need to help that boy."

"Someone will come along. It's war, miss."

Obviously this driver thought she was a bleeding heart. "He's been there two days waiting for his mother. Can't you make a call when you return to base? Please, could you do that?"

He hesitated. "Will do, miss."

HE SPED UNTIL THEY REACHED the outskirts of London. At a crossroads, a strange, medieval-looking shrine separated the routes.

"Is that what I think it is?" Kate said.

"Site of an old gallows. They always hung criminals at crossroads."

"Another one of your quaint English customs?" she tried, but he was already opening the back door.

"Oh, and before I forget," he said, and with lightning speed cuffed her wrists behind her back and slipped a bag over her head. "Sorry, miss, it's operational procedure. Another one of our customs."

Near Cockfosters

When Kate's blindfold was lifted and hands uncuffed, she was standing at a rose brick Georgian-style mansion, another manor house, no doubt requisitioned by Special Services. A soldier gestured to her from the wide oak door. He handed her slippers and a basket to put her shoes in, and put his finger to his lips.

Odd. But then a lot of what the Brits did struck her as peculiar, even after five years living among them.

She complied, clutching her carryall, and followed him down a narrow hallway smelling of walnut oil polish. They came to another long hallway. A door was unlocked, another hallway was walked, then another and another and another, as if they were descending into the bowels of the mansion.

Without a word, he led her into a high-ceilinged room, blue draperies kissing the floor. Kate took note of the blue upholstered chair and a Regency-style honey wood desk equipped with distinctly non-Regency headphones and a notebook.

Oh Lord, Kate thought. A test. And here she'd been up almost for twenty-four hours.

On the wall were several bookshelves full of cowboy Westerns. Kate spotted one book on Annie Oakley. A personal touch? This was someone's office. And not just anyone—a bigwig.

A buxom, dark-haired woman in a two-piece gray suit stood at a sideboard, a teapot in her broad hands.

"Milk and sugar, correct?" she said without smiling.

Kate nodded. "Who are you?"

"Call me Matron." She gestured for Kate to sit at the desk.

Kate sat and crossed her ankles, feeling like a schoolgirl. Her feet swam in the flannel slippers.

"Why am I here?"

"There's use for your special skills," Matron said. "You won't need that Webley anymore."

Kate pulled the clunky pistol from her pocket. Set it on the desk with a thump. "Look, I train agents in sniper skills. And I don't take exams."

Matron eyed her in that pompous British way. "You'll be listening to captured German POWs."

Kate set the cup down on the china saucer. Steaming tea sloshed over its delicate edges. "I'm from Oregon and my German is non-existent. Certainly you—or they—know that."

"Of course." Then, almost as a non-sequitur, "These are captured officers, high-level command. Elite."

Kate still didn't understand. But high-level intrigued her.

"Captured where?"

"Not pertinent."

Kate sipped the hot tea, wondering why in the hell she'd been chosen. The quick summons with no explanation had filled her with enough dread and uncertainty. German translators and linguists more skilled than her obviously existed. Something was off.

"Must be desperate to draft me," she said.

"Pay attention to this one," Matron said, placing a photograph in front of Kate. The picture revealed two men, one—the blond—in sharper focus, in front of a Bavarian castle. Handsome. The Alps shimmered in the background; a glass of champagne glinted in his hand.

Kate snorted. "A Kraut living the high life."

"That's Officer B. At the ancestral castle—in better days, mind you." She pointed at Kate. "Your job is to get accustomed to his cadence, his speech style, his voice. Write down what he says phonetically."

"What kind of test *is* this?"

"You've got thirty minutes. Press play." The door closed behind her.

The cumbersome headphones pressed tightly against her ears. Kate heard chairs scraping, two men talking, a woman's voice. "Lunch is served, gentlemen."

"*Das englische Essen ist für die Hunde,*" an older voice growled. *English food is for dogs*—that much Kate understood.

And figured exposing any German she'd learned to the Brits wasn't smart.

She heard the one referred to as B reply, and she wrote down what she caught amid the sounds of cutlery clinking and drinks being poured. Most of the conversation was sheer gibberish; what she could translate seemed desultory, entirely about food, and a waste of her time. She detected his slight lisp.

After thirty minutes, Matron reappeared and led Kate to a changing room, where she was given a cleaning smock.

"What's this for?" Kate asked.

"Cleaners are invisible," Matron said, shoving a pail into her hands.

"Listening to Nazis is bad enough. You think I'm going to clean up for them?"

Matron held her gaze. "You will if you want to save a life."

Kate's instructions were to mop up a spill on the dining room floor, and to take her time doing so. Then she was to return and list everything she'd noticed.

They were testing her—that much was clear. Right now all she wanted was to know why. This felt like a waste of time.

The smaller of the two elegant dining rooms, which were lit by wall sconces, held five linen-covered tables, a buffet filled with silver platters and lidded serving pans.

Fancy, like an exclusive London restaurant.

Only one table was occupied.

From the sidelines, she took in the man from the photo. Chiseled features, a sharp jaw and nose—he was even more attractive in person. This debonair Kraut held his cutlery in the European way; fork and knife working together on a piece of pinkish meat. His dining partner, a jowly, thick-haired man with an Adolph mustache, pointed to spilled red wine on the tiled floor without lifting his eyes to acknowledge her.

Invisible all right.

She got to mopping and swishing pine-scented suds, and bit her tongue so she didn't swear under her breath. Or kick their polished black boots. This whole fancy country manor was for captured Krauts?

Officer B's dining partner laughed at a comment Kate couldn't decipher. Mentally, she noted the room's warm temperature, the patterns of light from the window spreading in diagonals across the floor. She calculated her distance to the two men and how fast she could take a shot before disappearing out the dining room's doors.

The jowly one cast a glance at her and said something to Officer B. He chuckled.

She noticed a mole on Officer B's wrist.

Pompous POW pricks, she thought. From their tone and the few words she managed to understand, she knew they were mocking her and everything else around them—her figure, the food, the weather. She ached to send them to Berlin in a coffin.

Done, she left. She took off the smock as quickly as she could, changed into her jumpsuit, and joined Matron back in the blue room.

"State secrets?" Kate said. "As if I'd even understand them. What's this all about? Big surprise, too—they didn't seem very nice."

Matron showed Kate typewritten sheets of their dialogue.

That quick? Did little German elves work behind the walls?

"They called you a cow. Officer B said, 'Big-boned as a brood mare.'"

"Kind of you to share that," Kate said.

"Sorry, but that's who you'll be dealing with."

Kate's shoulders stiffened.

"How's that?"

"You'll find out," Matron said.

The door opened. In the threshold stood Stepney. Colonel Alfred Stepney, Great War flying ace and supposedly retired spymaster. Kate's former handler.

Who had recruited and trained Kate before using and betraying her.

Whom two years ago Kate had almost shot.

He'd aged. Probably she had, too.

Stepney's still-thick hair fanned in silver white waves and ran over his collar. She saw the slightest stoop in his stance before he straightened up, bracing himself on a malacca cane. A man always on his guard.

A man she'd trusted, once.

"He'll tell you." Matron rose and pulled the blue curtains

closed. "For the record, I disapprove of this plan," she said at the door. "But I'll leave you two to catch up."

Kate stared Stepney straight in the eye. "Didn't they throw you in the scrap heap, Stepney?"

Stepney, former head of the disbanded intelligence Section D, raised an eyebrow. He waited an excruciating beat before saying, "It's been a while, Mrs. Rees."

"Not long enough," Kate said. "Don't tell me they're resurrecting you, because you're well past your expiration date."

"Thank you for reminding me," he said, his mouth pursed. He lifted his malacca cane and pointed to the table. "Shall we get to the assignment?"

"What assignment? I don't work for Section D anymore. I train snipers."

"Your reports shine. Your skills grow more impressive all the time."

Surprised, she determined not to show it. Out in the training field no one had time for compliments.

"Flattery will get you nowhere, Stepney."

A smile curved his thin lips. "I'm also told you carry out the occasional assignment for Secret Services."

After the disaster in Copenhagen she'd vowed never again.

"Even if I did, you're the last person on Earth I'd work with."

He watched her with those curious eyes of his, a deep brown flecked with green. Those eyes that read inside her. He was always a step ahead.

"Of course, it's a problematic assignment, since you're one of the Reich's most wanted."

He had that right. The last time she'd been in Paris, her face was on posters all over the city.

Should have shot you when I had the chance.

"Better luck next time," he said and sat down.

Had she said that out loud?

Unperturbed, he hooked the cane behind his chair.

Now she saw clearer signs of aging—his body leaner, his spine crooked. But he was a tough old bird, with skin in the game.

"You and I, unfortunately, are the only ones able to prevent us from losing the war," he said in a quiet voice.

Did he think that would work? "Drama doesn't become you, Stepney."

"Plastic surgery's not an option since, as always, there's little time," he said dryly. "But hear me out, then you decide."

"If you think—"

"You'd disobey an order?" he interrupted.

"What order?" she said.

"Taking out a crucial target. Margo Pryce-Owen says you're the one for this mission."

The name stopped Kate. She'd trained with Margo, roomed with her when they'd first been recruited, before the Paris operation. But that felt like a lifetime ago.

"You, and only you."

Though trainees weren't supposed to communicate, Margo had woken Kate from her nightmares. Asked Kate why she screamed every night.

Ashamed, Kate had confided about losing her husband and child. Margo listened as no one else had. Pulled Kate out of despair.

Exhausted and lonely, Margo had revealed that her own fiancé had died at Dunkirk—and her shame: that she hadn't loved him.

Loss knitted them together. And in wartime everyone grabbed at friendships, especially with a woman who'd gone through what she had—almost.

Assignments and deployments made meeting up difficult, but there had been one memorable picnic at Oxford—strawberries and cream with champagne, though Kate had no idea how Margo had managed this treat. Margo abounded in secrets.

"Create an aura of mystery, Kate," she'd said. "It's half the fun. Femme fatale, a countess, a cleaning lady—I can do them all. People see magic while you obscure things in plain sight, move things around."

Margo's boyfriend, that rakish, I-can-charm-the-cows-out-of-the-dairy Gregory, had been the one who cleaned up the fallout in Copenhagen when Kate had botched her mission by trusting an informer. Gregory had kept his identity from her, though.

Which was why Kate had slept with him.

The rotten feeling came only later, when she'd discovered who he was. Margo had no idea.

Guilt swamped her. Kate swallowed. "Margo's in trouble?"

"She's in deep undercover. The operation's taken a turn for the worse."

Margo had saved Kate's life once. She'd thwarted a knife attack during a surveillance assignment. It was the first and last time they'd worked together in the field.

But no, Kate wasn't going back in the field after her Copenhagen disaster and broken arm.

Stepney's face remained expressionless. "Your skills will provide an effective outcome."

She owed Margo, didn't she?

"Shoot a Nazi, right?"

"Not just a Nazi, Mrs. Rees. The one who'll change the course of the war if he's not brought down."

Pretending not to be pleased, she stood and went to the window. Stop it, she told herself. Why did Stepney have this impact on her?

Outside on the grass, clumps of men worked in a flower garden. Beyond the wall she glimpsed rolling green hills. The place was so idyllic, who would ever think the men dining and drinking below were captured POW officers?

"What's Margo's assignment?" Kate asked without turning.

"It's complicated."

Complicated meant many things, rarely anything good.

"Complicated how?" Kate nevertheless asked.

"Margo will signal coordinates. Get you close."

That was all he was going to give her? Tension knotted her shoulders.

"I'm not agreeing to an operation I don't know anything about."

What if her nerve left her? Or the fear that woke her up in the night took over? The accident in Copenhagen—

"Tradecraft, Kate. What you don't know you can't reveal."

Under torture. She got that.

A KNOCK SOUNDED ON THE door. Matron marched in without a response.

"Not now," said Stepney, expelling an exasperated breath and raising a hand.

"Sir," Matron said. "You need to see this."

He frowned as she delivered him a thin file before bustling away without a glance in Kate's direction. He opened it. Kate could have sworn a perplexed look crossed his face before he turned away.

"Just spell it out, Stepney."

Flustered like she'd never seen him before, he motioned for her to sit down.

"I-n-v-a-s-i-o-n."

She stifled a gasp.

"May I remind you that you've signed the Official Secrets Act?" he said. "You never heard what I just said."

She still didn't understand what he wanted of her. "Stepney, you're not getting away with leaving me stumbling in the dark again. I imagine you realize by now that I work better when I'm not going in blind."

He pointed again to the chair. This time she sat down, glad to get off her feet. She picked up the notebook that was waiting for her, the pencil beside it. Ready.

"Here at Trent Park, we soften up German POW officers—the captured elite high command mostly," Stepney said. "Under the CSDIC, Combined Services Detailed Interrogation Centres."

She'd heard rumors that Latimer House and Wilton Park held deluxe accommodations for U-boat commanders and Luftwaffe crew.

"Of course, we put them through tough interrogations and intense questioning," Stepney continued. "Mostly a pretentious Prussian bunch. We know perfectly well we won't get anything out of them. But in this old country house full of comfortable chintz sofas and fireplaces, the lifestyle of hunting and billiards, taking walks on the grounds and having whiskey after dinner—they talk amongst themselves." He steepled his fingers under his chin. "That's what we're interested in."

"*We*, Stepney?"

His gaze remained fixed on her. A muted shuffle of footsteps from the corridor.

"We're sitting in the mock general's office. Multipurposed for interrogation and training. Behind you in the cabinets is the listening equipment and loudspeakers."

"This place is bugged?"

"I believe that's how the engineers termed it," said Stepney. "We removed the casings to fit the microphones into skirting boards, inside the false paneling, the ceilings, the fireplace, the light fittings. Even under the billiards table.

Everywhere you can think of in this mansion. They're wired to a junction box in the basement—wires running under the floorboards. Below us in three basement rooms everything is being listened to and recorded."

"And who listens?"

"Who do you think, Kate."

"Other Germans. Émigrés. "

"Putting these parakeets in a gilded cage like this gets them singing."

Smart. Sly. The Brits were good at that.

"So the Secret Service hauled you from retirement for a mission that would require your former agents?"

"Something like that," he said.

Or he'd never left.

"Fool me once, Stepney, shame on you. Fool me twice, shame on me."

"You signed up, Mrs. Rees. Took the chances. This is war."

"But I didn't sign up for you to set me up and betray me."

"I underestimated you. To my humiliation. My deepest apologies. But you were brilliant, Cowgirl. You will be again."

"I'm a rifle instructor up in the highlands," she said, ignoring the code name he'd given her. "Happy."

"Not according to reports."

His face said it all. She recalled the way she was watched, the tireless presence of eyes on her every movement. They had probably been keeping her in the wings to activate as needed. Every mission she'd ever been sent on she'd been scared to the bone. Spycraft wasn't her forte. Shooting a target was. Taught to shoot by her pa when she got old enough to hold a rifle, she'd learned to defend the ranch's livestock from prey and hunt for food in rural Oregon. She'd rate as Olympic caliber if they allowed riflewomen in the games, dammit. And she burned to get back at the Germans for what they'd taken away from her. If she could just use her skills—

She remembered Wilkes's speech to the new recruits:

The fallacy of training is the idea that skill is enough. Any mission is no more under your control than a game of cards. Bad hands will come your way. You must keep your focus on how to play each card, not on the outcome. That will keep you moving through a dark patch until the luck once again breaks your way. Use everything you've got, especially the most primordial gifts you were born with—your five senses.

Or in other words, fly by the seat of your pants.

"Margo saved your life," Stepney said. "And face it, Kate. You're itching to get back into the fight. Good Lord, I am, too. If it weren't for this decrepit body . . ." He trailed off.

She believed him.

"Margo hasn't a chance without your help," he said at last. "You decide."

Kate thought of Pa. Her brothers, scattered God knows where. Her husband; her baby girl, just ashes. Philippe, married with a family. And of herself, all alone.

As her pa would say, *Quit moaning and roll with the punches.*

The years since Paris had faded into mist in the Scottish Highlands, the comings and goings of agents from her training ground and out to the field, faces she knew might never return.

The training charades only simulated the real deal. Nothing replicated the pulse-pounding fear, the scream in her head, the gut-wrenching but glorifying, on-the-wire-edge energy of a mission.

She missed it.

Who was she fooling?

Stepney was right: She wanted to be out there, in the thick of it. Doing what mattered. Saving Margo. Getting revenge in the only way she knew how. She took a deep breath.

"On one condition, Stepney," she said. "You read me in. All the way in. No hidden agenda."

"I understand that it's hard to rebuild trust."

"Say yes to my request." She grinned.

"Not in my bailiwick, Mrs. Rees. This comes from the top."

"The top? Like who?"

"Not for me to say. Your mission's three-pronged; you'll carry an item and deliver it."

"I'm not a carrier pigeon."

"If I may finish, Mrs. Rees? You'll be carrying a quantity of penicillin."

"Why would you send a sniper to—?"

"It's economical," said Stepney. "The last courier died. But lives depend on this."

Kate felt a chill in her bones.

"As I was saying. The penicillin drop is a real necessity, but also a cover for your other two goals. They are to take out a target and to extract Margo. Will that suffice?"

As if it could. Seat of the pants, all right. But Margo needed her help, and she had nothing to lose; no one to come back to or for.

"Nah, not really," she said and stood to stretch. "Just don't throw me to the wolves like last time."

An Oasis South of Tobruk, Libya

⁓

Dismounting the camel, Rommel's favorite Afrika Korps captain, Kurt Lange, blinked sand from his eyes. He unwound the keffiyeh headdress protecting his face and neck—most of it, anyway—and spit out grit. The heat was so intense it wavered on the horizon. In front of the sheikh's tent a knobby-kneed boy in a tattered djellaba held out a pitcher.

Kurt extended his hands as the boy poured silvery well water smelling of stone. He splashed his face, rinsed his hands and scooped a mouthful.

Tepid and brackish, and yet thirst-satisfying.

German, he'd grown up in Alexandria until his mother moved back to Berlin. He'd been raised with a Bedouin servant, speaking fluent Arabic and several Bedouin dialects.

"*Shokran,*" he said, thanking the boy.

Kurt had come in response to a message the sheikh had sent him. He'd awakened before dawn to avoid the heat and ride here. These nomads' skill in tracking and guerrilla tactics in the desert was invaluable. He learned numbers of British troops and names of divisions, both those in the field and kept in reserve. He learned the British troops' state of training, numbers of tanks, their state of repair. Supplies of ammunitions, food and gas, who the commanding officers were. Most significantly, British strategic and tactical intentions.

Berlin had broken the code used in British radio dispatches—half the time the sloppy signalmen hadn't bothered to encrypt communications. But even the codebreakers couldn't beat Kurt's first-hand desert intelligence.

A gold mine, Rommel called it, and pressed Kurt for his source. It was Kurt's only advantage, so he kept his ace in the hole to himself. Without Kurt, Rommel wouldn't be the Desert Fox. Or have the Führer's ear.

Kurt rinsed his face again, noting the sheikh's men sitting in the date palm shadows. Watchful.

Kurt had saved their sheikh's life. Rescued him during a British ambush from the path of a tank that had caught fire. If there was one thing he'd learned about the nomads it was their fierce loyalty. They owed him. He hadn't just bought their cooperation, like the British tried to do.

Ducking under the tent's flap, he accustomed his eyes to the sepia light and took in the cool, musky scent of beaten carpets. A hint of orange shone through.

"*Salaam alaikum,*" said Sheikh Omar, whom his men called the Tiger of the Desert. His grizzled, white-flecked beard, walnut-toned skin and care-worn hands spoke to his age.

"*Alaikum salaam.*" Kurt returned the greeting and touched his hand to his heart.

"Sit down, *rafiq.*"

Comrade in arms.

A boy in faded blue appeared with a brass tray of steaming mint tea in small glasses.

"I have much to relate," said Sheikh Omar. "First, have tea."

"You are kind and I treasure your hospitality," said Kurt, the traditional response. He tucked his legs under his khaki desert Afrika Korps uniform with the SS lightning bolts on the collar. He'd feel more comfortable wearing a djellaba, but he was here on army business.

He savored the scalding hot, strong tea with date sugar and sprigs of mint. In the desert drinking hot things made you cooler. Kurt's men had laughed at first but now followed his example.

The sheikh sipped.

"As you know, the British plane crashed in the southern wadi yesterday."

"Have you got something for me?"

From behind his cushion, the sheikh pulled a brown leather attaché case, its buckle broken. Of course, he'd opened it and extracted what valuables he could. Inside were two files, one in English and one in French. The papers were useless to the sheikh, who could not read either language.

Kurt's pulse raced seeing CONFIDENTIAL—HIGHEST SECURITY stamped in red on the first page. A map of desert quadrants and British troop and gun emplacements along with supply lines. The next page outlined proposed Allied plans for an imminent invasion of Morocco and Algeria.

Operation Torch.

Gold, pure gold.

This sheaf of English paper was what military intelligence, the Abwehr, wanted.

"And the courier?"

"He's my special present for you," said the sheikh.

"Alive?"

"And waiting for you, *rafiq.*"

A real present.

"How can I repay you?" Kurt asked as a sign of respect.

"I owe you my life." The sheikh pressed his palms together. "Defeat the stinking British—that's enough for me." He smiled. "But my men did the hard work."

Nothing came free.

"Understood."

LANGE FOUND THE BRITISH COURIER tied to a stake under a date palm. Heat blistered the soles of his feet and bare knobby knees where he'd tried to crawl away on the baking sand. One leg, flecked with dried blood, twisted at an odd angle. His burned face and cracked lips testified to what a few hours in the desert could do. His swollen black and blue eyes were slits encrusted with sand flies.

"Where were you going?" said Lange, in English.

"Thank God," said the Brit, his voice cracking. His sunburnt arms reached out blindly. The man couldn't see his German uniform. "Please, some water. Get those natives to give me my things and let me go."

Pompous Brit. The colonial attitude would cost him.

"Why?"

"What do you mean? I'm in pain. Injured. Can't see a bloody thing."

"Answer my question."

Lange's hand moved to his sheathed knife.

"Look, we crashed en route to Cairo. My leg's broken, the pilot's a goner."

"Tell me the truth."

"Wait," the Brit rasped. "You're not English. What accent's that? Who the hell are you anyway?"

"You don't want to know."

Lange knelt down behind the man. Disturbed flies, the nasty biting kind, buzzed in a black cloud.

Lange let a trickle of water drop onto the man's lips.

"Oh, please—more. I'm so thirsty." His voice cracked again.

"Where were you flying to? It's simple; just tell me."

He let another few drops fall and the man's tongue stuck out to catch them.

"Malta," he said after a minute.

Lange drew his blade across the man's bony throat, ear to ear.

He wiped his blade on the man's pants. "I thought so."

FROM HIS CAMEL BAGS, KURT took out the Lee-Enfield rifles his men had recently captured from the British. "Many thanks," he said while passing out the rifles to Sheikh Omar's men. A smiling, gap-toothed man wore a Swiss Audemars Piguet watch. Exclusive and expensive. No doubt booty from the plane.

Should he trade his own for that?

Before he mounted the camel, he did. Later he wished he hadn't.

Lunchtime found him back at his desk in Tobruk, in the military compound, scouring the documents stamped SECRET. His English was almost as good as his German, or his Arabic, or his French.

On the fourth page he caught his breath.

Hitler believed the Allies would invade the Balkans, where Romanian oil fields at Ploiesti were vital to the Reich. Current intelligence, activity in the Mediterranean and troop movement hinted at an upcoming Allied invasion there.

But these reports and communiqués indicated the opposite. Instead of invading the Balkans, the Allies intended to invade North Africa. Brilliant, perfect strategy and what he'd do himself. Logistically, it could be the first step to invading Europe; once the British captured all of North Africa, they would use it as a base to attack Sicily, then go up the Italian boot to Europe. And win the war.

Mussolini floated the idea that the Allies could aim for North Africa every so often, trying in vain to get Hitler to protect Rommel's strongholds there. Yet the Führer remained deaf to anything but guarding access to the fields in oil-rich Romania and the Middle East—the lifeblood to the home front, which kept the forces rolling. Every report uncovered by the Abwehr, every decrypted transmission, aerial reconnaissance and shipping flow activity indicated invasion of the Balkans.

It was a well-constructed, thought-out ruse. But now Lange knew the truth.

For once the chubby little Italian seemed right.

HIS WARY SIDE TOOK OVER. He had to think it through. A French plane with British documents detailing a North African invasion. Authentic? Or what if it was a plant, a ploy with faux documents?

He had to float this by his connection in Berlin. Get their take.

Or would he?

This could get him a promotion. A seat at the big table. Even the ear of Admiral Wilhelm Canaris, chief of the Abwehr, who had the Führer's.

He'd tell Rommel later.

He answered his ringing phone absentmindedly.

"*Ja . . .*"

"It's me, *Schatz*," said the woman he knew as Magda.

Kurt started, knocking the paper to the ground. "Magda, how did you—?"

What sounded like a wet kiss over the line interrupted him. "Your boys here in Paris are so sweet. Especially Rolf. I told them I wanted to talk to you and they put the call right through," she said.

He was amazed she had been allowed to reach him

on the Abwehr line from Paris HQ to Rommel's HQ in Tobruk. Only a woman like her could charm the pants off German military intelligence. As she had him. Magda had a way about her.

"You're something else," he said. She made him hard already.

"I'm going to get angry if you're not here tomorrow."

"Tomorrow?"

"My suite at the George V," she said, a smile in her voice. "The one you liked so much last time."

That voice. That body.

"There's a war on, remember," he said. "Our battle front's porous . . ."

"Don't disappoint me, Kurt. The count's pressuring me, but I'd rather see you."

A thought entered his mind. He'd take these plans to Berlin in person. En route, he could stop in Paris, meet Canaris, recruit the agent he had his eye on—and it might be just right. He liked the thought more and more.

Trent Park, Outskirts of London

In a redbrick storage shed abutting the Georgian mansion's service entrance, Stepney handed Kate a multi-pocketed vest and pointed out a long table. "Tools of the trade. Easy to fit in your pocket."

"A dead rat, a hollow screw, dog turd, a rock, mustard?" She sniffed. "Seriously?"

"Apart from the rat, fresh by the way, you can use any of these to leave a message or find one."

"In dog poo? No thanks."

"Rubber." He stuck his finger inside and pulled out a red striped firecracker with a long fuse. "A bonus distraction. Quite effective. Mustard smeared on your right shoe indicates danger. Abort. On your left it means meeting changed."

She moved to the other end of the shed. The rat was getting pungent.

"What's with all your toys, Stepney?"

"Familiarize yourself, Mrs. Rees. You might need to find a message or leave one. Simple items found everywhere. They won't stand out and they're hollow."

He handed her a small brown button.

"Turn it counterclockwise. Like this."

It opened and inside was a small compass.

"More toys," she said. "And this?"

She lifted a small bag with dark red powder.

"Add milk and it resembles blood. Could save your life," he said. "Before we go back inside, get out your notebook. It's time for a refresher course."

"The rat goes or I do, Stepney."

He nodded. Picked it up by the long greasy tail, opened the pebbled glass adjoining door and tossed it out onto a garbage pile. He closed the door, lifted his wrist, consulted his watch and counted, "Four, three, two and . . ."

A loud crack and explosion. The glass door vibrated.

"Exploding rats?"

He gave a small grin. "What will they come up with next, eh? Now, let's get to work on refreshing your tradecraft, shall we?"

TWO HOURS LATER A TIRED Kate followed Stepney into another wing of the mansion. They passed what had been a ballroom while heading downstairs to a spacious multi-roomed cellar. Here sat men at desks wearing headphones. Signs in thick German script were taped to desks.

Kate's jaw dropped. She noted wall diagrams showing the mansion's layout and grounds—all over were dotted colored pins.

"Do you bug every bird feeder and bench?"

"Just about, Mrs. Rees. This is the M room."

"M as in microphones?"

"You catch on quickly."

She surveyed the desks, the listeners bent over their notes. "Where did you get all these German speakers to listen?"

"Jewish émigrés, refugees from the Nazis. Some were evacuated on Kindertransports," said Stepney.

"No women?"

"They recruited young men who fled fascism—got out early on and have been here for years. The government put them in enemy alien camps until Intelligence saw reason and we put them to work transcribing their native tongue, interpreting the nuances in conversations."

Only made sense.

A large fan whirled, and air ducts sucked out the moisture. The cellar felt oddly sterile, without the usual musty odors or damp. The place reminded her of a laboratory. Kate still wore her training overalls and wished she had a sweater against the chill.

"What about the man with the lisp, the one who I cleaned up for who called me a hippo?"

"I believe it was a cow," Stepney said. "What do you remember about him that wasn't in your report?"

"You mean what did I miss?"

"I believe they teach trainees in Scotland to use the gifts they were born with."

She remembered how the man had perspired. Then it hit her.

"Pine cologne. I thought I was smelling the soap suds, but the scent was stronger near him."

Stepney smiled for once. "You don't get a man's smell from a photo or newsreel. He's quite partial to his signature scent, as he calls it."

"But what's the point? What makes him special?"

"We need his cooperation and he's a top engineer. For now that's all you need to know."

Upstairs, in a dark, wood-panelled room, Stepney had her sit at a desk piled with charts and manuals.

"Mrs. Rees, as you've experienced on other missions, whatever can go wrong does go wrong."

What else was new?

"It's most effective to plan for positive outcomes and pre-pare for the worst-case scenarios," he said. "Any moment your contact could be compromised, your disguise dam-aged. You'll have to think on your feet. You're wanted and there's a price on your head, so listen closely."

He reinforced his dictum for in the field: Read the situation, Assess the options, Decide on one, and take Action—RADA.

She jotted notes. Rubbed her eyes. Finally, he showed her a photo of small test tubes nesting in a jewelry case.

"What's this?"

"You're delivering this penicillin to the Pasteur Insti-tute."

"Isn't that for curing battlefield wound infections and pneumonia?"

"This is all you need to know. For now."

"You keep saying that, Stepney," she said. "Margo knows I'm a sniper. Why did she ask for me by name?"

"You'll know when you need to know, Mrs. Rees."

She felt like Alice falling down the rabbit hole. Where was this going?

"Think of it as a stolen French weekend."

Kate paused, soaking it in.

"Who's the target?"

"Margo will contact you when she can."

"Don't you have some idea, Stepney? Why send me in blind?"

"In this case the less you know, the better."

He showed her another photo—a group scene at an outdoor café. At the table sat several SS, oak leaves on their collars. She looked closer and recognized the Café de la Paix's striped café chairs and in the background, the Opera Garnier. Margo sat with these SS with a glass of wine and holding the daily fascist *Paris-soir*. The Nazi next to her was grinning and pointing to the partially visible headline: CAIRO ABOUT TO FALL TO THE DESERT FOX, ROMMEL.

"When was this taken?"

"Not important. A good undercover legend is like a diamond. Crafted to meet the four Cs—the carat, cut, clarity, and color. They sparkle so brightly you can't look past them."

Diamonds were hard. Was Stepney saying something else here?

"Much of your mission depends on what happens on the ground after you land, and how Margo plays it. We can't know anything for sure."

Plan. Pivot. And re-plan. Hadn't Wilkes drilled that into the trainees?

Or as her pa would say, *ya gotta be ready to turn on a dime, Katie.*

"Then, as I mentioned, you'll extract her. You'll go via Meudon." He pulled out an aerial photograph of southern Paris and its environs. Pointed to a forested park. "Study this."

She did, noting the nearest roads, the paths and swathes of fields and treeless areas. As if they'd been cleared for runways.

Three jobs on one trip. The French were notorious for being frugal, but the Brits were just plain cheap. Deliver the package, take out the target and extricate Margo—it was a lot. And she didn't know if she could trust him.

"What aren't you telling me, Stepney?"

He opened a locket on a gold chain. "I'm equipping you for eventualities." There was an L-pill inside. "Cyanide. Hold out for twelve hours if you can."

She shook her head. "Been in the field lately?" Snorted. "Last time they stripped me and tied my hands behind my back. This wouldn't work."

"Good point, Mrs. Rees."

So this was a suicide mission. But she owed her life to Margo—simple as that. If her number was up, at least that debt would be squared.

Her one regret flashed in her mind. She'd never said goodbye to her pa. Now, she might never visit his grave.

Tapping his cane with one hand, Stepney dialed a number on the black melamine phone.

"Get a car out front," he said into the receiver. "Tell Elder we're coming."

WHEN SHE AND HER PA went hunting, he'd always warned, *you can't carry enough tools when it comes to survival, gotta use your wits and muscle.* He'd meant being caught in an Oregon blizzard, but the same advice applied in Nazi-occupied France. Yearning sliced through her. How she missed her pa.

In her Section D training days, she'd learned breaking and entering from a Cockney cat burglar who'd rewarded her lock-picking skills with champagne. Her makeup and disguise instructions had come from Peter, a royal Shakespearean actor. The techniques, imprinted on her brain, joined Stepney's refresher on surveillance, spotting a tail and evasion techniques.

This mission felt rushed. Seat of the pants. More than the usual wartime scurry. And Margo's life hung in the balance.

She pushed down her fear. Her hesitation. Killing the enemy was her job.

Barrage balloons filled the gunmetal sky. Batteries of anti-aircraft emplacements stood at the corners. Pedestrians in drab grays and browns stood in a bus line beside piles of rubble. Ash floated in the air, the odor of scorched brick and death emanating from the bomb sites.

En route to the airfield, Stepney instructed the car to park behind the Victoria and Albert Museum. In the rear museum workshops, unknown to the public, clandestine camouflage and sabotage devices were manufactured. Tested day and night to be field ready. Special Services' "operational" division had expanded into these new quarters where, Stepney had informed her, she'd get a "redo." A new persona. They couldn't send her back as herself—not with her face on wanted posters in Paris police stations. Or with the reward posted by German military Intelligence. The ongoing reward.

A twinge of panic fluttered inside. Was she really doing this?

The high-ceilinged workshop buzzed with activity. A large salt and pepper-haired man in a work coat that strained against his shoulders beckoned. He stood at a large table displaying what looked like kitchen utensils. To the right were several beauty stations, like in a hair salon: lit mirrors, swivel chairs, pots of makeup and brushes, wigs, hairpieces, mustaches and sets of false teeth.

"He's the head magician, we call him," said Stepney, under his breath. "Works in films and theater."

No wonder it felt like backstage. He smiled and shook Kate's hand as if delighted to meet her. Cheerful type. Big ears and rosy cheeks, like Joe, the ranch hand who'd found Ma dead in the kitchen.

"Wonderful to meet you. I always say it's you people in the field who show us reality. What works and doesn't. You're the stars."

Kate had no idea what he was getting at. But she returned the Hollywood smile he'd flashed. "Stars shine, though. We're not supposed to be noticed."

"We like you to think you're going onstage. And we're helping you play your part."

Only it's for real. No applause or raising the curtain.

"Came up with something, Elder?"

He rocked on his worn heels. "There's a few things you might want to consider. Plus, a makeover."

Stepney checked his watch. "Her flight's in a few hours. Let's go shopping, then you can work on her."

Somewhere in the English Countryside

⸺

The car pulled up on the pebbled roadside at the cross-roads, where a dairy truck was parked. A soldier opened the door for Kate. She'd been made up to look middle-aged, fitted with false teeth to fill out her cheeks and a dark shoulder-length hairpiece; her chest had been bound in a padded vest under a Red Cross uniform. The soldier escorted her across the dirt road and into the cramped, windowless rear of the requisitioned dairy truck. It smelled of sour milk. The Royal Army Forces driver, in a freshly pressed uniform, advised Kate to sit back and hold on. Little else she could do, squashed into a ledge by the milk bottle rack. Wasn't she supposed to be going on a mission?

"Where are you taking me?"

"Confidential, I'm afraid, miss."

"Missus. I'm Mrs. Rees."

"No names, please. No conversation. Sorry, missus, but that's orders."

After a while—she must have closed her eyes and slept—the truck ground to a halt. Peering ahead through the mud-splashed windshield, she could make out high stone walls, damp with splotches of moss and topped by twisted iron spikes. Her heart dropped. Prison.

A medieval prison stuck on what looked like the moors. Was this her destination?

Her heart raced as the back doors opened. The driver took her things and assisted her as she stumbled out the back. Dawn broke in a warm golden glow.

An Argus single-engine monoplane's wings glinted in the early morning on the rutted tarmac. The humming engine spit into a high rev. Someone shouted, "Hurry up."

She was sick of all this back and forth. Were they disorienting her on purpose—or just plain scrounging for available transport? Were the Brits this desperate? Were they actually losing the war?

A hand gestured from an open metal door.

Incredulous, Kate realized the rutted road was the take-off strip. They'd been waiting for her.

"Go," the driver shouted.

Then she was running, tossing her bag inside just as reaching arms pulled her into the plane. She landed face down on a gunny sack of Royal Mail. She managed to right herself, spit out the grit on her tongue and strapped on a harness. The tiny four-seater smelled of burned oil and damp wool as it bumped over the ruts in the road. The pilot pulled back the throttle, increasing the speed and sending her jostling on the mail.

"Open your mouth so your ears pop," the pilot shouted. "We're about to trot—"

She didn't hear the rest. The road vanished. Out the cockpit window she saw only gorse, pale purple heather and rocks. The jagged rocks were coming toward them. Her stomach jumped. They were going down.

Her scream was drowned in a bone-rattling shudder. The engine would catch fire and explode. She was going to die.

The plane whined, complaining in the throes of a metallic shaking. The pilot cursed and wrestled with the throttle. Somehow the bucking plane stabilized, heaving a last judder as if coming to after a spasm.

The plane climbed, barely skimming the rocky crags, and headed toward the clouds. Her stomach plopped back where it belonged. She hoped she wouldn't be sick.

The other two passengers were a man in an RAF uniform and a blindfolded figure wearing a flight suit, handcuffed to the seat.

The engine's noise made it impossible to talk. Not that she wanted to. Her thoughts drifted to her pa. He'd always told her to never forget who she was and where she came from. Stay proud.

Wasn't she?

Guilt hit her. If only she'd been able to go home to take care of Pa. The war had prevented that.

Now, rootless, she fought in a war across the ocean. If she ever made it back to Oregon, home wouldn't be the same without her pa or her brothers.

The pilot half-turned and handed her a thermos.

"If that didn't wake you up, this will. Pass it around." He grinned. "It's restorative."

Whiskey? This early? No wonder the plane got in trouble.

She sniffed. Tea. The English answer to everything.

She poured a stream into the tin cup chained to the lid and sipped. So steeped and full of tannin it woke her up all right. After spending half the day at Trent Park and the rest training with Stepney, she needed it.

He'd said she'd be in France three days max. *One dirty weekend in Paris. Drop the penicillin, hit the target Margo directs you to and extract her.*

She wiped the cup with the edge of her nurse's cape. Passed it to the RAF man. A mumbled thanks. The slumped, blindfolded figure's ankles seemed to twitch—she couldn't make out much in the dark plane. A prisoner, that much she gathered, escorted from one prison to another.

Like she'd begun to feel.

The prisoner's ankles continually twitched and the manacled wrists joined in making a metallic clanking. Shaking in fear, or . . . ?

The first rule in training was keep your mouth shut. This prisoner wasn't her business. The pressure in the cabin made her ears pop.

Sometime later, a swathe of landing strip appeared, bordered by dense forest. After the pilot's seat-of-the-pants takeoff, who knew if he could land the damn thing? Her nerves vibrated with the plane and she rubbed her neck, her skin moistened by perspiration.

The RAF man's fingers drummed on the cabin's metal ribs. The steady beat of *tok, tok, tok* put her more on edge.

Below appeared an airfield control tower resembling a child's stack of blocks. Lining the runway, faded khaki corrugated steel Nissen huts and men in dark navy flight suits.

A Royal Air Force clandestine site.

The plane dropped altitude and so did her stomach. Any minute she'd be sick. But a quick plummet, a heavy thump and the screeching of tires meant they'd landed. Finally. Her throat caught as they bounced over the runway while the brakes' force threw her back against the seat. Any minute she feared this tin bucket would go crashing into the forest.

A quick maneuver by the pilot pivoted the Argus into an open hangar. The plane shuddered to a halt. Bile rose in her throat—she had to get out. She unharnessed herself, grabbed her carryall and climbed onto the concrete.

The prisoner was hustled off and into a waiting transport truck. Another plane had taxied to the front of the hangar.

"We expect your cooperation," a man in overalls said.

She took a deep breath—kerosene odors and a soldering iron's acrid fumes. But thank God she stood on terra firma. Her stomach righted.

He handed her a new satchel. A plane's motors whined. A Lancaster model, the kind used for landings in the French countryside.

"Where's Stepney?"

"Haven't the foggiest," he said.

"But when's my updated brief?"

"Plans changed. You'll need to get going."

Sirens whelped, startling her.

"Changed how?"

Men in flight suits started running across the tarmac. An ominous droning filled the sky, getting louder.

That familiar flutter of fear danced up her neck. She remembered the sound of the Luftwaffe's planes bombing the Orkney munitions factory. Her two co-passengers were gone.

"The Luftwaffe's attacking, Sherlock," he said. "Time to hurry."

With that he whipped a blindfold around Kate's forehead. What in God's name had been the point of their first stop? And in the middle of an air attack?

Within two minutes she'd been strapped into the Lancaster. "Where are we going?"

Only the whirring of the propellers. The next moment she felt a sharp prick in her arm and a piercing coldness. That was the last thing she knew.

Paris Early Morning, the Right Bank

Kate perspired in the Red Cross uniform, her brown wig itchy and hot under her cap. She felt like a chipmunk with the false teeth distending her mouth and puffing out her cheeks. Smudged dark pencil aged her fifteen years with under-eye circles and crow's feet. So far no one looked twice at her.

She was unrecognizable even to herself after the magician's handiwork.

Invisible.

Falling yellow and orange leaves littered the stone walls. All of a sudden she was back in Paris—standing in that Parisian light reflected off the limestone. For a moment Kate let herself inhale the brisk air of autumn—just as she remembered it. A cloud of perfume wafted past, accompanying a chic woman wearing a couture pre-war mocha skirt and cardigan sweater, her wooden-soled platform shoes clicking over the cobbles.

Paris. Occupied and yet with an unvanquished spirit. She could almost smell it in the way this woman moved on the street, ignoring the strolling Wehrmacht soldiers, seeing right past them and the draped flags with swastikas.

In the Marais, the Jewish shops on rue Saint-Antoine were shuttered. Her heart clenched.

Could she do this? Pull it off?

Her nerves fizzed. For a moment she thought she'd lose it and jump out of her skin. Scream.

For her first mission undercover, Peter, the Shakespearean actor, had trained her to think:

Don't just wear the disguise, be the character.

And the most important thing he instilled in her:

Believe.

You could plan a mission down to the second, but things went well until they didn't. Prepare for anything, pivot and regroup.

Read, Assess, Decide, Act. RADA.

At her dawn landing in a field past Meudon, she'd woken up.

"What happened?"

The pilot turned back and winked.

"You enjoyed an anti-bacterial cocktail with enough knock-out drops to get you through the storm over the Channel."

"Why?"

"A lot of disease running rampant these days, miss. You'll thank us for it later."

She hopped out and the Lancaster picked up two silent men. Kate was met by an old woman who handed her a flask and grinned.

"Café nationale," she said.

What passed for coffee these days, chicory and ground chestnuts. Kate had been awake almost twenty-four hours, apart from the knock-out shot on the plane, which had turned out to be a refreshing cat nap. She needed this coffee, ersatz or not. Just as she needed the woman's old bicycle with a basket.

She'd save the pink pill, the one called Dexedrine, for when tiredness caught up with her.

Miles later, she'd finally cycled into Paris. A pawn ticket given to her by Stepney moistened in her damp palm. She breathed in the scent of cut, wilted grass. Heard that familiar flushing of the Paris street gutters, felt the still-warm October sun dappling her feet on the worn pavement in the Marais. So reminiscent of 1937, her first time. It took her back to the day in September she'd met Dafydd. Fell wondrously, wholly in love.

But that Paris was gone. Up in smoke, like Dafydd and Lisbeth.

This had become her war.

A small park and playground she passed held a sign: ACCÈS INTERDIT AUX JUIFS—Jews forbidden. Disgusted, she saw red flags with black swastikas like clinging spiders hanging everywhere. Passed a recruitment center for STO, *service de travail obligatoire*—the formerly voluntary work program in Germany but now mandated and hated by all.

KATE FELT THE FURTIVE GLANCES of passersby—their evasive air. The sullen resignation.

Ration signs hung in the windows of the few open shops with lines of those waiting in front. A baker set a sign that read *plus de pain*—no more bread—in the window and Kate heard a collective groan. Worse than what she'd seen in London.

Her weariness evaporated as adrenaline coursed through her—she was on the street in an enemy-occupied country. Searching for Margo, a package to deliver and a jack-booted target to remove.

A chance to get even.

Concentrate on that.

She scanned the doorways for watchers, cigarette

smokers, a couple who'd broken into singles. Faces she might have recognized. None. No one followed her.

That didn't mean danger didn't lurk around the corner. *Inside.*

This was her only way to make contact. The first step that would lead her to Margo.

Believe.

The pawn shop was below the Crédit Municipal marquee. "Auntie's," the Parisians called the government pawn shop, where they'd go when they needed cash. Kate pushed open the door. Certainly fancier than the pawn shop Pa had taken her mother's wedding ring to. Her nerves jangled.

A tilted chandelier and sagging floor-to-ceiling brocade draperies came straight out of the 1800s. The spindle-back chairs, too, she thought, sitting down in one and waiting for her turn.

Too nervous to sit, she stood back up after a few moments, careful to keep her gaze low. She needed to watch every step. Remain inconspicuous, part of the woodwork—fancy as this was.

The first rule drilled into her: *Never stand out.*

Who knew who was watching. *Trust no one.*

The man ahead of her showed his claim slip. The persnickety clerk put him through hoops to redeem his item.

She had no clue as to who'd pawned the item she was here to retrieve. But assumed it was vital to her mission.

"Next." The clerk at the window, a middle-aged woman, sported a mole above her lips. She looked bored, sour, and ready to make life difficult for anyone in her way.

Kate couldn't let that happen.

Take control, Stepney had told her. *Act assertive and expect compliance.*

The moment she opened her mouth she might be caught out. Denounced. Branded as foreign.

A spy?

Somehow she made herself talk.

"*Guten Tag, Madame,*" she said, trying for an Alsacienne accent. It was her best chance at passing as German among French, or French among Germans, as Alsace had ping-ponged between the two countries for years.

Her background—legend, Stepney called it—was that she'd worked in the Charité hospital in Strasbourg. She'd memorized the church she'd attended and characteristic items the local small grocer carried. Her mind stumbled through trivia about the famous Alsacienne baking powder, and the hair dye wealthy Parisiennes were all ordering from the Alsacienne chemist—things a local from Strasbourg would know. *Focus. Breathe.* "You speak German, Madame?"

The woman stiffened. "*Quoi?*"

Kate continued in her less-than-perfect German-accented French. "My boss at the hospital sent me to redeem this." She handed the woman the damp pawn ticket.

The woman studied it, then consulted a file. Her nostrils flared.

"Not here."

"What do you mean, Madame?"

"See this?" She pointed to a faded B in the corner. "This is from a different shop. Go to twenty-nine rue Bayen at the auxiliary Crédit Municipal. But this ticket is old."

Kate's antenna rose.

Something was wrong. What if this was an ambush?

Her heart was racing. Why had Stepney sent her here?

She couldn't hesitate—she was only drawing attention to herself. She turned and left.

WHY HADN'T STEPNEY KNOWN THE pawn shop ticket's location?

Had the Luftwaffe attack prevented her from getting an updated brief with the correct location?

Concentrate. Play her role. Think ahead.

Was this Stepney's redirection to throw off any surveillance she might have picked up? Keep fluid, he'd instructed.

He'd said the mission involved a lot of moving parts.

Quit overthinking. Keep moving. Hadn't that been drummed into her?

Standing still made you a target.

PAST THE ARC DE TRIOMPHE, not far from Place des Ternes, she found rue Bayen and through it a stone colonnade. This portal to the past was the remaining vestige of a chateau that existed when this was nothing but countryside. She pedaled around the block twice, checking for a tail, then made it just before the shop closed for lunch.

As she approached the claim window, she prepared herself.

Believe.

Knotting and unknotting her fingers, she clutched her damp ticket. How much narrower and more utilitarian this pawn shop was.

The woman took the ticket without a word, handed it to a gangling youth wearing a blue work coat. No wasting time when lunchtime was approaching. This was working in Kate's favor.

A recent notice above the counter listed new Occupation regulations pertaining to all pawn shops. She couldn't understand everything, but gleaned enough to realize that Stepney's contact had given her a ticket that was not only outdated, but that also had the wrong location. A double-cross? It could get her killed.

What in the world would this pawn ticket reclaim? A pistol? Keys to a safe house? A link to Margo?

A stiff portrait of the Führer, required in government buildings, looked down on them.

Pompous pumped-up jerk. He'd been in her crosshairs once—her biggest regret.

The clerk set a wooden box on the counter and tore off the pawn tag's bottom portion.

"That's 920 francs."

Just under five dollars. Not bad for whatever it was.

"Sign here."

Kate scribbled in the ledger. Was that too illegible? Would the clerk demand identification? How dumb.

She couldn't mess up the mission so early—leave Margo stranded and ruin the delivery to the Pasteur Institute. But her gut was screaming at her to get the hell out.

The clerk tore the tag into pieces and threw them in a bin. "I'm supposed to report every irregular transaction, but I often forget."

Kate stifled a grin. French bureaucrats, notorious as powers unto themselves, could make one's life easy or complicated. But it seemed this one had found her own way to resist the Boche.

Out on the street she ducked into the first doorway leading to a courtyard. Her frayed nerves made her knees shake. A small boy appeared lugging a wagon with a wire birdcage of chirping finches, and she pretended she'd forgotten her key. She smiled and followed him inside.

Instead of crossing the courtyard, which smelled of frying garlic, she sat on a stone staircase. Opened the clasp on the wood box.

A child's wooden flute nestled on worn blue velvet.

She swiped her finger inside the flute's ends, poked her bobby pin into the finger holes. Empty. Her fingers felt the worn crushed velvet, found a narrow slit on the side.

Inside she found a movie ticket.

Matinee at cinéma Le Champo. Seat 153. Great.

What kind of goose chase was this?

Nervous, she wondered if she was being set up and like an idiot, she was following poisoned breadcrumbs.

The theatre was all the way back on the left bank, heart of the student quarter; she remembered it had a side exit to the street by the Sorbonne. (Always scout exits, Stepney said.) She'd gone to a Charlie Chaplin movie there once during her brief student days.

If she didn't go she'd have no chance of meeting Margo.

What choice did she have?

Back at her bike she found the front tire punctured. Flat as a pancake. No pump or patch to fix it.

Was it sabotage?

Had someone followed her? Everything had taken too long and she was behind schedule.

It was time to move.

At Place des Ternes she hopped the first bus heading toward the Left Bank. A brisk gust of wind carried the algae scents of the Seine through the exhaust smell pumping through the open-backed bus. Several soldiers stood on the platform hanging to the back railing, smoking unfiltered German cigarettes, their gray-green uniforms a blot on a sunny day—just her luck.

Should she hop off?

One held a Pariser Plan, the mustard gold map given to the Wehrmacht on R&R. He had cameras around his neck. Tourists. She couldn't stand it. Still she smiled when he bowed as he squeezed past her.

He excused himself in bad French. *"Excusez-moi, Schwester."*

Was that what Germans called nurses—sister?

She wanted to kick him down the steps—until she noticed the pimples on his face. He looked eighteen. Like her youngest brother.

Stop it. Concentrate on your goal. Any little mistake and she'd get rounded up by pimple face or any of his ilk. It was all about keeping her mission front and center. Not making a mistake like Copenhagen. She'd taken her eye off the ball. The bus jolted as if to remind her to return to the present.

The traffic light changed. She alighted and caught up with pedestrians in the crosswalk on boulevard Saint-Germain. Kept step with a couple, flashed her ticket at the ticket booth, and darted into Le Champo. Posters lining the lobby advertised a Danielle Darrieux film.

"It's almost ended, sister," said the young usherette.

"That's all right," she said.

"Must be a Danielle Darrieux fan, eh?"

Kate nodded. The usherette tore her ticket, guided her into the dark theatre, and, with a flashlight, showed her toward a seat in the back row.

All Kate saw were heads silhouetted against Danielle Darrieux's blonde hair on screen. Kate stole a look down her row. Two women.

Neither of whom were Margo.

She pretended to drop something and felt under the seat. Smooth and metal but nothing there. She slid her hand on the sticky floor. Her palm came back with gunk.

Kate pretended to watch the screen and kept alert. No one came into the theatre or left. The film ended and no one had shown up.

The lights came up and illuminated the tatty red curtain, scuffed floor and threadbare velvet seats.

No Margo.

What in the world should she do? She checked her torn ticket, then her chair—152, not 153.

She waited for the lights to go down and the newsreel to start. The Luftwaffe bombing and strafing British troops in the Libyan desert. Rommel, the Desert Fox, directing a division of panzer tanks in Tobruk. Old news.

Horrific.

She slid her hand under the next seat and ran her fingers around. Felt something cylindrical stuck there. Carefully she wedged it loose.

Her fingers came back with a gray mechanical pencil, the type you refilled with lead. Quickly she unscrewed the top, slid out the cylindrical lead wrapped by a cigarette paper. Eyes down, she cupped the message penciled on the thin paper. Damn, she couldn't read it.

She lowered her head and ducked out into the aisle, heading for the rear exit.

Go out back. Lose your surveillance. Meet at Carousel in Parc Monceau.

God, what an idiot. She'd sat in the wrong seat. And she was being followed.

Parc Monceau on the Right Bank

Kate walked through the gilt-trimmed gates of Parc Monceau, past the manicured green hedges and nannies pushing baby carriages. She heard children's laughter, happy squeals from the ancient spinning carousel with painted wooden horses—watched it all from behind her ugly round glasses. There was a couple sitting on the bench, arms entwined.

Lovebirds that could have been her and Philippe.

Bastard.

The raw hurt opened. He was married with a family.

But why waste her energy? Forget him and focus on the here and now.

Stepney's warning filtered through her mind—*things aren't what they seem.*

Margo was in deep undercover, had sent the distress signal, and needed extraction.

Margo had requested Kate, saying only Kate could do the mission.

But there was something else. A niggle of doubt she'd been harboring since she'd seen that photo of Margo with the Nazis at Café de la Paix.

Ahead by the blushing pink of rhododendron bushes, her eye caught on a woman. Slender in a flowing lemon-colored tea-frock, with a familiar gait.

Was that Margo? Kate quickened her step.

She couldn't see the woman anymore. So many people stood in the way—mothers with children, an elderly woman walking her schnauzer, a one-armed veteran reading a folded newspaper. Kate scanned the benches and the paths for that familiar figure.

Over by the gilt-topped gate, she saw her. Barely. Only the rippling swish of her dress in between two black uniforms disappearing into a waiting Traction Avant. By the time Kate got through the gate the car had left.

Had she imagined it? Had she wanted to see Margo and so her eyes played tricks on her? Yet wasn't Margo supposed to make contact?

She'd sent a signal. Told Kate to meet her.

But was that her? Any woman whisked away by two SS boded danger.

The churned gravel and disturbed leaves in the gutter might indicate she'd resisted. An ambush. What if Margo had avoided Kate to protect her?

How could she be sure of anything? Maybe she'd read this wrong.

If there's only one thing you remember, make it RADA.

Burn it into your brain, make it second nature.

Kate returned to the carousel, bought a ride ticket, hopped on, and stood by a colorful unicorn. Her eyes swept the benches, the paths, the clusters of people, children. No Margo.

The carousel's organ music mingled with children's laughter. As the man collected tickets, she added her torn ticket stub from Le Champo. Shot a look into his worn, grizzled face.

He shoved a wooden ride token into her palm. As the organ's music swelled, the carousel began to turn. She didn't know what this meant.

Huge mansions bordered Parc Monceau with their backyards overlooking million-dollar views of the park. Not only aristocrats but *nouveau riche* lived here; their children played together in this charming park. She'd be easy to pick out in her Red Cross uniform among the nannies herding children and well-heeled strolling couples.

She slipped off the carousel, made her feet move over the gravel.

Whispered conversations reached her ears. Then several short shrill blasts of a whistle. She peered over a hedge and saw groups of French police, blue capes over their uniforms, questioning people.

On the nearby bench an older man with a handlebar mustache shook his head. "They're looking for someone."

Her.

The young woman next to him stood, gathered her bag. "Any minute they'll round us all up, Papa. Let's go."

Her heart dropped. She hadn't lost her tail. No wonder Margo hadn't made contact.

Kate looked for an exit. Found one and kept walking.

Keeping her breathing steady with effort, she ducked onto a lane and then up another. More cars than she'd imagined, and all of them were Mercedes.

She'd wound up in a Nazi enclave.

Bungled this already?

If Margo left a message with the carousel man—what if he was questioned?

The one-armed man she'd noticed reading a paper—odd in itself—turned the corner. His olive-green shirt caught in the dappled sunlight. He raised his arm. She wouldn't wait to find out if that was a signal.

Time to get out of sight. Figure out her next step.

Second rule Stepney drilled into her: if it ever feels wrong, leave.

Right now.

She heard voices. The toot of a police whistle. Good God, they'd tracked her.

She'd get caught with the penicillin, wearing a disguise, and get shot on the spot.

Kate looked around. Perspiring in her hot uniform, she spied a laundry truck with the lettered sign SERVICE DE NETTOYAGE DE BLANCHISSERIE standing in a driveway. The gates were open. In accordance with gas rationing, it had a *gasogéne* contraption resembling a tin pot stove on the roof.

After opening one of the truck's back double doors, she gathered her dowdy skirt to climb in and hunker down. As she tried closing the door, her fingers caught on a latch that made a soft click. It sounded like thunder.

Or maybe that was her pounding heart.

She realized the token the carousel man had given her felt strange in her hand. She finally thought to look it over—it was coin-shaped but hollow. She pried its two halves apart and found a scrap of paper.

Pasteur D 62. Read and destroy.

Had Margo planted this message? Or was it a trap?

Either way, her orders had been to deliver the penicillin to the Pasteur Institute. Apparently that was her next stop.

She prayed the thin rivulets of sweat didn't loosen the adhesive taping the drugs to her back. The damn tight vest she wore under the heavy outfit was soaked.

She inhaled fresh-smelling folded linen in canvas baskets, some wrapped in blue papered packages, some hanging tagged from rails running the length of the truck. The clipboard on the dashboard listed the delivery addresses, some checked off, some still to be completed. She lifted one of the cloth coverings and sucked in her breath.

Black SS uniforms with oak leaves on the collars, starched and cleaned. And women's uniforms, some an offensive gray. She'd seen pictures of these gray mice, as they were called—the German counterpart of the British FANYs who did all the work.

Third rule of training was using what you found. Fourth: use it to survive.

Escape.

Hating to, she searched for the largest size. God, what did these size numbers mean? Finally, she chose the largest jacket, the only one having a chance of fitting over her broad shoulders, and a skirt.

Stuffed them in her bag.

The truck's back door opened.

She ducked down behind the tallest canvas basket and reached for her small nail dagger, a triangular steel blade fashioned from a long nail with an oval grip, from where she'd strapped it to her thigh. The launderer, dressed in a blue work coat, stuck in two baskets of dirty clothes. She hoped he saw nothing inside but dark from where he stood in the bright sunshine.

Something was said to him in German. A short conversation ensued. She wished Stepney's intelligence had told her the Gestapo outsourced their laundry.

Her knees shook.

All of a sudden the ignition fired up. The *gasogéne* contraption shook the truck. The grinding of gears whittled her nerves like fingernails clawing a chalkboard.

Pressing herself to the floor, she wished she'd remembered the stops on the clipboard. Think, she told herself. *Think.*

After a few blocks, the driver made a stop. She heard

steps on the pavement, gravel crunching. He must be making a pickup.

She had to get out before she was discovered.

Keeping low, with her bag strapped around her shoulder, she slid and tried the back door. No handle. You could only open it from outside.

Just her luck.

Her pulse thudded. She made herself crabwalk past the baskets and the racks of clothes and partition to the driver's seat.

She opened the passenger door and climbed out. Heart thudding, she smiled at the gardener, who trimmed the yew hedge. She kept going.

All she could think was Margo had been rumbled. Unmasked by one of the smiling Nazis at the café table in the photograph.

She might be being tortured right now.

You were taught techniques to hold out twelve hours under torture to give time for others to get away. Or was it eighteen hours?

And who in the hell could do that, anyway?

Stepney said you gave in sooner or later unless you beat them to it with a cyanide pill.

Another rule was never assume. Margo might not be alive. She could be face-down in a tub at the Gestapo HQ, drowned in her own blood.

Kate's nerves tingled. Bile rose in her throat.

She was on her own.

At the corner, willing her nerves down, she hailed an approaching vélo-taxi. Once inside the flimsy canvas and metal pod, she waited until the driver crossed the boulevard before she told him her destination, hoping her voice didn't squeak or brand her as foreign.

"Métro Pasteur."

The Abwehr, Military Intelligence Headquarters, in Hôtel Lutetia Left Bank, Paris.

⏤

Dieter von Holz, a twenty-eight-year-old military intelligence officer with a trim fencer's build and dark hair crested in a widow's peak, checked his messages in his corner office overlooking boulevard Raspail. Contrary to all expectations, Dieter, who was of Prussian aristocratic stock, loved his work. Born to it, if he said so himself.

The only message on Dieter's belle époque desk read *Call home.* Never a good sign.

Dieter, on alert, scanned the bustling activity in the ornate Hôtel Lutetia suite, sage-hued rooms trimmed with gilt-edged wood boiserie. Each Abwehr officer was assigned to one of the elegant hotel's 233 guest rooms. The mailroom had been turned into a staff dormitory. The large banquet rooms had been converted into offices.

Dieter registered the irritating clicking of the telex feed overlaid by the chatter of uniformed young men. A *Blitzmädchen*, a Luftwaffe courier, scurried past his door in her navy-blue pleated skirt and double-breasted jacket. Like a hive of hornets outside this office worked the *Wehrmachthelferinnen*, the army auxiliaries in the drab gray that reminded him of the female guards in his grandmother's prison hospital.

His grandmother—from a line of Bavarian *Prinzessin,* and the bravest woman he knew—had said if the Reich wanted her ancestral castle, the Führer would have to carry her out.

His men did. And rehoused her in prison. A princess in prison.

Dieter's high-ranking Nazi brother, the engineer, would have gotten his grandmother released, but his brother was missing, presumed dead. So the task fell to Dieter. He walked a fine line to protect her, bribing the prison governor to obtain a better cell, more food, but it was never a guarantee. Eyes watched him everywhere. There was little more he could do. The sooner the coup deposing Hitler happened the better.

No one was paying him any mind. He dialed home.

The phone trilled. And again five more times. Why didn't she answer? Dieter's thoughts went to the baby. Last night he'd felt warm. Had he come down with a fever? Or . . . ?

Had the plot been discovered?

A breathless "*Allo*" came over the line as the maid answered.

"*Desolée*, Madame's out, monsieur," she said.

"Out?" At the doctor's? He grabbed a pencil. "Did she leave a number where I can reach her?"

Pause.

"Madame asked not to wait up for her. 'Softly, softly.' She said you'd understand."

Dieter's pencil tip snapped. The lead splintered with a sharp crack.

Softly, softly.

Their code for danger. A signal to implement the backup plan. He reached for the Luger in his desk. Slipped it into his tunic pocket.

Images of the baby, the documents and the suspected double-agent flashed through his mind.

As Dieter set down the phone, his boss, *Oberst* Schlüssel, strutted into his office.

Dieter stood. Shot out his arm in a Sieg Heil.

God, how he hated that. *Not for much longer,* he told himself. For now he masked his distaste.

As always.

Schlüssel brushed a leaf from his crisp uniform. "My quarters, von Holz, now. There's news."

Had Admiral Canaris's coup all come out, everything discovered? Hence the message from the maid? He braced himself, wondering how he could take over if he had to, keep Lange's assassination in play.

"The Führer's concerned about the Romanian oil fields. There's a cog in the works."

With supplies waning and the horrendous cost of reinforcing the Eastern Front, the military needed access to oil to keep going.

"What's that, sir?"

"That stupid Lange insists the invasion's set for North Africa, and that it's imminent. He's going to change the Führer's mind about Romania."

So Lange believed the recovered plans were real. Hadn't been fooled by the careful disinformation campaign to hide Operation Torch. Not ideal.

"Goering's all over this, too," said Schlüssel. "You know how he sticks his fat toes into everything."

Dieter expected that from Goering, the corpulent Luftwaffe minister, who lived at the Ritz. Dieter kept careful tabs on him and knew things about him his own wife didn't know. Goering liked dressing up in women's couture, according to Dieter's spy, the hotel's head valet. Dieter's spy network had entrée all over the city. Bell captains, hotel maids, taxi drivers, bistro owners, waiters, concierges, even several news agents were in his employ. Their kiosks made perfect vantage points for surveillance.

Whether they did it for money, a better position, or personal ideals—he paid if they delivered.

He could have done without Schlüssel's attention at this critical moment.

"What do we know?" said Dieter, straining for a tone of polite interest.

"I've been going through the Lorenz's decrypted ciphers," said Schlüssel. "Seems Lange's got proof. Or so he says. The Führer's interested."

Scheisse.

The Führer used the Lorenz machine to send secret coded messages to his high command. Only Admiral Canaris had access in Paris—or so Dieter had thought. Canaris had counted on Lange's using the encryption to communicate directly with him and Berlin without any meddling by any other players—like Schlüssel.

"Lange is Rommel's golden boy," Schlüssel grunted. "And an opportunist. I don't trust him."

Schlüssel got it right on that.

The more complicated this got, the more dangerous it was. Hitler's attention was to be avoided at all costs. Dieter had observed again and again that small matters that fell under the Führer's gaze would obsess him. The Führer would step in and override his generals and advisors, whether on the logistics of an offensive on the Russian Front, the race laws to be implemented in Norway, the Aryan business regulations in Paris. The Führer insisted on control in everything, then played each branch of his government against the others. Hitler had more lives than a cat, and an uncanny sense for danger. He intuited weakness. Between Hitler's meddling and the atmosphere of distrust he cultivated, no person or organization had any chance of functioning independently.

The Führer had promised to leave the security of the Wolf's Lair to visit the Romanian oil fields, rally the troops. There Canaris's sympathetic generals would stage the coup. It was the only chance of ending the war quickly. But a field visit was rare—Canaris had barely convinced the Führer to make this one. For the plot to succeed, Hitler must continue believing the Romanian oil fields were at risk—he couldn't be allowed to latch on to Lange's intelligence out of North Africa.

Canaris, a former Hitler supporter who had been awarded the Iron Cross in WWI, had grown disillusioned with the Reich. Politically savvy, he resembled a kindly, diminutive grandfather, despite the fact that he was a spymaster and saboteur who had already undermined the Russian campaign Operation Barbarossa by passing details to the British through his Polish mistress. Dieter only knew some of Canaris's activities, but the admiral had tentacles in Spain to Franco and a working relationship with Stalin, not to mention a rumored acquaintanceship with Churchill. The man spoke fluent English, ran military intelligence, and just reached Dieter's shoulder. No one would suspect the head of the Abwehr working toward Hitler's downfall. Unless . . .

Lange, a stumbling block, had to be removed. Once Lange was out of the way, their mission, months in planning, would proceed. With Hitler subdued in Romania, Operation Torch could unfold smoothly; the Allies would land in Morocco and Algeria and provide the needed North African foothold from which they could take out Rommel's Afrika Korps and launch an invasion up to Italy, and springboard the end of the war. So much depended on these few crucial days.

"*Jawohl, Oberst.*" Dieter's mind spun thinking of ways he could salvage this.

"Lange is arriving in Paris soon," said Schlüssel. "He

thinks he's kept it quiet, but I'll surprise him and throw a little reception. Must entertain him, you know, *ja?*"

Gottverdammt.

Abwehr communications hadn't even known of Lange's trip. Schlüssel wasn't as out of touch as he'd thought.

Someone in Dieter's office leaked information like a sieve.

Dieter had to be more than careful. He stifled his unease. Maybe he could somehow work this to his advantage.

"I'm at your service," said Dieter.

"Not needed. Lili's organizing," said Schlüssel.

Schlüssel's mistress. Bad news.

His boss had called on his mistress to pull together her "crowd": impoverished but titled aristos, louche socialites, the literati always hungry for a free meal, an actress or two who always spiced up the evenings.

Resolve came over him. Dieter wouldn't let the plan fall apart. He put on a smile.

"There must be some assistance she'd need. What can I do to help, *Oberst?*"

Schlüssel tented his fingers. Thought. "Start by helping me pick out my jacket."

Dieter followed him through his office into the suite of rooms rumoured to have been a *comte's*. The requisitioned suite, with its odor of sex, leather, and stale perfume, felt hollow, unlived in. This messy room matched this spoiled Prussian aristocrat, a distant relation of Dieter's on his father's side. The maids were under strict orders to clean once a week only. His hand-tooled leather saddle was splayed over a chair; his muddy-soled riding boots and crop were on the floor.

For Dieter he was an ideal boss, without particular ambition. He took his daily ride in the nearby Bois de Boulogne, visited his mistress, dined out and counted on Dieter running the bureau. Usually he showed not the slightest interest as long as Dieter's communiqués kept the Führer and Admiral Canaris happy. He was a high-ranking Nazi, due to the fact that his father ran the steelworks that provided the Reich's tanks. He felt he served the Reich already.

At least, that's what Dieter had believed.

Dieter slipped an evening jacket from the armoire, one of several bespoke outfits.

"What about this?"

He winked. "You have superb taste."

Anyone could, with a steel industrialist father footing the tailoring bills.

"Is this Lange a snob, sir? Expecting to see city nightlife?"

The usual Eiffel Tower and red velvet bordello tour that he gave to bigwigs. While Dieter's guest was occupied in the bordello behind Saint-Sulpice, any pillow talk was recorded via his arrangement with the Madame; meanwhile he had their rooms searched.

"*Nein*, Dieter, I'll handle him," Schlüssel said, unbuttoning his collar.

Alarm filled Dieter. He needed Schlüssel offstage so he could maneuver Lange into the sniper's target. His agent Magda's last message said the sniper was here. Ready.

"*Jawohl.* Shall I make dinner reservations?" said Dieter. "Pre- or post-reception at Tour d'Argent, brasserie Lipp or your usual?"

"They're boring. We'll slum it downstairs."

Only he would call it slumming with a chef who'd earned a Michelin star in 1939, the last year of the guide's rating.

Magda was Dieter's main connection to British intelligence. The British Allied Signals desk in Cairo had decrypted Lange's message hinting at a "recovery in the desert." The alert analyst in Cairo HQ monitored the crash of a courier plane carrying desert troop maps and plans for Operation Torch. The analyst connected this crash to

Lange's message and had sent a priority encoded message to London.

After London informed Magda, she'd lured Lange here from Tobruk and requested the assassin. The plan to shoot Lange would be staged as one of the random attacks happening on the Paris streets recently. Dieter would make sure blame went to the underground partisans. Through his network of agents on both sides, Dieter gave as free a rein as he could to the Francs-tireurs et partisans, the FTP, armed Communist saboteurs: a ragtag organization of Jews and Eastern Europeans. Dieter's own informant in Paris—a Communist—was meeting Lange.

As quiet as he kept it, Dieter's relations with London via Magda worked both ways. He helped the British and vice versa. When the war ended, he and his family would make a new life in the English countryside.

Lange had to be stopped before reaching Germany, getting the Führer's ear and showing him the Operation Torch maps. The sooner he was taken out, the better.

"My goal is to smooth out your evening so you can . . ."

"*Gott im Himmel,* Dieter, quit worrying and get Canaris to the dinner."

How could he work this to his advantage?

The hit needed to happen tonight. Here. And look random.

Dieter had to get the word out and gum up his boss's plans for monopolizing Lange. Dieter would appeal to his vanity, talk him around to another way of thinking. Something that usually worked.

The phone rang in the suite. Schlüssel picked it up, raised his hand and listened.

"For you, Dieter."

Him?

"Institut Pasteur." A woman's low voice. "Now."

The phone clicked off.

Rue de Vaugirard on the Left Bank

En route Kate had popped half a pink pill dry to stay alert. Forty-eight hours on the go. She ignored the rippling up her arms. Her jumpiness from the pill after little sleep.

Focus.

Bits of blue peeked out from behind the fat clouds. Disgorged Parisians flowed up the Métro steps and through the green metal art nouveau entrance, two orange flower buds atop cast-iron lampposts curving like plant stems. The lettering on the sign was old fashioned, reading PASTEUR and METROPOLITAIN. Men and women grabbed their hats before the hot underground updraft blew them away.

Keep moving.

Behind the Pasteur Institute gate she saw an enclave of shadowed, rose-brick buildings. She smiled at the *gardien*, wearing a worn blue cap, who peeked out of a sentry box.

Before she could speak, the *gardien* shook his head.

"We're closed to visitors, mademoiselle."

Wasn't this a medical research facility? She'd expected her Red Cross uniform would grant her access. She clenched her fist. Unclenched it.

"Monsieur, I'm expected at a meeting."

"So you say."

Had she come all this way for nothing? She reminded herself to keep calm with the pumped-up self-important *gardien.*

"Please understand, it's important."

"*Desolé*, I've got rules to follow. Who are you supposed to meet?"

She couldn't say Margo. What could she say?

Simple worked best, Stepney said.

"D 62."

He stared at her like a statue.

"Can you check, please?"

"Check what?"

"I'm expected. Can't you make a call?"

Reluctant, he turned back into his sentry cabin. Called. It felt like forever.

She didn't know whom he was calling. Room D 62? A secretary who verified appointments? The SS, to come arrest her?

Why did this have to be so difficult? Why did she get the runaround every time? Was she losing it?

Frustrated, she took a breath. Then another. Tried to clear her mind. Focus on the now.

Get real. She knew why these contacts were skittish and afraid. There were eyes everywhere.

The next moment the gate clicked open. "Second on the right," he said. "Go to building D and laboratory 62."

The magic phrases—an open sesame. Easy. Too easy?

No lights or activity she could see in the cluster of buildings. Weeds cropped between the uneven stone pavers.

It seemed deserted. Still, she felt eyes watching her.

BUILDING D HELD NO EXTERIOR windows. Reminded her of a dark tomb. The double doors yielded to a fluorescent lit entry lined by racks of hanging white lab coats. Kate continued until she found a door labeled 62.

Took a breath, then opened it.

A lab-coated scientist worked at a metal counter near a Bunsen burner emitting a blue flame. Kate remembered those from her one high school science class. She'd barely passed the class.

Racks of test tubes, empty and waiting, sat on the counter. She noticed the tall glass wall cabinets shelved with brown glass bottles, canisters, mortars and pestles, iron scales and weights.

"*Excusez-moi,*" she said.

He looked up in surprise, revealing a pale hollow-cheeked face.

She approached the scientist. "I think I have something for you, monsieur. Do you have a message for me?"

But the man raised his hands, a look of shock in his eyes.

"Actually, I do," said a voice behind her.

The lab scientist dropped a test tube. Glass splintered, shattering on the tiled floor.

Kate turned to see a man in the doorway. Her stomach plummeted to the worn tile floor. His black leather coat didn't conceal his silver SS rune collar pin.

Institut Pasteur Laboratory, Left Bank

She'd walked into a setup. Her own damn fault.

Her adrenaline shot into high gear. Margo must have been caught and tortured. Must have given her up.

Forget going down without a fight. She'd shoot this SS, take out as many as she could trying to get out. Down the cyanide pill before she let them put cuffs on her.

Hadn't she been told to prepare for a suicide mission?

Too bad she'd never have the chance to hit her main target. Screwed up her mission. Again.

Under her Red Cross cape she slid her 9mm Welrod's 12-inch cylinder, containing its bolt, barrel and baffle, down her sleeve. It took seconds, during which she never broke eye contact with the Nazi. His irises were a flinty metallic gray.

She held the magazine grip from the pocket under her blue cape and snicked it into place. This short rifle, nicknamed the "bicycle pump" because of its look, performed close contact shots by bolt action and had a six-shot magazine. Also quiet. Wilkes had said it best: she should never be unarmed.

Kate's finger pulled back the trigger.

"Margo sent me," the Nazi said, in British-accented English. "I'm her brother-in-law."

Kate's finger tensed on the Welrod's trigger. *Trust no one.* Now she was supposed to trust a Nazi?

"Put your hands in the air," Kate said, "and prove it."

His eyes never left her sleeve rifle as he removed his black cap with one raised hand and showed the gold crested ring on the pinkie of his other.

"Is that supposed to mean something to me?"

Cold light filtered from an overhead skylight, spreading a frost-kissed sheen over the chrome counters. The scientist, his hands still raised, stepped back, crunching over the broken glass on the floor. No doubt ready to bolt.

"Read Margo's message inside my hatband," said the Nazi.

Had he hidden an explosive device in there? Some trick to gain time?

She stepped over the splintered glass, motioned for the scientist to take the hat.

The scientist's hand shook as he rooted through the felt interior. She wondered about his work at this seemingly deserted facility. At the lack of German presence.

The scientist set a folded paper on the chrome counter. He blinked in fear.

"Go ahead, open it," she said.

The nervous scientist looked from Kate to the Nazi and back. He unfolded the paper to reveal a receipt from Café de la Paix. On it a penciled message.

> *Cowgirl: P for Pasteur, save one for me + Dieter. Adonis in Paris. Hôtel Lutetia 22:00h.*

Adonis.

The nickname she and Margo gave a training instructor—a small, mousey, sallow-faced counterfeiter with bad breath—pulled from prison, who taught them how to distinguish real and fake bills. He was the butt of their inside jokes. No one else knew that nickname.

Kate hoped her jaw hadn't dropped. She studied the German. "How did you obtain this?"

The German kept his hands raised. "Why does that matter?"

"I'm supposed to believe an SS officer is Margo's brother-in-law and delivering her messages—"

His brow furrowed. "I'm not SS. I'm Abwehr."

Like it mattered?

"Still a Nazi."

He shrugged. Fingered his collar button. "Member of the party, so technically, yes." He cocked an eyebrow, giving her the sense he was studying her, too. Didn't quite know how she fit in.

This man looked increasingly familiar to her—and suddenly she realized why. Officer B in Trent Park—the facial similarity clicked, and she remembered the picture of Officer B and his brother in front of the family castle. He'd aged a few years since that photo was taken, was maybe in his late twenties now, but the eyes were the same, the same widow's peak of black hair.

But why would Margo marry a Nazi? That didn't make sense; didn't she have a boyfriend in the military? That creep Gregory, who'd taken advantage of Kate's weakness in Copenhagen? Not to mention that fiancé who had died at Dunkirk?

"I don't get why Margo would send you," she said.

"Then you don't know Margo that well."

Well enough to risk her life for a comrade by coming here.

Keeping her gun pointed at the Nazi, she turned to the scientist. "My instructions were to deliver a package to a doctor. That you?"

The scientist's darting eyes looked about to bulge out of their sockets.

"I'm doctor in Poland, here I am researcher. Run the lab. You want to see my papers?"

The Nazi said, "Not important. All I need is the code word. Otherwise you're dead."

Kate heard steel in his voice. A long moment passed.

The clock in the hallway gonged.

"Janek," he said, his chin quivering as he spoke. "My name Janek."

"And Jaro's your cousin?" asked the German.

Who was that?

"*Ja.*" The doctor's face relaxed a little. "Jaro promised me penicillin cultures so I can manufacture myself." He pointed out the window overlooking the courtyard to the building across with a sign reading LE DISPENSAIRE. "We need it to treat sick children in the old dispensary. All orphans."

"You're keeping orphans in the dispensary?" Kate clarified.

"It's warmer there. Insulated walls."

That sold her. Kate had to put down her gun to unbuckle her belt, grapple with the case taped to her spine under the cumbersome nurse costume. She wiped the perspiration off it. Hoped to God none of the tubes had broken. Or leaked.

Inside the small jewelry case, the cork-stoppered test tubes glistened in the light. Dr. Janek sucked in his breath, excitement on his face.

"Cultures," said Janek. "I'll start growing these today. The Germans requisitioned our sulfa drugs for the Wehrmacht."

Like businesses and apartments, along with everything that wasn't nailed down.

His face clouded. "But . . . we need penicillin right now. Didn't you bring treatment for the children?"

Dark circles cratered his eyes.

"You mean these?" She folded back the leather belt's interior to reveal penicillin tablets, like black and yellow bumblebees, packaged in the lining.

"Thank you," he said. Janek executed a stiff bow, a vestige, she imagined, of the old life he'd once inhabited.

"That's my job, doctor."

One task down. Two to go. She felt lighter.

She jerked her thumb to the Nazi, who picked up his cap. No Abwehr insignia on him, but she remembered they went plainclothes. In training, she'd had to memorize all the branches, ranks. Was this man really a double agent within the military intelligence? Could she believe him?

He led her out of the laboratory and into a sleek, coved art deco office space with white walls and a black grille. It reminded her of a stage set.

"This place is haunted," he said.

Not what she'd expected him to say. "Pasteur's ghost?"

"Something like that. Look, what's your name?"

"Jane Doe."

"Dough as in you make a pie?"

She grinned. "Why not? And you're . . . ?"

"Von Holz. Dieter." He almost clicked his heels. Stepped closer. "You're experienced, or they wouldn't have sent you. Margo told me about you," he added. "You look older in your disguise."

That's the point, she almost barked back. Did he know she was wanted?

"Where's Margo?"

"Plans changed. She sent me with your instructions."

Trust no one.

Kate eyed the Nazi aristocrat, trying to figure out her gut

instinct about him. "I met your brother a few days ago," she said.

For the first time he looked shaken.

"*Nein*, he's dead," he said. "There must be a mistake. My brother, Margo's husband, is dead."

"Your brother's very much alive," she said.

"Alive? Impossible."

Now she knew why she'd been tasked with observing Officer B, catching his speech patterns, his traits. So she'd be able to prove it when she needed to gain Dieter's real trust. "He's got a faint lisp, and a mole on his wrist."

Unimpressed, Dieter von Holz expelled a rush of air. "Easy to say. That's in all the reports."

Kate swallowed hard. "He's rude, too. Called me a brood mare." She watched his eyes narrow in suspicion. She tried the last thing she remembered. "When he eats he perspires. His pine cologne stinks."

Dieter's eyes widened.

"*Mein Gott.*"

She almost smiled at his reaction.

"Sound familiar?"

His knuckles clenched. "Where?"

"Can't say," she said.

"A POW?"

He'd figured that out. It couldn't hurt to confirm.

She nodded.

"He's four years older than me," Dieter said. "Spoiled—indulged his whole life as the wonder boy first son. He's smart, it's true. But we disagree politically. I spent two years in England when my father was stationed in the embassy. Attended Cambridge—only a year—but I met Margo there, and introduced her to my brother."

"Cambridge?" Kate repeated. Margo had attended Cambridge?

"My brother was . . . is an engineer. Margo's older brother went to Cambridge, too; she'd visit him on the weekends. Young and impressionable then."

"When was this?"

"1936. That's when she got political in Cambridge and so did I. Life-changing."

Kate felt her own suspicion reigniting. "There's no way Margo has been with your brother for six years. She was engaged to a man who died at Dunkirk."

Dieter shook his head. "A cover story. They married in secret. Her family tried to break it up—the earl didn't want Margo marrying into a German family, no matter how many castles we owned."

Earl—so Margo was an aristocrat? Like people in the pages of that hoity-toity magazine *Tatler*. Kate's scalp itched under her wig. Why hadn't she known any of that? Why had Margo been so secretive about her past?

"They ran away and lived in Germany for a while. You know she speaks flawless French and German. Her mother was European, grew up partly on the Continent. But things got . . . complicated for them . . ." Dieter trailed off, then added, "Now it's too dangerous for her."

What kind of double life was Margo living?

"What's too dangerous?"

Dieter averted his gaze. Sighed.

"Like I said, I walk a fine line coordinating with London."

There was something wistful and cunning about him at the same time.

"Margo's ill. She needs help. And she's under surveillance. But once you remove the target tonight, I'll get her to the plane. I'll figure out a way."

She'd have to take what he said as true. For now.

Trust no one.

"Who's the target?"

"An officer named Kurt Lange."

"I'll need a photo. Can you get me one?"

Dieter nodded. "There will be a party at the Hôtel Lutetia in a reception room off the bar. That, however, could change."

"Any windows?"

Dieter shook his head.

Kate's confidence ebbed. Wasn't this Dieter risking his life meeting her?

Or was it an elaborate ruse?

"I'll need his room number."

"The hotel's Abwehr headquarters are highly guarded. I can try to get him near the window in my office, which faces boulevard Raspail. Second floor. Right across from the Cherche-Midi prison."

Hard to set up a position for a good shot. "Better if we do it outside the hotel."

"You mean out on the pavement?"

"Right in front of a crowd. It will look like a random attack. Can you get him drunk? Ask him to join you for a cigar. Say your mistress is giving you trouble and you want his advice or something. You'll figure it out."

"At ten o'clock. All right. What's your backup plan?"

Seat of the pants, she thought but didn't say. "Can you get me a floor plan? Showing exits, offices, service doors. Can you do that?"

"Yes."

What was the name of the square across from the hotel? It came to her.

"Meet me in Square Boucicaut opposite Bon Marché," she said. "Third bench from the statue. Thirty minutes."

He glanced at the time. "Forty. If I can't stay, I'll have taped what you need below the bench."

"I want contact with Margo," she said.

He showed her a thick vellum card. Kate read the embossed black letters. *Dr. Fabien, le Centre hospitalier Sainte-Anne.*

"Leave word there where she can reach you."

Kate memorized the phone number and stuffed down her worry. Right now she had a target to take out.

"Are you prepared?"

She nodded. With a shoulder mole containing cyanide, a lipstick gun and wood-soled shoes filled with explosives, she was ready.

Left Bank

⌒

Kate's hands shook as she walked down narrow streets. She was aware of eyes watching her. Within a few hours she'd be out of Paris. She just had to shoot Lange and get Margo.

And survive.

She had to keep a low profile, stay invisible. Her disguise worked so far. She could do this.

Focus, girl. Concentrate.

She found herself turning down a cobbled passage—one she remembered well. Cool air emanating from the old stone that rarely saw daylight chilled her arms. On the stone wall, she saw the familiar painted blue *DUBONNET* ad for the popular apéro. Those red geraniums spilling from the windows, the limestone portico leading to another crooked passage. Why had she turned down this passage, of all places?

She inhaled the baking scents, felt the uneven cobbles under her feet—all of this reminded her of Dafydd. They'd walked here hand in hand. She felt his warmth, the joy when he made her laugh. Remembered how he'd stopped to sketch the striped cat by her feet.

The café was still there. Where that gorgeous man

picked her up on a warm September afternoon and never let go.

Someone was tugging Kate's arm, pulling her hand. Jolted from her memories, Kate realized a young boy was speaking to her.

"Sister, it's an emergency." His voice echoed off the limestone walls.

"What do you mean?"

But ahead by the café, someone was shouting into a group of German soldiers. "Stand back, make way for the nurse."

Good God, they meant her.

Fear tickled her spine.

The passage widened here to a flower shop and a boulangerie. Instead of the usual line forming for bread by the boulangerie door, she saw a woman lying crumpled on the cobblestones. The skirt of her gray suit rode up her thighs. Kate recognized her outfit as that of the Wehrmacht female auxiliary, the type of uniform she'd stolen from the laundry truck.

The enemy.

The German soldiers, two of them, beckoned her. She didn't see any other help coming. The cobbles under the woman's head were red with blood.

She couldn't make her feet move forward. "Has anyone called an ambulance?" Her French came out stilted.

"Ambulance? Do something." The voice with a schoolboy French accent came from the tallest Wehrmacht soldier, a worried-looking blond. "Isn't this your job?"

Her job? This woman was the enemy.

Kate felt like she was underwater. Her flushed face sweated profusely.

"What's the matter with you?"

One of the soldiers was shaking her. "Do something. Help her, before she bleeds to death."

Abwehr HQ at Hôtel Lutetia

⌒

The Hôtel Lutetia manager's thick eyebrows beetled at Dieter's request.

"Monsieur, I'm not sure I can help you," he said.

Dieter didn't care if this hotel manager resented the Abwehr's requisitioning his hotel and subordinating his duties to the Reich, or if he thought himself a French patriot. "This isn't a request," said Dieter. "And I think you will."

"My predecessor moved everything around, stored things I don't know where. *Desolé, monsieur.*"

The manager's demeanor changed now to placating, helpless and the typical Système D. Dieter would normally have admired this passive-aggressive resistance. Not today.

Not when Lange was about to arrive on his doorstep.

The man had to be taken out. And his information destroyed.

Dieter pulled out cash from his pocket. Swiss Francs—the only stable currency going. Slapped it on the mahogany desk.

"Please take this for your trouble," he said. "We'll keep this between us."

The hotel manager took in the wad. Within the blink of an eye had swooped the cash into his pocket. Stood up, took a binder from the shelf and handed it to him.

"This should meet your requirements."

Dieter thumbed it open to see the building plans, floor by floor. "One more thing," he said. "See that Herr Lange is given the corner window room on the third floor. He likes that room."

The manager's brows had a life of their own, Dieter thought.

Before the man could reply, Dieter doffed his cap, clicked his heels and left.

A Passage on the Left Bank

—

"Please get this crowd away," Kate said, aiming for calm authority.

She hoped no one would pick up on her shaky French. Her accent. Or the tremble in her voice.

Oh God, why did this have to happen now?

Her stomach tightened with apprehension.

Step up, girl, she could hear her pa say.

She snapped her fingers and pointed to a woman. "Get me water, napkins." She knelt down on the cobbles.

"She's bleeding," a man was saying.

Monsieur Know-it-all stating the obvious. There was always one in the crowd.

Struggling out of her navy cape, Kate spread it over the cobbles, careful to slide the cartridge casings into her pocket first. She hid the Welrod and kept her crossbody duffel bag, which held her dismantled sniper rifle, across her chest. She turned the woman to lie her straight and flat, loosened her collar and gray tie and elevated her legs on the step. Go with simple and work from there. An ambulance should arrive soon.

The young woman could have fainted from the

unseasonable heat and hit her head. A heat stroke complicated by a head injury. Maybe a concussion.

Kate smoothed back the woman's hair, took the arriving
napkins and applied pressure on her forehead to stop the
bleeding.

"Don't let her swallow her tongue if she's an *epileptique*,"
said that irritating voice from the crowd.

One of Pa's ranch hands suffered from epilepsy and it
hadn't looked like this—no mouth foam, limb stiffening or
restlessness.

"Forget those old wives' tales."

Kate remembered seeing another ranch hand, Tom,
pass out from overwork and dehydration in the barn outside Salem. Kate had been six years old, hadn't known what
she was seeing. She'd watched her pa pinch Tom's skin.

"Shoulda noticed," he'd said.

Now Kate pinched the skin on the back of the woman's
hand. It tented, stayed raised—a telltale sign with her sweating.

"She's dehydrated."

That bought her some time as someone went running
for water. But what if the woman had a concussion? Hell,
Kate wasn't a nurse.

Finally the water arrived and Kate lifted the woman's
head. She stirred, opened her drowsy eyes. Sipped.

"Hope you know what you're doing, sister," said the same
irritating voice.

So did she. Sound authoritarian and often the hecklers
back down. She looked into the faces of the Wehrmacht
soldiers.

"Has this happened before?"

They shrugged.

She discovered a wrist bracelet with a medical tag, matted by sleeve threads. It read *Blutgruppe A*, her blood type.
No help there.

In the woman's pocket she found an ID. Useful. Kate slid this into her own.

Kate tugged the woman's skirt down over her knees with one hand as she kept applying pressure to the wound. Soon the bleeding stopped, and Kate managed to get more water down her. Thank God. But a limp lifelessness clung to her. Kate cradled her, worried that she'd passed out again. Passing out was never good. If the woman had suffered a concussion she had to be kept awake.

What could she do with soldiers watching her?

Worst case scenario the woman's heart stopped.

She imagined the blame. The interrogation. A firing squad.

"She needs the hospital. Quickly. Where's the ambulance?"

A soldier shrugged.

"Ambulance!" Kate's voice rose.

Worried, he looked around. For a moment confusion painted his face. Panic in his gaze.

Just like how she felt.

Then suspicion sliced his eyes.

"Don't you have antiseptic in your bag?" he said, edging closer. "Bandages?"

Terror clutched her insides. Her throat tightened.

Believe.

"This woman's suffered a concussion," she said. "If no ambulance is coming, get a taxi."

She had to make him buy it. Pointed to the street. "Taxi." She summoned authority in her voice. Barked, *"Now."*

Obediently both soldiers went to the corner. This gave her time to think.

She had to get away before they discovered she wasn't a nurse.

The woman blinked listlessly. Kate could tell she was coming around.

Thank God.

She'd be taken for care. Kate removed the navy cape, sat the woman upright against a planter. The irritating voice was carrying on a self-important conversation with someone.

Now was the time.

Before anyone noticed, she slipped into the boulangerie behind her. She put a finger to her lips, passing the baker in his white cap at the oven, walked right through to the rear and left by the back door.

She had to hurry to meet Dieter. All this business had taken valuable time.

But not entirely useless. She'd pocketed the poor woman's ID—and her military pass booklet, which contained ration coupons, passes to restricted buildings, transport vouchers—you name it.

Everything Kate would need to enter Hôtel Lutetia and infiltrate the Abwehr HQ.

Right?

The plan formed in her mind.

Now if she could just fit into that damn uniform she'd stolen from the laundry van.

Square Boucicaut, Left Bank

—

Kate made it to Square Boucicaut, the leafy hedge-lined green square across from the Hôtel Lutetia and the fancy department store le Bon Marché, without incident. But on the dark green bench where she was supposed to meet Dieter sat a svelte woman with a navy cloche hat over one ear. She wore a matching wool jacket and wide-legged trousers. Kate had seen trouser suits like that in British *Vogue*'s wartime fashions as "utilitarian chic."

The woman was striking in the latest couture, with her pearls and Hermès handbag. Was she a fashion model?

Don't get distracted.

No Dieter. Maybe she was late and had missed him. Or maybe this was a setup.

Concentrate.

Wary, she approached the bench. Stepney had told her, nine times out of ten, meetings in the field were a waiting game, showing up in the agreed window at the location hoping the contact showed and that they weren't under surveillance. Or got so nervous they gave themselves away.

But not here. Not now. Every minute counted.

She sat down next to the chic woman in her cloud of *L'Heure Bleue* by Guerlain.

Had the woman sat here reading a newspaper by chance? She could be a look-out. A collaborator.

Kate reined herself in. Stepney's rule etched in her brain—*never assume.*

So far, no Dieter.

The woman lifted the newspaper, *Paris-soir*, blocking the view of her moving mouth.

"What's the code word?"

A deep Polish accent.

Code word? Kate's mind scrambled. What else had Stepney neglected to instruct her on?

Children ran past crunching over the gravel path.

She took a chance. "Janek?"

The woman set down the *Paris-soir* paper. The front page rustled in the breeze.

"About time," she said. "You're late."

This woman was straight out of a magazine, with full red lips, light mascara and a porcelain complexion. Double agents meant double trouble. Kate felt for the lipstick gun in her pocket.

From an open window across the square floated an operatic voice practicing the scales.

"Dieter sent me."

Why hadn't he come himself?

"Who are you?"

"Call me Jaro, for now," she said.

The Pasteur doctor's cousin?

Before Kate could ask, Jaro smiled and set her gloved hand on Kate's wrist, leaned forward. Intimate.

"The Hôtel Lutetia plans are inside the paper."

The woman knew Dieter and had the plans Kate needed. Could she trust her?

Stepney had said trust no one.

Kate folded the paper and slipped it inside her cape. She'd go with this for now.

"Where's Margo?"

"It's complicated."

What else was new?

"I'm tired of hearing that," she said. "All I'm getting is the run-around. If she's in trouble . . ."

The woman silenced her with a tight squeeze of her wrist. "We might be watched." Jaro leaned closer, pecked both of Kate's cheeks and whispered, "Later."

And like that Jaro glided away over the gravel. Disappeared behind the thick clump of linden trees.

Kate's nerves tingled. She wanted to get the hell out of here. Now. Forget this mission more fraught with complications by the minute.

Was she being strung along? Was Margo even alive?

Kate lowered her gaze, still scanning the square for anyone who'd eyed them, for any sign of movement. No one.

Kate gave it another moment. Took a deep breath. Unless you were looking for it, why would you suspect a middle-aged Red Cross nurse with a lined face and support stockings to be a twenty-something American sniper?

Two men in black SS uniforms strolled into the park. Their high black boots crunched the gravel in unison. And they headed right toward her.

Square Boucicaut, Left Bank

—

Kate's fear was palpable, like a wire brush raking down her spine.

Idiot. Go. Move.

She stood and walked toward the trees, keeping to a measured pace, her insides screaming.

The sleeve gun's metal shank gave her goosebumps. She had to get away.

Had the woman who passed her the plans pointed her out to the Gestapo, too?

She flipped open her compact. In the mirror she saw the Gestapo striding toward the boulevard Raspail. In the other direction.

She felt a wash of relief. Still her anger bubbled at Dieter for switching things. Bringing Jaro, an unknown, into the mix. But he hadn't turned her in yet—that was a good sign, right?

Time to control her emotions. Otherwise she might as well hand over her weapons and surrender. Give up, bite the cyanide pill.

How could she rescue the woman who'd saved her life by letting fear rule her?

Keep Margo front and center. Operate on the original plan—Margo was alive until Kate had proof otherwise.

She forced herself to cut off those thoughts. Focus. Find a place to read what she'd been given.

Down the Métro steps. She headed down the tunnel to the other exit across boulevard Raspail. Everything about the Métro bothered her—the close quarters, being underground and the high chances of getting picked out for questioning.

She pretended to consult the large Métro map displayed on the tiled wall. An *indicateur d'itineraires,* one of the fancy ones that lit up the stations with little red lights to the destination. She chose a random station, hit a worn black button and when the stations lit up she walked in the opposite direction.

Then a whoosh of air shot through the vents into the tiled tunnel and Kate found herself alone. Alone until the next train let off passengers. She opened the paper, saw several pages of the plans clipped together. A note in pencil:

Garage on rue d'Assas. Ask for Odile.

She stuffed the plans into her waistband.

All she had to do was keep walking, go up the steps, blend in with the crowd on the street. Don't look back.

Ahead on the right loomed the Cherche-Midi prison, to her left sentries at the Hôtel Lutetia's steps. No way she'd get in there. Beyond lay the neon sign: GARAGE.

Rue d'Assas

———

Wary, Kate entered the dim garage. She scanned the area for guards. Saw no one.

Hôtel Lutetia, across from the Cherche-Midi prison and opposite Square Boucicaut, formed a point in the triangle bisected by boulevard Raspail and boulevard Saint-Germain and rue de Sèvres. All close and within one hundred yards of each other. An easy shot.

Now she stood dwarfed in a cavernous place under an arched ceiling with dust-coated skylights. Surrounding her were Michelin tire signs, bare shelves and parked cars, Renaults and Citroëns, dust on their hoods, some outfitted with the *gasogéne* contraptions on top, among a real potpourri of police vans from the prison opposite and Mercedes staff cars for the Abwehr headquartered practically next door. Even some Kubelwägens, German jeeps, property of the Wehrmacht. This must be some kind of depot.

Her mind ticked over an idea.

Old oil slicked the stained floor. The smell of burning rubber lingered in the air. Kate saw a lit, glassed-in office overlooking the shop floor. By the time she reached the door, it was opened by a stocky man in a blue cap.

"*Bonjour.* I'm looking for Odile," she said.

A petite woman at a typewriter looked up in the neat office. Frizzy hair escaped her bun; the woman was about five foot tall when she stood. Her thin, penciled-in eyebrows matched her narrow, pursed mouth.

She nodded at Kate, cranked the typewriter's black rollers to spool out an invoice.

"Take this to the Renault, Emil," she said, handing him the invoice.

Emil made motions with his hands.

"I explained the repairs, Emil," she said. "Monsieur Gault understands."

Emil's hands moved again. Signing, he was signing. A mute mechanic.

Odile, assuming she was Odile, signed back. Transfixed, Kate watched the hand and finger ballet. A now seemingly reassured Emil took the invoice and disappeared on the shop floor.

"You're Odile?"

"No names, please. This way," she added, in a thin, reedy voice. Kate followed her through another door, then another and into a cavern. Humid and metallic smelling. Odile unpinned part of a tarp draping the arched stone.

Another tunnel.

"You're English? Dutch? Polish?" asked Odile.

A moment's indecision hobbled Kate. But she'd walked into the belly. Might as well deal with the beast.

"Let's say Canadian."

Odile expelled air from puffy cheeks. "Hopefully your cover's that you nursed overseas and forgot how to conjugate verbs properly. You couldn't even pass as a Québécoise."

That bad? Kate shot her a withering look.

"Let's get to work."

"Do you have something to show us?"

Show us? Who did she mean?

"It depends. Who's us?"

"The others need to meet you."

A coldness seeped into her bones in the dark tunnel. Filled with unease, she caught hold of Odile's elbow.

"What others?"

"If the decoy plan works, you won't have to open your mouth."

Already it sounded like too many people. She worked alone. More than herself and it was one too many.

"No one mentioned a group."

"Think of it as a team. I'll explain."

They'd reached some kind of pump house, or a part of the sewer. Huge tanks connected to pipes crisscrossing the ceiling. The greenish light filtered from above, striping the concrete. A faint whiff of chlorine reminded her of the high school pool in Beaverton.

A man perched on a red velvet high-back chair. On the table in front of him were a set of chalk diagrams, and a steaming bowl next to a red and silver tin of Viandox, the cheap meat broth served in cafés. Celery salt beside it. Medieval. A poor man's feast in the greenish glow.

The man gestured to an empty chair and shoved the steaming bowl across the table. Accompanying it was gravel-gray bread—probably made from chestnuts.

She hadn't eaten since yesterday. Only had the chicory coffee this morning. Even this looked good.

"*Merci.*" She sat down, longing to get the hot wig off and scratch her scalp. For a moment of peace to study the hotel plans.

Then she felt something sharp at her jugular. The razor edge of a knife from behind her.

"Who the hell are you?"

Couvent des Soeurs du Sacré-Cœur

⁓

At the convent gate, Dieter smiled at the nun who handed him a small woven willow basket of chestnuts, which obscured the plans in the bottom.

"*Merci*, sister," he said.

Chestnuts meant danger. Code for dismantle and move out.

The nun nodded. "We've got too many chestnuts, monsieur. But I'll just take one, *merci*."

Code for the mother was gone. The baby remained.

He knew the baby would slow her down—she had to escape quickly. Yet in his heart he wondered how she could do that. Leave her own child. A tiny thing, completely dependent on her.

Never mind. The baby would be safer here. He'd move him later.

Dieter blamed her difficult birth—a hemorrhage and a long hospital stay. He questioned whether she'd bonded with the baby at all. Dieter knew what living through this war was like—nerves scraped raw, constantly alert, so careful of every detail, action. Margo never let on. But how did mothering a newborn fit in?

Dieter would worry about the baby later. For now, all that mattered was Lange.

But would the American be able to pull it off?

———

Lange parted the heavy drapes, his fingers moistened by musk oil. His favorite aphrodisiac. Around him the brothel's flickering candlelight illuminated writhing bodies. He heard gasps of pleasure, in the corner the crack of a whip. Slaps. All tastes were catered to here; everything was available for a price. This brothel, which catered to the Tobruk elite, offered girls, boys, young women and old and everything in between. When bored with young girls, Lange would savor Madame Leila, who'd grown up in a harem. He imagined the old hag—with her heavily kohled, lazy-lidded eyes—was his mother. He'd make her moan. Her flabby thighs, her cries of pleasure, her massages excited him like few did.

Except Magda.

Magda taught him new games and never bored him. She was a sexual chameleon. He couldn't get enough of her.

Magda, an English aristocrat, manor born, had been raised tri-culturally between a Bavarian castle, a Swiss finishing school and a London townhouse. Magda was a rare and unique English woman, cold and crisp on the outside, but hot and insatiable inside. A product of her upbringing and some class system he didn't understand. But he didn't need to.

He felt her rubbing his thighs. The spreading heat. Madame Leila was gone. Magda's hot breath on his—

Screeches, thumping. A blast of cold air.

The Ju 52 transport aircraft landed, yanking Lange from his dream. Drool dripped from the corner of his mouth as the plane taxied on le Bourget's runway. Quickly he wiped his lips. He was sitting on the hard trestles in the cargo bay used for Rommel's reinforcement divisions. The Ju 52, escorted by two Bf 110s over the Mediterranean, had been a bumpy flight, thanks to the sirocco.

But lured, as he let Magda believe, to Paris, the city of light in the darkness of war, he'd be able to kill two birds with one stone. He didn't care if this liaison was a *scheiss* Bolshevik.

Then a rendezvous with Magda. His reward.

Or maybe he'd reward himself first.

No one would know he'd arrived. He'd leave no trace. Nothing official, no proof to sting him later. He was tired of being only known as Rommel's golden boy. He was more than that and Berlin needed to know.

But if Rommel heard Lange had gone AWOL from his Libyan post and not shared the Allied plans discovered by the sheikh he'd be court-martialled. Or worse. The Gestapo.

Not like he hadn't done it before. The thrill excited him. That surging adrenalin coursing through his veins at doing the unexpected and risking everything.

Let that fool Schlüssel think he'd wine and dine him. When the Abwehr in Paris twigged on his coded message, he'd given a false arrival time. Once he made it to Paris he'd vanish like smoke. Going AWOL meant he had to cover his tracks.

Afterwards, he'd report to the Wolf's Lair in the Polish forest. Maybe the Führer would bestow on him the black iron cross for bravery.

His mother would be proud of him. For once.

Down the airstairs and onto the oil-stained tarmac. He breathed in the smell—gasoline, pine, coffee from the canteen, the soft breath of wind carrying an autumn chill. Europe.

He had never felt at home here. He belonged in the desert.

"Transport, sir?" asked a Luftwaffe mechanic.

Lange nodded.

"Through the terminal and to the left."

He found a military staff car to take him into the city. Lange dismissed the driver.

"That's irregular, *Kaporal*," said a non-smiling man at the staff pool. "We require drivers to accompany all commissioned staff."

He needed this to be a trip he'd never taken. Under the radar all the way.

"You'll need to sign the logbook, sir."

"*Ja, ja*, of course," he said, scribbling something unreadable.

Once the driver pulled onto the main motorway into Paris, Lange had him drive to the local train station near le Bourget. By the station he gave the driver a pack of cigarettes and fifty Marks, and told him not to report for duty and to meet him here tomorrow, same time.

"*Verstehen Sie?*"

The driver pocketed the money and cigarettes and left.

Lange took the wheel and pulled away. He avoided the motorway, used back roads. Soon he grew aware of a gray car following him. Watched it in the rearview mirror. Instead of rejoining another entrance to the motorway into Paris he kept to the back road. Not five minutes later the gray car popped up in his rearview mirror.

Did the Gestapo have spies at the *aéroport?*

Of course they did. Himmler's henchmen had their noses in everything.

Just their style, too.

But what did the Gestapo want from him? And how had they found him? The constant rivalry between the branches vying for Hitler's favor was something he hadn't missed.

He couldn't lose the car on this narrow provincial road winding through villages and farm fields. He scanned the horizon, the looming Parisian outskirts. He considered returning to the airfield and hopping a plane to Berlin. But forget Paris? His goals? Magda?

Fail before he even made it into the city?

To the left, bordering a furrowed field with abandoned carts, a cleft of trees hugged the roadside. He pulled under the trees and parked, then jogged over to a weather-beaten two-wheeled hay cart. Awkward, heavy, the cart fought him each step of the way.

By the time he'd lugged the cart to block the road, he could hear the car's engine approaching.

He stood on the roadside, waving to flag down the car. "Help, *s'il vous-plaît.*"

The gray Traction Avant, the Gestapo car of choice, slowed.

"*Problèmes?*"

A man wearing a wool cap pulled low on his brow emerged from the car with those strange backward doors. This was a French stooge hired to surveil Lange. He could smell it.

"A big one."

"That's crazy." Now the man replied in German, a light accent. "Who'd leave a cart in the road?"

"No idea. Can you help move this?"

The man looked around. "Where's the farmer?"

He didn't seem to buy it.

Lange eyed the vacant field, a clump of cows in the distance. Otherwise empty land until the next village.

"Hey, I'm late, mind helping?"

Lange gestured for the man to push the wheel. As he hesitated, Lange leaped forward and grabbed the man's right arm, shoving him to the ground.

"Who sent you?"

"I don't know what you mean."

A rumbling engine, like that of a truck or bus, drifted across the field.

"I'll ask for the last time. Who sent you?"

Lange had pulled the long desert knife from its sheath on his calf. He held it just above the apple on the man's throat.

"Last minute." The man gasped. "All I know, I get a call, answer and do the job."

"What's the number?"

"What?"

Lange pulled him tighter.

"How do you contact them? Get paid?"

The man's Adam's apple bobbed as he swallowed.

"My notebook."

Lange searched his jacket pocket. Found a thin brown notebook with a phone number followed by a column with dates and amounts.

Convenient.

"You keep busy, eh? This the number you call?"

The man's eyes bulged. His words came out in a rattled stutter. "Let me g-go. P-please, I won't s-s-say anything."

"No, of course you won't."

Lange slit the man's throat from ear to ear. The sharp

blade slid through skin and sinew easily. He kept him face down so the blood dripped onto the road. Still, he'd have to clean up later.

Lange dragged him to the Traction Avant trunk. He removed everything from the man's pocket—*Carte d'identité* and a Métro pass.

An amateur. Contracted by the Gestapo for small-time jobs. Lange counted on being out of the country by the time they IDed the corpse.

Le Garage on rue d'Assas

Kate's tongue, dry as sand, stuck in her throat, a whisper away from the blade. The dental prosthetic altering her mouth bit into her gums.

Caught. And she'd walked right into it. Why hadn't she kept alert?

Only herself to blame.

Which didn't help.

She wished she'd trained in the barehands killing techniques with Wilkes.

She was angry. Her own damn fault. Scared. She felt the blood draining from her.

This mission had reeked of amateurs—it was thrown together, not thought out. Without directions, people made mistakes.

Focus. She had to concentrate. Wiggle her way out of this.

Or die trying.

She tried controlling her breathing, aware her nostrils flared in terror. If only she could reach her sleeve gun.

"Answer me," said a man's heavy-accented voice. "Who sent you?"

She managed to swallow. Breathe. Had to talk her way out of this.

"People sent me to take out a target," she said, almost in a croak. "But you know or you wouldn't be here. Who are *you?*"

A clanging noise, followed by a shout in German, sounded before he could reply. The man at the table pointed a gun at her. A leaded window cast thick green light.

"Did they follow you?" he asked.

"Me? Odile brought me."

Perspiration dampened her neck. Odile had disappeared. The loud footsteps were approaching.

"Let me go," she said. "Hurry."

No one moved. Couldn't they reason out that this would feel different if someone had betrayed them? As she listened, the footsteps faded away.

Odile had returned. "It's the pool maintenance and German guard on rounds. As usual."

She felt the pressure lessen as the knife came away from her neck. Instinctively, she reached up. Her index finger came back with a bead of blood. The man with the knife stepped away. Her eye caught on a thin volume sticking from his pants pocket titled *Poèmes.*

"So you're the poet?" she said, steadying her voice. It was a gamble.

His eyes narrowed in suspicion. "How do you know?"

"I'm a mind-reader." Tempted to tell him his tradecraft was bad, she pointed to his pocket. "Aren't you my contact?"

"It depends," he said.

"On what?"

She had no time for games. Or stupid partisan infighting, which seemed the Résistance hallmark lately. "Either you're against the Boche and will assist with my mission or—"

"Assist you? Our unit's independent. We're the MOI, *main-d'oeuvre immigrées.*"

Another splinter underground movement?

"Which is what?"

"We're workers and partisans loyal to the party. Following socialist guidelines."

Communists! She hated politics. Couldn't care less. But the Commies she'd dealt with were pricklier than cactus. Self-important, too.

Just what she needed right now.

Before the argumentative poet could go on, Odile shushed him. "We must hurry." She nodded to Kate to eat. As Kate hungrily spooned up the broth in the bowl, Odile unfolded a black tarp with a chalk diagram and Xed a spot. "Here's the Hôtel Lutetia. Notice the quartier, the streets radiating in front. We're on this side under the pool."

No wonder it smelled like chlorine. She imagined Dieter taking her target for a swim—no, too many variables.

Kate reached for a piece of chestnut bread. Vile as the broth tasted, she welcomed the warmth trickling down her throat.

As Odile continued chalking out locations on her map, her low voice carried quiet authority. Calm, controlled, emotionless. It took something for a squirt like her to command the unruly Commies. Something Kate didn't have.

Learn and listen to her, Pa would say.

But wasn't Odile scared inside, like she was?

"We need your MOI team to create a disturbance at this corner," she said, making an X by the hotel entrance. "Draw manpower away."

"This plan's new to me," said Kate.

Odile shot her an irritated look.

"Once MOI creates this disturbance, the target will be in position to be taken out."

Target . . . Her target? Dieter had seen Margo's message.

He'd agreed to get Lange, her target, out front of the Lutetia at 10 P.M. How did these guys fit in? Was Dieter in on this group? Their leader?

"Where does this tactic come from?"

"The same person who gave you the Lutetia maps." Odile's mouth pursed.

Dieter. Or Jaro.

Kate turned to the poet.

"What kind of disturbance?"

The poet shrugged as if it weren't his problem. As if working together wouldn't disrupt his plans. Kate's shoulders tightened.

"Our attack will be like the others," he said.

Attack?

"What do you mean?"

"My disturbance will seem random. A distraction for the main show. You."

Unease traveled up her spine. The more who knew about a plan, the more could spill it.

She stared again at the Xs. "On whose orders?"

"Random as wildflowers in the field. Old Armenian saying," said the poet with a wink.

"You're not French?"

"We're all mongrels here," he said, "with three strikes against us."

"That's not my business, but why do this?"

"We fight fascists."

So these were saboteurs. Down and dirty, on-the-ground recruits. Could she attempt to trust them?

Trust no one.

"No one runs us or thanks us," said the poet. "But if we don't act, who will?"

Kate kept quiet. Her eyes on the men at the table. A disparate group she couldn't get a handle on.

"We're workers, Communists, some Jews, and all foreign."

Kate wondered if that was why Margo had teamed up with them.

"That's four strikes," said Kate.

KATE HUNCHED AT ODILE'S DESK in the garage office, dialing the number she'd committed to memory. The number Dieter had shown her on the embossed card.

"Dr. Fabien, please," she said.

"Not here," said a muffled voice.

Kate couldn't tell if it was male or female.

"Margo?"

Quiet.

"Tell her Cowgirl's at . . ." Kate read off the number on the black rotary phone dial face. "ODE8444."

The phone clicked off.

Nothing felt viable. Or sat right with her.

When something felt off, it usually was, Stepney said.

Yet Margo had sent her a message using Kate's code name and referred to Adonis—which only they knew. She'd need to work with this bunch: a ragtag group of Communist partisans, Margo's Nazi brother-in-law and Odile the garage owner. Make a plan B. Somehow prepare.

Remember her instructions.

She unpacked her supplies, unwrapping the vest with its pocket of small explosives and carborundum. Took out the rest from her hollowed-out wood platform shoes. Twenty pounds lighter, she breathed easier. She demonstrated to the MOI partisans how to use the items; explained how to add and mix carborundum, a mineral silicate in grease form, into a grease cylinder in an SS truck. The poet jeered at the small explosives she took out.

"About as useful as firecrackers," he said.

"Firecrackers are great distractions. Didn't you say you were going to cause a disturbance here?" Kate pointed to where Odile had drawn the X. "Set the timer switch and stick them inside a dead rat. Do you understand?"

Odile shook her head. "*Attends,* if the trucks break down, the garage will be at the top of the list for reprisals. That's a death warrant."

Kate had seen this stuff in action. An abrasive that took its sweet time—hence the beauty of it.

"This gritty compound cycles through before it's absorbed and clogs up the engine. The breakdowns occur miles away from the starting point."

Odile set down the chalk and flicked the dust off her hands. "How can you know that?"

"I've used it before. To the Germans, you're just a parking garage. They wouldn't expect sabotage here."

Odile's eyes blazed. "How long before they'd blame us?"

Kate almost said she wouldn't suggest this if it were dangerous. But she couldn't lie. It was.

Le Garage on rue d'Assas

In the garage, Kate opened her bag in the creaking cabinet ready to change into the *Wehrmachthelferinnen* uniform. Sickening Nazi symbols decorated the sleeves. Would it fit her big-boned frame? With this uniform and the stolen ID, she'd have credentials and blend in unnoticed.

But the few phrases of German she'd picked up left a lot to be desired. Face it: the moment she opened her mouth she'd be dead.

She removed the dark brown wig and brushed it out, letting her scalp breathe for a minute. She stepped into the skirt, pulled it up her thighs. Held her breath and tugged it over her hips. Let out her breath. Not bad. Snug, but she could live with it.

The crisp light-gray shirt buttoned—just. She looped the dark tie around the collar and knotted it as best she could. The fitted gray jacket with darts clamped her ribs like a straitjacket. Damn—it hurt to breathe.

Using her teeth, she broke the jacket's inner seam, unpicked where it followed the lining. She did this on both sides until she felt breathing room. Better. She'd have to

keep her arms tight to her sides to disguise the looseness—
and the sleeve rifle.

Next she pinned up the wig into a relaxed half roll low
on the back of her neck, like she'd seen German women
wear their hair. Put on small round dark frames. The thick
lenses masked her age, made her look myopic and vulner-
able, the disguise magician had told her.

Were there regulation shoes? She tried to remember. So
much whirred in her head.

This had to do for now.

But it was the small things that pointed one out as a foreigner or a spy—looking left instead of right to cross the
street. Not using both knife and fork to eat. Details got you
killed.

She'd step into the lion's den.

Believe.

Be this person. Inhabit this world.

Accomplish your mission, then disappear in the woodwork.

Concentrate.

She stuck the dismantled Lee-Enfield pieces into
her skirt's rear waistband. It hurt like hell pressing on her
spine. As soon as possible she had to get a regulation German bag.

Kate grew aware of Odile's voice in a side office. She was
talking on the phone, words rolling off her tongue, semi-
guttural yet sing-songy.

German.

Alarm bells screamed in Kate's head.

Trust no one.

A Roneo duplicator machine, its metal roller glistening
in the dim light, stood on a makeshift desk fashioned from
an old door. Dull gray paper sheets printed with vile smelling purple-blue ink held calls to action: *Vive la Résistance.*
Seems they ran a clandestine press down here, too.

Right under the Nazis' nose. Still she didn't trust any of them.

Odile hung up the phone, turned, and without a change of expression handed Kate a note.

Two words on it:

Room 312.

Odile nodded, set the paper in an ashtray and lit a match that flared with a *thupt.* Seconds later, it was ash.

If this was Kate's mission, why wasn't Margo in the picture? Or was Odile a double agent? Maybe even sending her to kill the wrong target, someone vital to the Allied war effort?

"Where'd you learn to speak German? You sound like a native."

Kate watched her for a reaction. Odile only smiled.

"Me? I grew up in Basel, where we speak Swiss German. My father ran a garage just like this. Didn't you hear my Schweizer accent?"

The words had sounded less harsh to Kate. The consonants rolled.

Every agent is involved in the war for their own reason, Stepney had taught her. Agents must share ideals or there could be no trust—the mission would not succeed. *Ascertain your contact's motivations. It boils down to Money, Ideology, Coercion or Ego—another acronym for you. MICE.*

What were Odile's motivations, she wondered?

"Our group speaks many languages: Polish, Armenian, Spanish, Italian," Odile said. "But you Canadians and Americans don't speak other languages, do you? I read about this."

Calling her a country hick? In rural Oregon's harsh winters, survival was the language one learned.

"Who gave you the info, Odile?"

"Same one who gave you those plans."

Jaro via Dieter? The chlorine smell overpowered Kate. It permeated her clothes.

"You've worked with them?"

"You mean do I trust them? That's funny coming from you because I sense you don't."

Astute observation.

"They check ID at the Abwehr," Odile said. "You'll be stopped at the door."

Kate pulled out Elke Moeller's ID. "Not with this."

Odile nodded. "Smart. Then you're on your own. For now." She paused. "But yes, I trust the poet, and so should you. You need his people. And I trust Dieter. He is German but there are people he cares about involved in this."

Play dumb.

"I don't understand."

"You'll find out. You're receiving a package tonight."

KATE SPENT TEN MINUTES MEMORIZING the hotel plans, which included the pool area diagram, before she climbed the rungs of the metal ladder.

Focus. Breathe. Believe.

She found herself in the women's changing room. On target. She remedied her shoe situation by stealing what looked like a regulation black leather pair of brogues with laces from a locker—almost her size, thank God—along with dark colored tights to cover her old lady support hose and a canvas khaki shoulder bag.

She stowed the disassembled Lee-Enfield pieces inside, re-arranging the Welrod sleeve gun to shoot from inside the bag.

Kate rubbed off the mirror's condensation with the jacket sleeve, stepped back and surveyed herself. A middle-aged Frau with full cheeks—but she needed something else to complete the look. What was it?

A quick rummage in a locker found a cake of black

mascara and tiny lash brush which she moistened with her tongue. Young or old, the German women she'd seen wore discreet mascara despite the Führer's edict that Aryans have fresh scrubbed faces and no lipstick. Brushing the cake mascara back and forth, she teased out her lashes to show her eyes behind the glasses.

She angled the narrow cap over her forehead, a few inches above her right brow. Regulation, like the women she'd seen parading in the street.

No one knew *all* her plans. She was a lone operative.

Given all the players, she liked the odds better.

Abwehr HQ at Hôtel Lutetia

Where was Lange? Why hadn't he arrived? Dieter needed to know.

And to update the sniper.

Outside the door to his office he heard his latest *Wehrmachthelferinnen*—these auxiliaries came and went like ants—talking on the outside line. Dieter drummed his fingers on the thick blotter, then picked up the phone and called his Luftwaffe contact at le Bourget airport.

"The Marseilles flight's delayed," his contact said. "The weather report indicates sandstorms. The sirocco's blowing bad."

"Grounding flights?"

"As of half an hour ago."

Dieter ran through the possibilities. Lange could have taken the train. Worst case scenario, he'd headed straight to Berlin.

"What about an earlier flight?"

He couldn't leave anything to chance.

"*Nein*. No, wait. The daily military cargo flight arrived an hour ago."

"Any passengers?"

"Not supposed to be, but there was a last minute add on the manifest. K. Egnal."

"K. Egnal?" Dieter repeated the unfamiliar name, and it clicked. Lange spelled backwards.

Kurt Lange was in Paris.

"*Danke.* I owe you."

"Of course you do. Dinner at Maxim's?"

Hôtel Lutetia Lobby

———

"*Papier, bitte.*"

The smiling military man, handsome apart from his pitted cheeks, gave an abbreviated bow, like a short forward dip, and stretched out his hand.

Kate, standing in the heart of the Third Reich's Parisian military intelligence headquarters, swallowed hard, her knees trembling. Pulled out Elke Moeller's ID with her thumb over the photo.

He took it from her grasp and checked it.

Kate willed down her panic, the cold fear clutching the roots of her hair, making her teeth hurt.

If she was caught with a bogus card and mismatching photo she'd be arrested, sent across the street to the Cherche-Midi prison and shot in the morning. Probably after having everything she knew about her mission tortured out of her.

"*Alles in Ordnung*, Fräulein Moeller." He slapped it back into her waiting hand. Winked. "*Schöne Frisur.*"

Didn't that mean nice hair? Was he flirting?

Ducking past him, she glanced at Elke Moeller's photo and then herself in the glass door. Her loose chignon was a definite improvement over Elke's severe bun.

She found herself in the middle of the art deco hotel bar, which was thronged with Germans. Glasses clinked; cigarette smoke spiraled up to the dropped stained glass ceiling. On the other side of the exquisite mahogany bar, a singer in a simple black dress sang a German *Lied*, accompanied by a piano-playing officer. The bar's ambiance took her back to before the war. Almost enough to forget battles raged and the men sitting here were enemy occupiers.

The Abwehr "dormitory," as well as their headquarters, it appeared. Men with duffel bags and room keys hurried by, showing that it continued to function as a hotel. Across the lobby, the elevator and stairs swarmed with Abwehr clutching papers, chatting and laughing. She didn't stand a chance of getting upstairs with this crowd.

Her heart thumped so hard she thought it would jump out of her chest.

Breathe.

Think positive. These weren't the dreaded Gestapo. Small mercy at least.

She'd gotten this far, she could do this.

Couldn't she?

Act on her information. Move.

If she went to room 312 now, she could wait there until 10 P.M. when Dieter would get Lange outside on the pavement, the Commies would stage a distraction and she'd get him in her crosshairs. However, no guarantee that Lange wouldn't return to his room with someone, and then she'd need to kill both.

Eyes down, she kept to the outer tables, aware she was the only female besides the singer. At reception, she consulted the Abwehr directory and realized that there were two Dieters. Panicked, she made herself calm down. Think.

One worked on the first floor and the other, Dieter von Holz, on the second. Was that him? Two high-ranking officers stepped up beside her—she noticed their lapels and shoulder insignia and the oak leaf on their collars.

Her fear mounted. Fizzed down her spine. Every nerve tingled.

Kate avoided the elevators. She climbed the staircase into the enemy's hive of intelligence. The nest of spies.

Conversations hummed, teleprinters droned and cigarette smoke stuck in her nose. A mundane office where they greeted each other with Heil Hitler. No one paid her the slightest attention. On the first floor, the gray mice worked at desks in an open-plan meeting room, scurrying in and out of offices like they were hunting for cheese. Off the corridor was the telephone exchange with a row of operators.

Look busy. Don't stand like a lump on a log.

Kate scooped some swastika-stamped papers from an empty desk and kept walking.

Brisk busy steps took her to Abteilung I, Lt. Kol. Dieter Kretchmar's division. The man behind his desk had white hair, a limp. Not the Dieter she was looking for. Still she'd had to check in case she'd bungled his name in panic. Kate kept walking.

The fading tinkle from the piano drifted from downstairs. Applause. She needed to hurry.

On the second floor—what would be the third floor in America—she noticed a quiet had descended. Only a few desks were occupied. She followed the arrows for Abteilung II for Dieter von Holz. She kept her eyes straight ahead, as the others seemed to do. She headed past what seemed like inter-office memo slots, looking at the papers inside. As if she could read them—German gobbledygook with a lot more swastikas stamped on them like thick evil spiders.

"Ist fertig für den Abend."

Kate looked around. It was a young woman addressing her.

What in God's name did that mean? Her disguise would
pass scrutiny only until she opened her mouth. She nodded. Winced. Touched her jaw, which she'd puffed out
with false uppers. Moaned for effect.

Behind the young woman she spotted Dieter von Holz's
office.

Kate nodded at the young woman. She tried for her best
German accent. "*Ja, ja.*"

And she kept going. Striding purposefully and holding
the random papers she'd picked up. Act like you belong
there.

Phones were ringing and when the young woman didn't
stop her, she started praying she could reach Dieter's office.

Abwehr HQ at Hôtel Lutetia

———

Dieter's boots clicked over the art deco mosaic in the hotel's entry. Exquisite. A boat on choppy water. Each time he walked over it he remembered the Romans had called this river outpost that would become Paris Lutetia, inspiring the hotel's name. The mosaic illustrated the centuries-old motto of Paris: *Fluctuat nec mergitur.* She is rocked but does not sink.

Dieter headed upstairs, careful to avoid the offices of the foreign service espionage department, the counter espionage and especially Kommandur Oscar Reile, responsible for the sabotage and counter-sabotage counter-espionage services *Abwehr Leitstelle* III.

He had to work with them. And trusted none.

Kommandur Reile prided himself on his double agents. Dieter kept his eye on Reile's every report. Reile scared him. Smart—frighteningly so. A short Prussian with an axe to grind. They'd been in the same school, Reile a year older and top of his class. He was quick at fitting disparate pieces together—at taking advantage of circumstances.

If Canaris's plan didn't work soon, Reile would figure it out.

Admiral Canaris's latest memo warned Dieter to keep

Lange's visit under the radar. From whom was left unsaid. Dieter's orders were to remind his boss, Schlüssel, that this site was a military HQ, restricted to military staff and the Reich's *Kommandantur*.

Just another thing to deal with. That wasn't his job. Dieter snorted. Schlüssel snuck his mistress and her cronies in all the time. He wasn't alone in that. Canaris paid lip service to regulations and turned a blind eye.

Up the broad stairs to the mezzanine overlooking the bar atrium and the dining room. He checked a small banquet room. Then another.

Where were they?

The film stars and starlets, hungry aristocrats, anti-Semitic intellectuals and poor writers whom Feldstaffel Gerhard Heller dragged along with his approved publisher, Gallimard. Gallimard printed books on requisitioned paper Heller had found forgotten in a government storeroom. Vile stuff.

Had Schlüssel's mistress, Lili, changed the plan? Or had his boss changed his mind? He still needed Lange's agenda to plan and to get to the sniper.

What an odd one, he'd thought seeing her at the Pasteur. Nervy, big-boned and watchful. Could he trust her ability? He'd need to stay extra alert.

Dieter just missed colliding with Marcel, the maître d', supervising a waiter loading a trolley of Christofle silverware, Baccarat crystal tumblers and delicate Sévres porcelain.

After apologies were exchanged, he padded down the lush carpeted hallway.

Elegant dining was another perk. The Abwehr, Schlüssel reminded him, had to keep up their standards. Surrounded by this excess all his life, Dieter had had enough of it. Time to change the guard.

Squeals of laughter erupted from somewhere ahead.

"Star anise? *Mon Dieu, non.* Never. I'm allergic."

Lili appeared in a pale rose sequined dress that looked as if it had been sewn on her. Maybe it had. Her long blonde hair curling on her shoulder had a tousled, wind-blown look. Contradictory and seductive at the same time. But that was a Frenchwoman, wasn't it?

"Where've you been, Dieter?" She waved what looked like a menu in her blood red lacquered fingernails. "I'm hopeless at organizing, can you help?"

Lili, a conniving opportunist, used her assets to get by. No different from the others in her entourage. But smart and one who had an instant take on people.

An alluring little viper.

"I'd like to, of course," said Dieter, "but you-know-who told me hands off. I can always reserve upstairs at brasserie Lipp for backup."

Lili moved close. Her perfume drifted over him like a net. Her nostrils flared as if smelling him like primates did to ascertain friend or foe.

Everything about her was primal. Intoxicating. Oozing raw female power.

Her lazy smile answered him.

He wanted to crawl inside it. To feel the small of her back arched, her long legs wrapped around his waist . . . What was the matter with him?

"Of course you will," she said.

Will what?

Admiral Canaris beckoned him down the hallway. Some-how Dieter snapped back to himself, shook off the cloud of perfume. He clicked his heels.

"Excuse me," he said.

Almost too late, he'd registered what she held in her hands; the menu for hors d'oeuvres, underneath it notes he recognized as a schedule.

"Don't be silly," she said, "you're more organized than me."

"Of course, I'll help you." He nabbed her notes and turned to greet Canaris.

Admiral Canaris grinned. "You're blushing like a school-boy, Dieter."

It showed. Why did this woman affect him so? He loved Renate, his wife. But he hadn't felt this shiver with her for a long time, not since their honeymoon on the Baltic. A cold, sexless marriage. No children. He'd been guilty of taking comfort in the arms of another.

Dieter wanted to sink into the plush hotel carpet as Admiral Canaris took his arm. The chief, a short older man who exuded warmth and steel in equal measure, led him toward Dieter's office.

"That's the problem with this place, Dieter. Everyone warned me. Use a fancy exclusive hotel as HQ and you're asking for trouble. But look at the top brass requisitioning the Crillon, the George V, the Meurice—*Gott im Himmel*." Canaris took him aside under the sconce before the elevator. "Watch out for Schlüssel, Dieter." He looked around the hallway. "Our plan is imminent. Stop this Lange. Prepare."

"*Jawohl*, Admiral." Dieter's chest expanded. Proud to be part of Canaris's coup to overthrow the government. The Führer wouldn't live to see the new month.

Abwehr HQ at Hôtel Lutetia

One of the carved double wood doors to Dieter von Holz's office stood ajar. Kate kept moving through the corridor, eyeballing the outer office for a clerk, staff, or an Abwehr officer. Tried to keep her breathing even and her fear in check. To look busy.

So far no one.

Don't overthink. Find Dieter, get info on her target. Insist Dieter cough up Margo's location.

She might not need to go to Lange's room. She preferred to assassinate Lange on the street. Easier to get away and grab Margo.

Playing it by ear, she slid inside Dieter's office. Took stock of the natural light from the window to the street, the view of the Cherche-Midi prison with its sentries opposite. She considered Dieter's office layout: his ornate Louis quinze desk and the period chair positioned across from it, the metal file cabinets. The porcelain light switches, lamps, and paucity of electrical outlets. Only two she could see. Examined the room for any furniture or mirror that would reflect the sun or streetlight. Scanned it again for a possibility—shoot Lange from here? What was the clincher item she could take advantage of?

Footsteps creaked on the wood floor coming this way.

No way she could hide behind the door for long. No time to move and get behind the file cabinets. She dove under the desk, hoping to God her butt didn't stick out. Why didn't the Louis quinze desk go to the floor, instead of just halfway?

Voices. Rustling papers. Dieter?

She could see two pairs of shoes—a woman's and a man's—from where she hid under the desk. They stood right in the office doorway. Her heart thudded in her chest.

"*Entschuldigung*, but Kaporal von Holz has gone to a meeting." A woman's voice came from the office entrance. "You can give me your message."

One of the mice, evidenced by her black shoes, who spoke English with a thick accent. The man in brown tooled leather shoes answered.

"That's disappointing." A deep voice with a cut-glass English accent. An Englishman in a nest of Nazi intelligence? "Can I wait for him?"

Kate's stomach dropped. These damn spindly gold-leafed legs wouldn't conceal her for long.

"Against regulations."

"But he needs to see this, it's important."

"I'll see that he gets it."

No pushover, this mouse.

"Better yet, let me leave it here for him. Sealed and waiting on his desk."

"As you wish. Your name again?"

"He knows it."

Why couldn't he be done and get out of here?

"I'm required to make a note for Kaporal von Holz."

"Just tell him Starr."

Kate held her breath while this altercation wound down and hoped to God they wouldn't spot her.

The door closed. They'd left.

Close shave. She couldn't count on another one. But who was this posh Brit Starr?

Dieter von Holz's Office

———

Kate crawled out from under the period desk. Daylight was fading; she knew she couldn't wait for Dieter. Or get caught by whoever walked in here again.

Dieter had told her the Lutetia was now fully under the command of Berlin and the Abwehr's admiral, Wilhelm Canaris. As military intelligence headquarters, the Lutetia certainly housed interrogation work. At least it wasn't SS headquarters, where Kate knew there were torture chambers in the basement. One British agent had suffered Gestapo interrogation, escaped from a camp and survived—his accounts were included in all agent training.

Kate wanted to talk to Margo. Suddenly, dark thoughts took over. Why had Margo requested her help and then vanished? Dieter had said she was ill—was she even alive? Was she captured?

Kate needed to find her.

She picked up the phone to call Dr. Fabien again and heard, "*Bitte*, Kaporal von Holz."

A switchboard. Terror-stricken at her stupidity, she managed an "*Entschuldigung, danke.*" Hung up.

Maybe it made more sense to go to room 312. Hide

before she'd get discovered. Could the schedule be there? Had she been stupid not to head there first?

Margo's note said only 10:00—inside the hotel or outside was the crucial detail. Without the target's schedule she would be operating in the dark. A successful assassination took planning. She'd had little, but the plan B, outside on the pavement with the partisan distractions, might work.

Her gaze fell on Dieter's open calendar, some scribbles and curlicues in the margins. The letter the Brit Starr had left for Dieter.

She used a paper knife and slit the side open. Loud voices in German came from outside.

Her hands shook. Open it, she urged herself. Hurry before someone comes in.

A typewritten sheet containing a code key for a radio operator. And a note.

Dear Dieter,
I'm hoping our arrangement continues. My rent's due.
If you want more like this, you know where to meet me.
Evenings at 7.

Creep. Starr was selling out a British radio operator.

Kate couldn't dwell. Hard as it was, she must focus. She had a mission in two parts. Either one felt as strong as jelly.

She couldn't wait any longer.

She tore a page from last week's calendar. Wrote, *Agenda?* Slipped it inside the envelope after removing Starr's letter. Replaced the envelope on Dieter's desk as the slime Starr had left it.

Kate opened the door, picked up a file from the top of Dieter's cabinet. Before any of the women looked up, she strode across the outer office with purpose. Mounting the stairs, she answered the courteous *"Guten Tag, Fräulein"* with a nod. Prayed she'd reach the third floor without having to open her mouth.

No worries there. None of the officers seemed to expect a reply. She found room 312 on the rue d'Assas side facing the Eiffel Tower in the distance. Below lay a café and a boutique selling gloves, on the horizon blue slate rooftops and pepper pot chimneys—postcard pretty, except for the enemy who thronged the pavement.

Her target could be here, and she'd take him out. Or not, and she'd wait in his room.

Her insides churned. Was she killing the right man? Or was she a pawn of her enemies?

Yet her target was a man who was serving the country who'd killed her husband and daughter.

It's them or us, Katie, her pa had told her when they hunted wolves in the snow. You know what to do.

Kate pretended she was about to knock as some men crossed the hallway.

She slid her lock-picking kit out. Toggled the tumbler. But something was wrong.

The door was unlocked.

Room 312, Hôtel Lutetia

Kate turned the doorknob, her lipstick gun in her left hand. The first thing in her line of vision was a maid, who looked up from fluffing the bed's duvet.

"Ah, *excusez-moi*," said Kate.

A cursory glance revealed no one other than the startled maid. Kate looked for signs of habitation—a bag, unpacked clothing, toiletries. Nothing. A pristine room with chintz-covered furniture awaiting its guest.

The room phone, black and old-fashioned on a wire stand, trilled. Kate should back out, pretend this was a mistake.

"*Attendez, s'il vous plaît, madame,*" the maid said, addressing her formally.

Kate went with her gut feeling. She'd been expected.

The maid turned to answer the phone. Kate pocketed her lipstick and waited.

"*Oui?*" the maid answered. "Room 312."

She turned and handed Kate the phone.

Swallowing hard, Kate put the receiver to her ear.

"Follow new instructions."

Kate didn't recognize the voice.

"Who's this?"

"Not important. New venue Hôtel George V, modify plans accordingly. Target in suite 1413. Execute and remove briefcase."

Her heart dropped.

Another network? There were spies everywhere here. There was no one she could trust.

Kate felt the maid's eyes on her.

She lowered her voice. "Wait . . . what about Margo?"

"More soon."

Click.

The maid pulled a photo in color from her pocket. A dirty blond-haired ruggedly handsome man, tan, full lips, piercing blue eyes and sharp cheekbones. "He's your target. Medium height, slim. Got it?"

Kate nodded. Committed it to memory. The maid slipped the photo back into her smock and accompanied her to the door. At the armoire she took out a knee-length black coat. Folded it, slipped a piece of paper into the pocket, then handed it to Kate.

"Go to the rue de Sèvres service exit," said the maid. "Follow those directions, then destroy. Wear this the minute you leave, keep your bag under it. Wait at the corner of rue du Cherche-Midi for ten minutes. If your contact doesn't appear, proceed with your new telephone instructions."

She took a duster and followed Kate to the corridor, pointing her toward the exit.

After the maid's whispered "*Bonne chance,*" Kate padded down the stairs past the men coming up, keeping her head down until she reached the rear service stairs diagramed on the paper. Past the steaming laundry, the black coat tucked under her arms. She wondered if the Commies in the garage had sabotaged the trucks and put the explosives in the rats yet.

She'd find out.

By the time she reached the corner, she'd belted on the black coat with the dismantled rifle in her bag under it. She felt glad of it covering her uniform. She put on the thin wool cap she found in the pocket, stuck her straggling chignon inside. After several hours, her makeup had started to flake off and had required an urgent touch-up. In the rear service stairwell, she'd reapplied the foundation and redrawn the age lines. Now she could be any middle-aged woman waiting for a bus or headed to the market.

A cutting wind had risen. Momentary sadness flickered in her when she saw the empty pedestal at the cross street—once it had supported a metal statue, but the Nazis had melted it down.

Kate wished she had a shopping bag or some other prop to blend in. Nervous, she kept her hands in her pockets and tried to melt into the buildings.

She waited ten minutes and no contact approached her. She walked up rue du Cherche-Midi toward rue d'Assas and the garage. Should she check in with Odile and the Commies?

Kate had to focus. Her job was to shoot the target, get the documents. All the rest was up to Odile at this point.

So caught up with her thoughts she tripped on the pavement. A hand caught her and pulled her into the doorway leading to a courtyard. Spindles of fear danced up her neck.

"Were you daydreaming?" Dieter hissed. "You're being followed."

Her heart clamped. Idiot.

He pulled her further into what appeared to be a long *porte cochère*, a carriage entry for what would have been a coaching inn. Now they were hunched on the floor of the concierge loge, vacant and musty, behind a stained floral curtain smelling of grease.

"I just followed the instructions."

He put a finger to his lips. Flicked his lighter to illuminate a card with an address, a name written in ink, and Dieter's signature.

Whispered: "Whatever happens—I mean whatever—go to this address, pick up the package, and get it on the plane. *Verstehen Sie?*"

Kate nodded. Slipped the card into her shoe. "What's wrong?"

"Everything's heating up," he said. "This isn't the only thing happening."

"Meaning what?" Kate wanted to hit him. First, he'd been late, then he'd scared her out of her skin. "Quit hiding things from me."

He looked around. Refocused his intense gaze on her. "It's better you don't know."

A cold pall settled on her. He was right.

"But I haven't reached Margo and she's why I'm here. What's wrong with her?"

He glanced at his watch. "She'll tell you. Just go with the instructions."

"Where's the target? And if someone's following me?"

"If they haven't come in here by now, you're fine. Just take off that *Dummkopf* hat."

He stood up, peered out the smudged concierge window, and came back to her.

"Wait two minutes then go out."

He buttoned his black leather coat with the Nazi insignia and was gone. Her pulse raced as she watched the seconds tick by on her watch. She had forgotten to ask him about the package.

Two minutes passed and she made her way to the door. Checked.

Nothing screamed out at her. Keep going. Follow the plan.

She reached the street and turned right. At that moment, a sickening thud echoed, followed by a crash, the tinkle of glass, a scream. A body was lying in the cobbled street. A shopkeeper in an apron was pointing at a car screeching down rue d'Assas. For a brief second she saw a face and then the car was gone. An old woman turned away. Motioned for others to do so, too.

"Lock your doors," she was saying. "Close your shutters before the jackboots come."

A bubble of fear rose in Kate. Then she saw the body, the black leather coat still belted. The man in a pool of blood. Dieter.

"There's going to be German reprisals. Get inside," the old woman was telling Kate.

Bile rose in her throat. Two minutes ago he'd been alive. Saved her from whoever was following her.

But they were rumbled. Him, her, and whoever had put them together.

"Dirty *Boche*," a man was saying. "Why don't they run them all over? Then it would be worth it."

"You know they're going to take hostages. Last time it was ten for each *Boche*. Then the executions."

Sickened, Kate watched the men lift Dieter's body like it was a sack of potatoes. Soldiers were arriving. Acts of sabotage and resistance came at a price—always to innocents, bystanders.

As sick as she felt, it meant she had to move. Go. Get out of here. Now.

Like the old lady said.

Her legs obeyed; she was moving down the street as a crowd gathered. Breathing hard and trying not to panic, she turned the corner and saw the garage. But it was closed, the big doors shut. What should she do? Behind her a voice said, "Madame, madame?"

Kate's heart fell to her feet. She kept walking past the shuttered garage door. Every bone in her body, every sinew and muscle, every part of her screamed *run*. But she kept her back straight, wove along the pavement with her eyes trained ahead of her.

Get to the Métro. Hop on a train. Double back.

A hand grabbed her elbow. Terrified, she took a breath.

Always have a story ready, Stepney said. Always.

"Madame, we missed you." The poet half-smiled as he guided her to the crosswalk. Into the square she'd sat in earlier. They kept walking past the Bon Marché department store and onto rue du Bac. "Listen first," he said under his breath.

"Not here."

The first rule of undercover she'd learned was don't go back to the same place. There could be surveillance. A stakeout.

"Keep walking," she said.

"Where are we going?"

"To church."

Left Bank, rue du Bac

Inside the Chapel of Our Lady of the Miraculous Medal, a glass-sided coffin held Saint Catherine Labouré's uncorrupted remains. The saint, clothed in a simple habit, was leathery and shrunken. The Virgin Mary had appeared to her—a miracle—in the 19th century. Today the faithful made pilgrimages day and night while nuns presided.

Kate gestured to a side chapel. Votive candles flickered at the side altar, and the quiet murmurings of prayer competed with the clack of rosary beads. Kate kneeled, bowed her head, and looked for watchers out of the corner of her eye.

"Pretend you're praying, poet."

"I'm Jewish."

"Don't Jews pray?"

"Not like this, with a corpse . . ."

She nudged him. Had to get him on track. Find information.

"Why's the garage closed?"

"First you tell me why you killed the Kraut in daylight, right where we're trying to orchestrate diversions."

"I didn't kill him. Someone ran him over. I thought it was your group."

"Why would we dispose of Odile's contact?"

God, this got more twisted. What the hell happened?

"Before I tell you more, why is the garage closed up?"

"Odile got a call. The signal to leave."

"Betrayed?"

"Can you think of anything else? We escaped with the goodies. Even managed to sabotage some trucks. We scattered and then I saw you."

"You followed me coming out of the Lutetia. That was you?"

That's who Dieter had seen. Had it cost him his life?

"Good thing, too, so I could warn you. But you disappeared and then . . . the body, you hurrying away . . . I thought you'd shoved him under the car."

Who had run Dieter down? And why?

The melting candlewax aroma permeated the side chapel. For the second time the poet sneezed, wiping his nose on his stained sleeve. As the poet sniffled, Kate closed her eyes and said a quick prayer. For Dieter. That she'd accomplish it all. Though not religious by any means, she hoped being here among the faithful and being sincere counted in the big book.

She needed to figure out what was going on, though, or God wasn't going to be able to help her. There was much to coordinate, to synchronize—maddeningly she'd learned nothing from Dieter before he'd been murdered other than to pick up a package. Dead not two minutes after she'd last seen him. Her hands trembled.

Her dread mounted. They were running out of time.

The poet whispered, "Tell me whether the target's still in Hôtel Lutetia. Whether my men should continue with plans for incidents."

"He was never there. He's across the Seine at the George V. But if you don't cough up what you know so I can plan and take action, I'll find others."

He averted his eyes. Quiet for once. Around them the low hum of prayers and tang of incense.

"Quit stalling."

Then it made sense. He and his group had their own agenda. No intention of going along with a new plan.

Kate couldn't count on them. Odile and the garage were compromised. With Dieter dead, it was time to go it alone.

"Hand over the plan and we're done here."

She crossed herself.

"Now, poet."

He leaned closer to her head. "The men don't want to work with you."

"The feeling's mutual."

She extended her open palm below the kneeler.

"De Gaulle's Free French are a joke."

"Not my concern. The target's my concern."

He took a deep breath. "We're Communist Party members."

Politics.

"So? You say that like it means something to me."

"Communists aren't part of the Free French or the Allies."

Now he was telling her?

Enough was enough. "But you're happy to take British supplies and guns. Hypocrite." She got to her feet.

He gripped her wrist so hard it hurt. Tight like iron.

"She said you were coming."

"Who?"

"That one you called Margo. I know her as Magda."

Kate kneeled back down.

"Prove you know her."

"Why should I? You're the one nobody trusts."

Pompous little Commie.

"I don't owe you an explanation," she said. "But here it is. I'm here to take out the target and rescue her."

"Thought so."

Then why give her all this aggravation? Politics again? His nature?

"We got the message to scatter. That's all I know. I'm to call her contact later."

"Who's the contact?"

"That's not important."

"Not important?"

"No names, you understand."

Kate balled her fist. Angry. "We're wasting time."

"I spit on de Gaulle."

"Be my guest. I don't work for him."

A nun shushed them. They'd stayed here too long.

She gestured for the poet to stand and follow her.

Beyond the coved porticos with hanging medals for sale, she headed toward a wooden side door. Hoped it led to the courtyard garden the nuns had made famous with their medicinal herbs.

Grass. A statue of the Virgin Mary in blue robes. Beyond she found a bench under an overhang of spruce branches. He sat, and she shoved him to the far side of the bench with her derrière.

"I don't get you, poet. If you're not interested in aiding the Brits, why would you work with me? What's in it for you besides the weapons?"

The poet expelled air. Shrugged. So Gallic.

"Maybe it's because you're an American. Don't you see that when the war's over there'll be a scramble for power?"

Kate shook her head. "Like that's my business?"

"Only a small group, a minority, have any faith in de Gaulle, who's safe in London. It's us, the underground, who strike against the invader occupying this country.

Us, the Socialists and Communists, who will run France when the war ends. Until then . . ." The poet shrugged again. "We're here, you supply the ways and weapons, so killing Nazis is what we do."

"And Margo?"

He averted his eyes.

"Ask her yourself."

"I intend to," she said.

"Meanwhile, we've got disruptions to engineer. Look." He pulled out a map of Paris imprinted on parachute silk and pointed to the two ends of avenue Georges V. Both with Métro stops. "Easy enough at the métro George V, but we hit that a month ago," he said. "Alma-Marceau's better. Fast access to the bridge, the riverbank, the sewer. Fewer locals at night. But plenty of Nazis. They love the golden triangle."

"Then you need to refocus their attention."

"They parade on the Champs Élysées daily. Could have events lined up tonight."

They worked out details. All the while her mind was turning over evasion techniques. A way to escape and get the "package," Dieter's dying wish. And hoping to God she'd grab Margo in time.

Hôtel George V, Right Bank

———

Jaro knocked on the hotel suite's door. No answer. Winked at her portly *Kommandant* and knocked again.

The door opened to a dark suite of rooms.

"Ah, *meine Liebe*, Magda, hope we're not interrupting."

Jaro waltzed into the suite, dragging her *Kommandant*. "*Schatzi's* so thirsty. Needs a drink, don't you?"

Magda's complexion, normally porcelain-like, looked unearthly pale. Distracted, she kissed Jaro's cheek in a mechanical motion. Her rose-hued silk robe swished around her. As if on autopilot, she uncorked the champagne.

Jaro saw no evidence of Lange.

Madga poured everyone a flute. Jaro shot her a look and motioned her to the bathroom. Once inside the marble-tiled *salle de bain*, she turned the sink faucets on, then huddled close to Magda.

"Where's Lange?"

"No idea. He's en route."

"What do you mean? You said he was joining you then going over to the Lutetia at ten o'clock."

"He'll arrive any minute. His bags came."

"Where?"

"The butler put them in the armoire."

The invasion plans Lange carried—he wouldn't have let them out of his sight, would he? Their destruction was critical. Jaro felt in her pocket for the matches she'd brought to burn them and noticed Magda's pallor.

"What's wrong, Magda? You don't look well."

Magda squeezed Jaro's arm.

"I know you're concerned. So sweet."

"Haven't you healed yet?"

Magda's lip quivered.

"Dieter's dead. Run over. A hit and run behind the Lutetia."

Jaro's insides cramped. Someone knew.

And they were next.

Hôtel George V, Right Bank

———

Kate's lock-picking set opened the Hôtel George V suite's door.

The inhabited room, evidenced by tousled sheets and a black Gestapo jacket with lightning bolts on the collar near a trail of women's red underwear. She held her lipstick gun ready.

Laughter, splashes and occasional moans of pleasure indicated some love in the tub.

The suite's balcony overlooked the outdoor courtyard. Perfect.

An ideal shot to the room opposite. Suite 1413. Her target.

In this room were two empty bottles of Dom Pérignon—whoever was inside would probably break into the third one chilling in the ice bucket on the table. She uncorked it, twisting gently. Not a pop but a sigh, then mist. No over-spill of bubbles.

Just how Philippe taught her.

Stop it, he had a wife and child. She had to put him out of her mind. For good.

End of story.

Kate took an empty flute, poured from the sweating bottle. Sipped and savored it. If she was going to die she'd savor the Dom Pérignon first. The bubbles trickled down her throat like velvet.

Why let the Nazis drink it all?

She set two flutes on a tray along with the now-white towelled champagne. Took a deep breath and knocked on the bathroom door.

"Housekeeping," she said. "*Excusez-moi,* may I make up the room?"

Without waiting for an answer, she got on her knees, opened the door and slid in the tray. Because she kept low, her face didn't appear reflected in the bathroom's mirror, her only view the soap suds.

"Leave it . . . ah, *danke*," said a slurred voice.

After closing the door, she set a chair against it, knotting the silky underwear around the door handle and the chair. It wouldn't hold for long, but she didn't need much time. Hopefully she'd get in and out without having to shoot them.

Who knows, she thought, *those two might not surface until tomorrow, after all the Dom Pérignon.*

Or they might come out right now.

Never assume.

Kate used her sleeve to cover her fingers and dialed 9 as the engraved Hôtel George V phone instructed, then the suite number, 1413.

"*Allo?*" A woman's muffled voice.

Margo?

"Get him on the balcony overlooking the courtyard. Now."

Kate hung up.

She removed her black coat, opened the bag she'd got in the women's pool locker room and assembled the Lee-Enfield parts within seconds, then attached the custom-made cigar-like suppressor. She checked the cartridges, opened the balcony doors. Almost ready.

She spread the Gestapo jacket on the floor in front of the balcony, then crawled on her stomach into position. A perfect view.

The brisk air cooled her cheeks, which felt rosy from the champagne. Her head cleared, but a nice sensation lingered. *Joie de vivre*, the French would say. Or as Pa would say, *you only live once, so what the hell.*

It could be worse. She'd either make her shot and escape or make her shot and get captured. But she'd go with a champagne buzz, the image of her Lisbeth and Dafydd in her mind, and a quick swallow of cyanide.

Opposite on the facing balcony, a hundred and fifty feet away, the glass door had opened. Easy. Propped up on her elbows, she aligned the rifle's sight. Calibrated the target as he walked onto the balcony. She recognized him from the maid's photo and description. Lange, all right.

Teutonic and tanned, he was striking with his red-blond hair and sharp nose. His hawk eyes swept across the landscape as he looked out from the balcony. Almost as if he was waiting for someone.

For something to happen. A sniper, perhaps. Had he been warned? About her?

Several floors below in the mosaic-tiled courtyard, a few guests sat drinking at a table served by waiters. She had to take the shot before Lange turned.

She cocked the trigger, aligned the sight. Too late. He had moved away, was going inside.

She'd have to take a back head shot. Recalibrated. Then a woman's arms were around him. They were moving together against the balcony door frame. He'd lifted her in his arms.

Margo.

In a flash of a second Kate registered Margo's pale face, her intent expression, and how she tossed her head back. Inviting, seductive.

Then Margo was kissing Lange's neck, his shoulders. Keeping her head down. Laughing, he was laughing. His hand caressed the back of her neck with warm intimacy. The watch on his wrist caught the light, a fancy Swiss one costing more than any military salary.

And then his eye zeroed in on the balcony across. At Kate.

Kate inhaled. Perfect head shot.

She squeezed the trigger on her exhale. Without waiting for the outcome she re-cocked and went for a second shot. Margo, a trained agent, would get out of range.

Wouldn't she?

The low crack of the shot was distinctive, reverberating over the courtyard. She doubted it would be attributed to champagne. Margo still held him in her arms, but he'd slumped. She turned to Kate, a mist of blood on her hair, an unreadable look in her eyes. Then she went inside.

Kate sensed the people dining in the courtyard looking up.

She needed to move. But her stomach churned. The bile rose in her throat.

Sounds came from the bathroom.

Get with it.

She stood quickly. Dribbled champagne from an almost empty bottle over the rifle she left on the balcony and the jacket. Hopefully it would appear, at least at first, as a drunken mistake. Implicating the Gestapo with gunshot residue would be a nice touch. A bonus.

That would buy her some time.

She stuck his Gestapo-issued Luger in her pocket— much easier to handle and conceal—and scrunched up the woman's citron silk scarf trailing from the armoire. Paused. The Lee-Enfield was too valuable and could come in handy. Within seconds she'd disassembled the rifle.

The bathroom door rattled. A woman laughed and said, "Don't worry, silly, have more champagne."

Kate left the room, padded barefoot down the carpeted hallway to the rear EXIT stairs. In the stairwell, she removed her coat, then the tight *Wehrmachthelferinnen* uniform, which she balled up. She pulled back on the Red Cross outfit, looser now, stuffed the woman's silk scarf in her pocket.

Useful for later.

After putting on the short blue nurse's cape, she slung the khaki bag across her chest, then slipped her arms back into the long black pre-war coat.

The poet and his crew were supposed to engineer disruptions here. So far, despite them, all had gone smoothly. But that voice inside told her to get it together. Focus.

From the lobby phone Kate dialed nine, then Margo's suite. It rang and rang. Finally, someone answered.

"Meet me on Pont de l'Alma in fifteen, unless the doorman gives you a note."

Kate looked around. "But do you have the documents?"

Margo's voice came back steady. "Lange switched half of the documents to another case he sent to Schlüssel at Hôtel Lutetia."

Avenue George V

⌒

Kate had sensed the difference in Margo at first glance. Twig thin, and pale—such a vacant look in her face. Or had it been horror? Margo had held her lover while Kate shot him dead. They'd both been trained, though, to do whatever it took. Full stop.

Still, who could prepare for the murder of a living being? Kate's assassinations hadn't inured her to the toll of taking a life. Even if it was a Nazi in lust. But wartime didn't give her much opportunity for reflection.

Her nerves jittered. Dieter's death had shaken Kate to her core, and she had barely known him; she could only imagine how Margo must be feeling. Lange had been her assignment; monster he might have been, and now she had his blood sprayed all over her.

But Margo had signed on, taken the oath. They'd been told to harden themselves for tough decisions. Taking one life could save thousands.

Kate crossed the lobby, past the floral sprays. As the doorman opened the double door for her, he slipped her an envelope.

She began walking to the Métro but paused in a doorway and opened the note.

Inside she found a photograph of an Abwehr officer with the name Schlüssel written on the back. Below that in small letters in Margo's handwriting:

Cowgirl's new target. 23:00 outside Hôtel Lutetia as before. Explosives set in garage as planned. Destroy briefcase. Meet me after at le Centre hospitalier Sainte-Anne.

Her heart skipped. Damn Lange. Complicated things even in death.

Stepney's instructions replayed in her mind: deliver the penicillin, shoot the target and extract Margo. But now she had Dieter's package to take—his dying wish—and a new target dictated by Margo.

Whatever game Margo was playing, Kate didn't like it. But it seemed she had no other choice except to follow the plan and Margo would meet her.

Fifteen minutes later, Kate stopped dead in her tracks as the German vehicles pulled up at the Hôtel Lutetia's entrance. Her pulse raced. She checked her watch. 22:58.

This was wrong. None of it according to plan. The vehicles should be in Odile's garage—set to slow down.

Why hadn't the Commies known the vehicles would be used tonight? But the garage had been closed.

She pushed the questions aside.

Think on her feet, that's what Stepney said she was good at. Adapting.

So why couldn't she do it now?

Focus.

She'd improvise. Take the next best action.

Her original plan to shoot Lange outside the Lutetia now centered on Schlüssel, his contact or superior. It still could work, after all. She hurriedly searched for another vantage point to avoid the flying bomb detritus.

Several streets converged in the thoroughfare. There was the park, the two Métro entrances and exits, the Cherche-Midi prison, a closed café and the shuttered glove boutique. No one at the bus stop on boulevard Raspail. It was quiet and dark with blue glows from the streetlights, which had been painted against the air raids. Curfew.

How could she make it to meet Margo after? Steal a bike, ride the hushed streets and pray to avoid checkpoints?

She'd worry about that later.

The metal rails of the fence were gone. Taken, like the statues, by the Germans, and melted. Ridiculous, like the scrap metal donation drives for pots and pans in English villages. How were people supposed to cook?

She scurried to the niche covered by bushes. Saw the fence post she'd scouted earlier and climbed, using it as a foothold. Reached a toehold and climbed high to a birch tree branch, inside the park. The closed park had a watchman who patrolled every so often but for now she'd stay here.

Dim azure winked through the green leaves from the regulation blackout blue-painted streetlights. And for a moment, with the red from the Métro sign, it felt like a Christmas tree.

Kate checked the ammo in the Nazi's Luger from the room at the hotel. A full clip. Nice grip. Not too heavy.

Pistols like this 9mm parabellum only reached up to forty or fifty yards accurately. And that was stretching it. Still, it could be handy later.

But thank God the poet had followed instructions for once. He'd taped extra ammo for her Lee-Enfield on the tree branch. If she lived she'd thank him.

She assembled her rifle in seconds, loaded it and was

ready to fire. Kate's view took in the Lutetia's front steps with the red carpet opening to the distinctive mosaic floor. Her eyes roamed the crowd for Schlüssel, the officer who had the rest of Lange's documents. Lange, as smart agents did, must have hedged his bets.

She gave a soft whistle and heard the bushes rustle. Kate paused and looked down, noticing the poet's dark curls contrasting with the flat opaque leaves.

"Climb up here. Can you see him?"

More branches rustled. A grunt. Then he was on the branch beside her.

"He's the only one with a briefcase."

The poet nudged her. And there he was. Schlüssel. Prussian-looking with a dueling scar and a weak chin, thin legs and a large chest. Something was familiar.

She put the telescopic sight to her eye. Recognized him and gasped. The face from the car that had run Dieter down.

The Nazi deserved what she was about to do.

Never let emotion or vengeance sway your aim.

He was about five foot nine or ten. She adjusted the scope. On his arm was a woman, her blonde hair piled high with glittery pins like a tiara. A chiseled, leonine face and a predatory gaze from deepset eyes per the Lee-Enfield's telescopic lens. The blonde-haired mistress. A collaborator the poet had mentioned.

Hit your target. Only your target.

Schlüssel was doable in two swift head shots. The sniper signature. She'd shimmy down the tree, steal through the park and disappear into the Métro entrance on the other side. Or into the guard's little sentry house near the gazebo. She'd bribe or overpower him. Hide out, then escape.

But the documents needed to be found. Destroyed.

Kate waited, counting down the time.

No explosion. No flash of fire.

"Where's the explosion, poet? Your distractions?"

"Any second now," answered the poet, "unless the stuff is damp."

They waited. On the pavement the Abwehr officers, with their collabo girlfriends on their arms, smoked and awaited their vehicles.

Kate counted the seconds.

Five . . . Four . . . Three . . .

The women's clinging shimmery evening gowns glimmered under mink stoles. Or fox wraps. Ready for a night out or a soirée at the Folies Bergère.

No curfew for them.

Kate heard the poet breathing, his uneasy intake of breath.

Two . . . One . . .

Nothing happened.

Two Mercedes pulled up at the Hôtel Lutetia entrance, a troop truck escort behind them.

"What the hell happened?" the poet was saying.

"Maybe you didn't set the explosives right," Kate said.

"You gave us crap. Everything is defective."

A bad workman, her pa used to say, blames his tools.

The light had faded. The figures were still smoking but soon would mount their cars.

Never mind that nothing had exploded. Or that the Commies were inept. She had to take Schlüssel out now.

Avenue George V

—

Jaro smiled at the receptionist at Hôtel Athénée on avenue Montaigne. He knew her. She greased his palm often enough.

"Right this way, mademoiselle," he said.

He showed her to the telephone cabins off the lobby, all lush cherrywood and gilt handles. The deep maroon velvet cushions absorbed sound.

"I'll organize your telephone line. Only takes a moment."

She slipped an envelope into his pocket. Cash. The next moment he'd palm her a telegram.

Jaro had no qualms about paying for service. Or buying loyalty. He risked his job doing this. His life, if he had half an inkling.

She used most sources only twice. Any more was deadly. But this receptionist had been referred by his aunt in Poland, and his chubby cheeks reminded Jaro of her little brother's. Also, the Athénée was only a block away from the George V.

Lange's body should be on a cart on its way to the local school's incinerator. The sooner her contact knew, the better. Plus, her next instructions were waiting.

Jaro perched in the closed telephone booth. Suddenly exhausted, she wanted to curl up, even felt her eyes closing . . .

Bringgg . . . bringgg.

Jaro sat up. Alert now, she picked up the receiver.

"Line four's waiting. I'll put you through."

A clicking noise signified the line was listened to by the German at the switchboard. The telegram the hotel receptionist palmed her was addressed to a non-existent hotel guest. The ruse was simple. Effective.

Most of the time.

The telegram relayed, in code, London's message on the flight pickup in a few hours. She'd memorized the script. Coded and prepared it this morning. Thank God the shooter had taken care of Lange.

To keep up the charade that she was on a phone call and not reading the coded telegram she said, "Darling, are you there? I can't hear you. A crazy connection but if you can hear me I'm sorry I didn't say goodbye . . . What? Can't hear you. I'll try later, darling."

She lit a cigarette. At the same time, she put the match under the telegram. Watched it burn, watched the black edges curling and crinkling. She stabbed out her half-smoked cigarette on the ashes, turning them into soot.

She dunked the cigarette back in her case.

Her upper lip perspired. All that false gaiety, all the energy to keep up this front—after thirty-six hours awake, she felt fatigue hit her like a brick.

O mój Boże. Oh my God. She had to keep up. It was almost over. Just a few more hours.

Ever so careful now. Tired and groggy was when you got careless.

She took another Pervitin, even if it made her jumpy. No, just a half. That should get her to the plane. She dry-swallowed. Hated the chalky taste. If only . . .

Bringgg . . . bringgg . . .

The receptionist's signal that it was time to leave. People were asking questions up front.

A wipe of the receiver with her scarf, a spritz of Chanel No. 5 on her pulse points. The next moment she'd slipped out through the hotel's kitchen exit. Waved down a velo-taxi. Was gone.

In Front of Hôtel Lutetia

The red-faced Abwehr officers mingled, smoking, talking. Their loud drunken laughter drifted over the street. Kate couldn't get a clear head shot. Or chest shot, for that matter.

Kate watched Schlüssel's head bend as he escorted his mistress to the car, then he was leaning inside.

Time to improvise, or they'd lose their chance.

She whispered to the poet: "Where did you set the explosives?"

"Rear tires, trunk."

Kate fired once. Hit the left rear tire. Reloaded and quickly shot into the trunk. Nothing.

People were looking around. Their reaction time seemed dulled by liquor. Suddenly the officers were pushing the crowd off the pavement.

Schlüssel's car had started. She couldn't let him get away.

Kate shot again into the fuel tank. Reloaded. Again. People were shouting. Bystanders ran to the hotel entrance and were repulsed by the guards.

Kate aimed, breathed. Exhaled. Shot again.

Shouts and flames erupted.

Kate reloaded. Perspiration beaded her upper chin. She fired at the second Mercedes that was pulling out. Schlüssel was getting away. Troops spilled out of the back of the truck. Several going to offer help and douse the fire. Others fanning out and looking for where the shots came from.

It wasn't planned like this. In five seconds it should have been over—Schlüssel shot and one of the Commies nabbing his briefcase.

If she didn't hit the damn fuel tank they'd find her within a minute. Schlüssel and the documents would get away.

She fired at the front tire of his Mercedes. Then the fuel tank. Again and again, drilling shots into the trunk.

The Mercedes kept going, its flat tires wobbling on rue de Sévres.

Had the Commies screwed up or had she brought dud explosive powder?

"*Schnell . . . hier.*"

A soldier was pointing the others toward the park. To the tree above the Métro from which she was firing. They were in the middle of boulevard Raspail, getting their sights and finding their aim. Another soldier rushed out of the truck shouldering a bazooka. The poet was returning fire with his Sten gun.

A gunfight battle in the middle of the city and any moment a bullet would find her. Meanwhile, Schlüssel's car disappeared in smoke.

The soldier knelt so another could mount the bazooka on his shoulder. He pointed to the tree. To her.

She breathed out and peppered as many shots as were left in her cartridge. Go out shooting, she told herself. Leave in a blaze.

A crackling explosion thundered the ground, shaking the tree. Kate tried to hold on for dear life. But a force took over as a pressure wave sucked the air. She fell, knocking through the branches to the park.

The flash and fire blinded her. She tried to catch her breath. As her vision cleared the scene unfolded in slow motion. Flames danced. Debris rained down. Car bumpers, a tire, a woman's beaded handbag, an arm in a black sleeve with silver insignia. The stench of burning rubber, accelerant, fuel, burned flesh. She coughed.

A horror show. A complete horror show. All in less than fifteen seconds.

The Commies had come through.

And the target had gotten away.

Square Boucicaut, Opposite Hôtel Lutetia

—

"You all right?" The poet was helping her up.

Kate's ears rang. Everything sounded so far away.

He was pulling her hand. "Hurry. We need to go."

Bodies, cries, the piercing wail of a siren. Her hearing was returning. The swathe of destruction sickened her. On the boulevard, officers snapped orders at the soldiers to help victims.

Looking down rue de Sèvres, she saw the burning shell of the Mercedes.

Thank God. Relief flooded her.

But there he was: Schlüssel crawling from the burning wreck, pulling himself to his feet, gesturing for help. Damn him. She'd blown up his mistress but missed her target.

Kate took off her coat. She adjusted the Welrod rifle in her Red Cross uniform sleeve and her lipstick gun, then shouldered her bag.

"Get that ambulance from the garage. Right now. And bring it over there."

The poet had joined her. "Not enough time if you want to get Margo and make the plane."

Her mind went to Margo, then the package. She didn't

want to decide between them and the target. A difficult decision and seconds to make it.

But if silencing the target and recovering the documents would change the course of the war, she had no choice.

"Schlüssel's still alive. There." She pointed. "And with the documents. Do what you need to do. But I'm finishing this."

The poet's eyes hardened.

"I've got my knife," he said. "Together we'll take him."

Bewildered and injured people stumbled or sat dazed and hurt on the pavement as the officers attempted to take control. In the general chaos and confusion, Kate pushed herself through the crowd. Pointed toward the park as an officer came up to her.

"Make way, attention, ambulance arriving," she said.

Act like you belong. Believe.

The officer nodded, spoke in German, and motioned to a soldier.

Any moment they would have summoned troops from the prison or the casern barracks. But who would they be searching for?

Focus and act.

Anger painted Schlüssel's face. Aside from a bloody arm, he seemed untouched by the blast. He pulled the driver's charred body from the smouldering Mercedes with surprising ease. His mistress was a bloody corpse on the road.

Horrified, Kate turned away. Bystanders hurt and the target unscathed. This wasn't supposed to happen.

She had to focus on her target. The documents. If she didn't get them it would all have been for nothing.

Kate lowered her head, making as if to help with victims. Schlüssel was taking charge. He spotted Kate and gestured to her.

Panicked, she froze. All her training gone.

Now Schlüssel pointed to her. Barked an order to a soldier.

She was going to be found out, the documents would go to Hitler and she'd be shot.

Buck up, girl, her pa would say. Think.

The ambulances and troop trucks were arriving. Officers and soldiers swarmed the park and side streets. Mayhem.

Kate had to act now. She strode toward an injured woman in a singed evening dress lying on the pavement by Schlüssel. The Abwehr had covered the windows in the hotel's resto; Kate was grateful for the dim lighting.

The poet crept closer to the burning car. Schlüssel was kneeling by his dead mistress now, unleashing a tirade of German. He turned to Kate, commanding her to do something.

Now. Shoot him now.

In Front of Hôtel Lutetia

⁓

The lipstick gun was a 4mm, and its effectiveness depended on close range. Distasteful as it felt to get so close to Schlüssel's head, Kate did, and discharged the lipstick gun. Folded it back in her palm and nodded to the poet. Schlüssel, still kneeling, keeled over, clutching his temple. Kate hoped the man's yell masked the deadly pop.

No time for a double tap.

A face in the crowd turned; a young soldier looked up. Alerted by the gunshot, he caught her eye. She kept her head low among the pushing crowd, amid frantic cries for help, the moans of the wounded whom she had to step around on the blood-soaked pavement.

Get away from the target after the hit—that's what she'd been trained to do. But she needed the documents. And suddenly the poet was nowhere to be seen.

The peal from an air raid siren penetrated the night. Almost as if in response to the emergency.

Searchlights crossed the sky in wide arcs. From the outskirts of the city, white beams searched for planes. Any minute, Kate expected the pounding of anti-aircraft.

At the reeking charred car, she bent to peer in at the burnt leather. Saw the briefcase.

For once something went right.

She rolled her sleeve down over her hand, pincered the melting handle in her fingers and hotfooted it toward the arriving ambulance. The injured throng made toward the hotel's ABRI, the shelter in the basement where the staff were gesturing. Last place for her.

They needed to get out of there. Immediately.

Out of the corner of her eye, she saw the poet kneel and check Schlüssel's pockets. Pickpocketing Schlüssel, bold as brass with the Nazis all around? Where had he been? Hadn't he seen her grab the case?

She couldn't wait for him. But she needed his help to get to the plane.

The next minute he'd caught up with her, grinning.

"Found a nice watch. And a telegram."

"And it's from the Führer?" She couldn't keep the sarcasm from her voice.

"Should I check right here in the street?"

The piercing siren whooped again.

"Can you get your men to open up the garage and get a truck?"

"Why?"

"It's our only way out at curfew, with an air raid and this mess."

They kept to the shadows on rue de Sèvres, darting from one to another and making slow progress. Any moment she expected a bombardment.

Rue de Sèvres

Kate had delivered the penicillin, shot Lange, shot his contact Schlüssel and secured the documents.

Now, could she find Margo and the package and reach the landing strip in time to board the plane? She glanced up at the sky—soon it would be a full moon. That's when the drops and pickups happened.

She'd save her own hide but . . .

If they missed this flight, she'd get the radio operator to contact London and arrange another pickup. She remembered the dismal RAF statistics of cross channel flights able to avoid the Luftwaffe squadrons and antiaircraft. So many planes, pilots, couriers and agents were lost.

"My men made it," said the poet. "Hurry."

A flash of headlights. In the air came the dawdling engine sounds of an Opel Blitz military utility truck, the rear draped with khaki canvas.

One of the poet's crew, the slit-eyed one, sat in the driver's seat. A huge gaping wound oozed from his leg.

"Take over," he said, his voice cracking in pain. "I can't shift or operate the clutch."

Poor man.

The poet's eyes widened. He shoved a shock of curly hair behind his ear.

"I can't drive," said the poet. "I don't know how."

Kate shook her head. "Good thing I do. Help me."

Kate and the poet hefted the driver to the passenger seat. From her bag she took the silk scarf and tied it as a tourniquet. His face tightened in pain.

"Sorry," she said.

Rudimentary, but it would do for a while. If they didn't get out of here, it wouldn't matter anyway.

She slid the charred leather case under the seat. It reeked of smoke but the papers inside were safe. She'd checked, amazed at the maps of the desert inside. Next, she stretched out her arm with the Welrod snug against her sleeve. Made sure the trigger mechanism was handy on her wrist.

She'd driven tractors and farm vehicles. How different could a German truck be?

She stretched her leg and pressed down on the clutch, her other foot reaching and pressing on the accelerator. The clutch stalled and the engine died.

Typical. As if the Germans ever made anything easy.

Trying again, she settled the shift in neutral. Turned the ignition key, grabbed the shift and found first gear. She eased up on the clutch as she pressed the gas.

Said a little prayer.

The truck jerked forward. She smoothed down on the gas pedal and then said another prayer as she shifted into second.

Shouts came from the side street. A German military medic with two stretchers was beckoning the truck.

Kate turned to the slit-eyed man. Wasn't he called Rudi or Roger?

"Rudi, did you just steal this?"

"I'm Roger. You think they'd give it to me for my good looks?"

Definitely not.

Kate heard moaning. "How many injured are in back?"

"Two of ours. Maybe two or three others."

Kate kept her eye out for patrols. She'd have to come up with a story if there was a checkpoint or they were stopped.

First she had to drive this thing out of here. Meet Margo at Sainte-Anne's. That's what the message said.

Her heart juddered.

"What happened? Why didn't the explosives detonate in the garage?"

"Who knows?" Roger's voice sounded weak. "We set the timers. Followed protocol. With our luck they'll go off tomorrow."

"Check out the back, poet. Anyone following?"

She figured they were lucky to be driving an official German vehicle; they wouldn't be stopped unless the Germans noticed a female was driving. Or until the medic alerted the military to the hijacking of a truck.

"Where am I meeting the plane?"

"No one told me," the poet said.

"Liar. You've got to know or . . ."

A scrunch of his shoulders as he peered out under the windshield glancing at the sky. "Same as where you landed. The moon's rising, it's a good sign."

Faster. She had to drive faster. She wanted to scream at the truck's regulation dimmed headlights. She could hardly see a damn thing in the blackout. The truck was cumbersome and difficult to maneuver; she was constantly bumping over the curb.

Plowing a field with a backhoe on the tractor was a breeze compared to driving this clunker.

"The side view mirror's broken," she said. "See anything?"

Kate didn't hear the poet's reply. She was so busy shifting, clutching and driving she barely registered the commotion behind her.

"Do you see anyone following, poet?"

She turned to see why he wasn't responding and realized he'd slumped on the passenger seat, a dark red stain spreading over his chest like a flower. His throat had been slit.

She gasped.

Roger's throat was a gaping, open bloody slash. In the rearview mirror a wounded soldier knelt directly behind her with a knife in the air. Her heart thudded so hard she thought it would jump out of her chest.

She was next.

In a split second she eased up on the pedals, stalling the truck into a jerking stop. The soldier slammed into the back of her seat. Kate turned, deflected the knife with her left hand and with her right shot him in the chest with the Welrod. The stench of gunshot pervaded, the metallic smell of blood and death everywhere. His eyes were wide open.

Behind his corpse, the injured moaned on their stretchers. The truck was stopped in front of the Jardin du Luxembourg and the casern of the Luftwaffe.

Great. Like sitting ducks.

The air raid sirens whooped. Vehicles poured out of the casern. Right now all she could do was keep driving.

She started the truck up. Ground the gears but managed to get into first and turn off of rue de Vaugirard. Gasping, she took deep breaths, trying to keep her mind off the poet whose blood soaked the floor.

Her hands trembled. It took all her strength to hold the steering wheel. Keep the whale of a truck on course.

After reaching the narrow, dark and hilly streets of the Latin Quarter, she knew her way.

Didn't she?

She remembered of the many hospitals in Paris that here they went in a row; the military hospital of Val de Grâce, then the maternity hospital across from the Hôpital Cochin, past the observatory, and then the walls of le Centre hospitalier Sainte-Anne.

Ten anguished minutes later she reached Sainte-Anne. The gate was closed.

Kate honked, gunning the engine while keeping it in neutral.

No one.

She couldn't leave the poet's body, slit-eyed Roger or the German in a truck on the street. The wounded needed help.

She kept honking. Finally, a guard, rubbing his eyes, came to the gate.

"Go to the German hospital at Lariboisière," he said.

"There's wounded in the back. It's an emergency. Please."

If the truck or Kate's uniform convinced him, she still had to wait while he called a superior, then unchain the high gate, and move it aside for her to drive the truck through.

"Where's surgery?"

"Pavillion C."

Kate nodded. "Tell the doctor to meet me there."

She cursed to herself as she peered out the window trying to follow the small signs and arrows to the Pavillion.

She needed help to dispose of the bodies without the Germans knowing. Needed the poet's radio contact. His slumped form threatened to overwhelm her. For all his obstinance, he and his men had come through. She had to fight tears. Such a brutal waste.

How could she find anyone to help her? Or who'd lead her to Margo? Get the contact to get them out?

The heavy truck bounced over the cobblestones, its dim headlights striping the shuttered hospital wards, causing a ruckus.

The waiting doctor, coat over his green scrubs, looked unhappy. Thank God he was there. For the life of her, she couldn't remember the doctor's name Dieter had told her.

Finally it came.

"Dr. Fabien?"

"That's me." He shifted his feet in the night's cold and approached her as she stepped onto the running board of the driver's truck door. "Who the hell do you think you are, nurse?"

"There was an explosion. So many hurt."

The doctor's flashlight illuminated the dewed black-green foliage lining the rutted service road. Groans came from the truck. Kate heard one German man crying for his *Mutter*.

"We're a psychiatric hospital, nurse. I think you must know that. The Cochin would help you better."

Kate put her finger to his lips.

"Dieter told me you can help."

His eyebrow rose.

"First I need to meet my contact," she said. "Then you've got some bodies to bury."

Le Centre hospitalier Sainte-Anne

⸺

After parking the truck, she slipped through the trees and shadows to the building the doctor had pointed out to her. Margo stood by the wall. Finally.

A thinner, paler Margo, with her black hair held back by combs, rope of pearls over her sweater collar, and a lopsided grin on her red lips. Kate hurried over and hugged her.

"My God, are you all right?"

Margo hugged her back. Gave another weak grin. "Fine. You know me."

Did she?

There was so much to say. But more important things to deal with right now.

Kate opened Schlüssel's charred briefcase—thank God leather didn't burn—and handed Margo the papers. "Schlüssel's taken care of. He won't come after these."

"Good job, Kate. I knew you'd come through." Margo scanned the documents and hugged her again, shivering. Kate felt her bony shoulders under the sweater.

"What's wrong with you, Margo? Besides being obviously anemic."

That came out so wrong and so blunt.

Margo folded the documents and handed them back to Kate. "Carry these for now. I'm afraid you've got to do the rest."

Kate noticed how hollow her cheeks were, how deep her green eyes were in their sockets. Her skin translucent and everything about her fragile.

"I don't understand."

"It's up to you now."

What did that mean?

"To get you out of here, sure. But what happened to Lange's corpse? You mean to go back and clean up?"

"Not on your life. Jaro and I shoved Lange down the laundry chute; we wiped down the suite."

"Good. Hand me the rest of Lange's documents. I'll put them together and we'll get out of here."

"Jaro's got them."

After all this?

"How does that make sense? Who is Jaro, anyway?"

"She runs the Prague network."

"You trust her?"

Flustered, Margo rubbed her arms and pulled her sweater tighter around her thin frame. "Dieter says you met her. She handed you the hotel plans."

"Plans that we didn't need. Useless."

"She's good, Kate." Margo's voice rose with impatience. "Listen, what you did tonight was crucial. Lange was evil—a born predator. He kept everyone off balance. Even me." Suddenly Margo scrubbed her eye with the back of her hand. "Still, he charmed me. Part of me . . . well . . ."

Kate nodded. "Cared for him? Understandable. Deep undercover's difficult."

Margo shot her an annoyed look. "As if you know."

She'd put her foot in it.

"Sorry, didn't meant to sound condescending." She

checked her watch. "Look, we have to move. Show me where Dieter's package is and then we'll meet the plane outside Meudon."

Margo put her head down.

"I can't. You must go ahead."

Kate's blood drained to her feet. It took the wind out of her. She made herself breathe.

"Who is it? Who's got something on you that's so important you won't leave?"

Margo gave her a long stare. "Dieter's gone, so now it's up to me to run the underground network."

Duty? Or . . . ? Kate sensed something else behind the words.

"Time you took a break, Margo. Rested up. Look, no one's indispensable."

That came out wrong, too. She kept putting her foot in her mouth. But Margo hesitated.

Kate put her arm around Margo. Led her farther from the doctor and nursing staff who unloaded the wounded. She remembered Stepney's words: *Margo's cover's delicate and under constant scrutiny.* She looked drained. Who wouldn't after the double life she'd been living?

"No matter what, London's orders were simple," said Kate, trying to soften her voice. "It'll be all right. You'll get on the plane with me, Margo. You don't look well. London will figure out a fix. You can't be the only undercover agent here."

"It's complicated, Kate."

"You mean your Nazi husband complicates things?"

"You're reading this wrong."

"Then help me read it right," she said, struggling to keep her temper. Chilled, her body ached with exhaustion. Her legs throbbed from running. Stress knotted her shoulders. Nazis were on her tail. They didn't have much time.

Why was Margo being so obstinate? Wasn't this supposed to be the easy part?

Never assume.

"What's with you, Margo?" Kate said. "You're the only reason I took this mission. Like I wanted to see the city under the Nazi jackboot? There's a price on my head. No way you're bailing on me now."

"You Americans." Margo sighed. "Such cowboys. No subtlety."

Was that a bad thing?

"I get the job done. And I'll do what I have to do to make that happen."

Margo lifted up her bag, adjusted her dark green cloche hat. She checked her lipstick in a hand mirror she pulled from her purse. She looked like a different person than she'd been moments ago.

"You're too stubborn, Kate."

Stubborn as a mule, according to her pa.

"That's why I'm good. Get things done. And I'm not leaving without you."

Margo looked around, sighed again. Her feet shuffled in the leaves. "Sorry, but plans have changed. I wanted you to hear it from me. But I'm more than undercover."

"Meaning a double agent?"

"A little more, Kate. Best leave it at that."

"What the hell does that mean?"

All this wild goose chase to find her and now she was, what . . . deigning to tell her in person?

"What's changed?"

"Don't be tiresome." Her voice was dry, brittle, upper class. A new persona. "Time for me to get going. It's for your own good."

Kate's mouth dropped. She shook her head. "I risked my life for you. You owe me an explanation, Margo."

"Look, I'll tell you this and you must go. I work for the Soviets, Kate. Now leave and get out while you can. I don't want you on my conscience, too."

Courtyard of le Centre hospitalier Sainte-Anne

⁓

A Commie agent? Kate blinked in disbelief, but a sinking in her stomach told her Margo wasn't kidding. A reluctant awe filled her, seeing how Margo compartmentalized.

"Does London know?"

"Not yet. Well, I don't know, really."

They must suspect. But Stepney had seemed so gung-ho on this mission and rescuing Margo.

"So that means, what, you're a triple agent?"

Married to a Nazi, and now this?

Margo slapped her green gloves on her bag.

"Just get the hell out, Kate. Tell them you never met me. Understood?"

"Not until you spill, Margo. Tell me what this is about." She took Margo's hand, encircling the thin wrist within her fingers. "You can't think I came all this way to return empty handed. I owe you my life, sure. But it's time you level with me."

Margo shook Kate's hand off.

"It doesn't matter now. Take Jaro to London with the documents, we've got them all now. Lange's neutralized, Berlin will never know. Your mission's a success." Margo gave a brittle laugh. "The big fat accomplishment you needed after Copenhagen."

How did Margo know about the Copenhagen fiasco? Her stomach twisted. Had Gregory told Margo?

"Meaning?" said Kate.

"Don't get holy with me, Kate. You slept with Gregory, for God's sake. But you didn't tell me. Weren't going to, right?"

Hot shame ran up Kate's face.

"When was I going to tell you, before or after I shot your Nazi lover?"

Margo raised her hand to slap her. Kate caught it.

"That's cheap," Kate said. "I'm sorry."

"Lange was *my job*. Pleasurable, it's true," said Margo. "I cultivated him and worked hard to gain his trust and infiltrate his network."

Kate remembered Margo's memorable picnic at Oxford—strawberries and cream with champagne. How Margo abounded in secrets.

"Create an aura of mystery, Kate," she'd said. "It's half the fun. Femme fatale, a countess, a cleaning lady—I can do them all. People see magic while you obscure things in plain sight, move things around."

Kate chewed the inside of her cheek. "Look, I had no idea Gregory was your boyfriend. It wasn't even a one-night stand, just a sordid quickie on a cold, wet Copenhagen street." She tasted coppery, bitter blood in her mouth. "I shot an innocent man. A Dane. I didn't know how I was going to live with myself."

"Operational hazard." Margo shrugged. "You assassinate Nazis, that's *your job*."

"But this one wasn't a Nazi. And Gregory was . . . a distraction. A stupid attempt to forget what I'd done." Kate swallowed. "Is he—what is he to you?"

Hadn't Margot's fiancé gotten killed in Dunkirk? Or was that her cover to gain Kate's trust in training since she'd been married to Dieter's brother then?

All Margo's relationships swirled in Kate's head. The unease and creep of fear didn't help. The shadows and dark got to her. Like a stain of doom.

Why couldn't they just get out of here?

"Gregory? An ex," said Margo, looking away. "We were together a long time ago."

Then why did she sense Margo was jealous of her? Was there more than romance at stake here? Was Gregory a triple agent, too?

"I don't get it. Are you some romantic or a Commie idealist?"

"I'm a realist," she snorted. "You know what they say, war makes strange bedfellows."

So cynical. Brittle. Where had the Margo she thought she knew gone?

"There has to be a reason you're in trouble," said Kate. "Do they have something over you?"

"Of course they do. That's how this game works," she said. "At least now I've severed contact with Odile so the network can continue."

So Margo had organized with the socialists. She didn't know her network was in shreds. Kate pointed to the doctor's team taking bodies out of the truck.

"I'm sorry, but the poet and Roger didn't make it."

Margo's hands trembled. She blinked rapidly and Kate thought she fought tears.

"Margo, it's hard to believe you don't want to return to London."

"You just don't want to believe it."

The night wind rustled the damp leaves sending a scent of dank mildew. Sirens whined in the distance.

"So it was all a ruse?"

Margo sighed. She was so thin the wind could blow her away, as Kate's pa would say.

"Lange needed taking out. I could only trust you to do it."

"Me?"

"You owed me after I saved your life. We're done. Regardless, I'll make it here," said Margo. "I know too many secrets."

"Nazi secrets?"

"They're corrupt. Users. Both sides, I'm talking about. Stepney and his crowd of old school British politicians in Whitehall and Nazis in Berlin. They use us, and everyone pays the price."

The wind rose, blowing the leaves around her ankles, deepening the dank chill.

"Why did you—?" Then it dawned on her. She'd gotten emotional; hadn't looked at it with a clear head. "Did the Soviets ask you to take out Lange? It wasn't all about the battle plans he was carrying to Berlin—there was someone else?"

She remembered Starr, the slime smooth Brit who'd left the letter in Dieter's office. Obviously he was an informant who wanted paying. Was he the link? Some Commie connection who worked for the highest bidder? The tangles were unravelling; it was making sense now.

"Wrong. The Cairo decrypts made it clear to London Lange was a problem. I take care of problems, Kate." Margo shrugged. "But dealing with the Soviets is not so different. Yet they have ideals."

Ideals? What happened to King and country?

"It's betrayal." Kate shook her head. "You're a traitor."

"And you're going to get shot by the men picking you up if you talk like that."

That sobered her up. Muted cries drifted from the stretchers as more wounded were unloaded.

"It's not really betrayal, Kate," Margo said, softening her voice. "We're allies. I'm against the Nazis completely. But the Soviets are the ones who will win Europe."

"Dieter was run over by Schlüssel. I saw him. How does that fit in?"

Margo's eyes changed. Kate read hurt in them. For the first time she seemed like the Margo Kate knew.

Margo looked around and lowered her voice. "Several elite officers plan to remove Hitler. Dieter is . . . was plotting a coup. But Dieter's boss betrayed him."

Kate swallowed hard. This was taking too long. Margo's eyes darted around—she looked like she'd bolt any minute. Escape.

"Where's the package, Margo?"

Le Centre hospitalier Sainte-Anne

⌒

Before Margo could bolt, Kate gripped Margo's arm in hers tight and walked her through the dirty banana yellow leaves in the chill night air. All along Sainte-Anne's block-long stone wall. Lanterns reminding Kate of drooping tears cast dim light in the sprawling, nineteenth-century complex of stone pavilions holding wards connected by glass-awninged walkways. Every so often she heard shouts from the pavilions.

The looney bin, the ranchers called the state mental hospital outside of Medford.

"Dieter told me to call you here but I never got through," said Kate, as they crossed the hospital grounds via the windy walkways.

"News to me," said Margo.

"Did Dieter tell you what's going on with this package?"

Margo's elbows jittered and her eyes were like pinpricks. "Only that he'd use the safe house as last resort. It seems now he has. There."

Safe house?

Margo pointed to a faded red door. Through it, Kate

found a nurse's station inside a long wing of the hospital. Quiet as a convent, she thought.

"Sister, we're here to pick up a package."

Kate slid Dieter's card across the metal intake reception desk.

"How can you confirm that?" the old nurse asked.

Kate turned the card over. Dieter's signature showed along with a symbol Kate couldn't decipher. "He signed it. Regard this as confirmation."

The nurse's crow's feet crinkled as she studied Kate and Margo.

"Both of you must wait."

"But—"

The nurse had already shut the glass divider and left the reception cubicle. Kate was a sitting duck again. This late at night Kate saw few staff. But someone could be looking for them.

Margo pointed toward the restroom with a large black WC sign. "Back in a minute."

"I'll go, too. Hold on."

"Someone must wait for the nurse." Like that, Margo was gone. Kate wondered if she was ever coming back.

Kate stood in the green linoleum waiting room. The tall windows were screened by iron bars. Frustrated, feeling trapped, Kate didn't know what to do if Margo wouldn't cooperate. Her orders were to get Margo, or "Magda," back to London. Regardless of whom Margo really worked for, Kate had a job to finish.

This was her way of getting back at the Nazis who killed her family.

Something had changed Margo. Her emotions flip-flopped from stubbornness to compliance. Pale, thin and jittery—she didn't look well. Tuberculosis?

In the hallway Kate saw a passing orderly escorting a

patient—on his arms dressings mottled by dried blood, a vacant look on his bearded face.

No sign of the nurse.

Kate paced back and forth. Would Stepney treat Margo as a traitor—have her shot for treason? Was that why Margo didn't want to go to London with Kate? Could Kate extricate Margo from the Nazis' jaws to send her to death in her own country?

Bad to worse. She should have known. When had Stepney ever played straight with her?

More than anything she wanted the truth.

She sat down, but couldn't sit still on the cheap green leatherette couch.

This was taking too long. Fear tingled up Kate's arm.

Just when she was ready to pound on the glass, she heard scuffling and turned.

Margo held a pistol to the nurse's neck, one hand pushing her forward toward Kate.

"She's an informer," said Margo.

Kate noticed Margo's wild eyes. "How do you know?"

"I heard her on the phone speaking German. I disconnected the line."

"Good." Kate grabbed the loose phone cord hanging from Margo's pocket. Tied it around the sullen nurse's wrists.

The nurse hissed. "They're onto you."

Just their luck.

Kate stuffed the nurse's pocket handkerchief in her mouth before she could scream. Looked around. "What do we do with her?"

Margo snicked the cartridge. "Let's deal with her now."

"Too many bodies, Margo."

"There's not much leeway. I don't know if I stopped her in time."

Plan for the worst. They had minutes, maybe less.

"We'll tie her up there in the closet." Kate rustled the woman toward the closet door. "Hurry, get those tourniquets. We've got to go. Now."

Margo's face had paled again. Perspiration dotted her brow. She was shaking. What was wrong with her?

"Get it together, Margo."

The woman struggled, kicking at Kate while she tried to secure her ankles with cleaning rags. The rattling and banging would alert staff. The woman swatted Kate and Kate hit back. The woman caught her arm.

"Don't you remember training, Kate?" Using the raised heel of her hand, Margo chopped at the woman's neck under her right earlobe. The woman fell back in the musty small closet. Unconscious.

"It's not how hard you hit," said Margo. "It's where you hit."

"I missed that class," said Kate, tying the nurse's wrists by a tourniquet to the wall hooks.

She didn't know how long the woman would be out, but hoped it acted like heavy sedation.

With Margo's help she pushed the couch in front of the closet door, turned off the waiting room lights and, pulling Margo along, prayed the quick and dirty job would give them enough time.

"We should have shot her," said Margo.

The hall side door opened to a petite nurse beckoning them, an intense urgency in her large eyes. "You're late."

She sounded young. Was she in cahoots with the other nurse? Another plant in the hospital?

"If you're here for the package, you must hurry before they raid us."

Kate went with her gut.

"Let's go, Margo."

Kate pulled Margo's hand, cold and clammy, to follow the nurse to the next pavilion along the covered walkway glistening with mist and damp, dead leaves. A door opened as they passed, emitting a rush of sweaty hot air, moaning and screams. Horrific.

The nurse whisked them down another walkway and toward the incinerator building, heralded by a tall brick tower chimney. She pulled them into an arched alcove mottled with black mildew.

"*Alors*, our fault. *Désolée.* We'd suspected the nurse might be an informer, since her father's a patient."

"I don't understand," said Kate.

"He needs medicine. That's the Gestapo's new technique—hold something over the staff to get them to inform."

Kate tried to put this together. What could she believe?

"How many more know about the package? Us?"

"I don't know." The nurse shrugged. "You don't want to find out, right? You need to get out of here. Your package is right inside the incinerator's entrance, where you'll be guided ahead."

"Guided?" asked Margo.

"Into the catacombs."

Kate's mouth went dry. "Catacombs?"

Underground.

The nurse leaned closer. Handed her a folded map.

"When you get to the plane, give this map to the pilot. *Compris?* No one else. And if something happens, destroy it. We're near the city's outskirts. Some of the tunnels from the old rampart fortifications connect to the catacombs. Just remember, it all leads up and out."

Perspiration dampened her spine. Could she even trust this nurse?

Kate didn't like enclosed spaces. They reminded her

of the Orkney bombing; the panic of being trapped, the dread, the grief.

Margo was moving ahead. More erratic behavior. A bad feeling hit Kate. Whatever the package was, Margo wanted it.

Incinerator, le Centre hospitalier Sainte-Anne

———

Kate followed Margo into a brick, high-walled incinerator building. A toasty, woody smell—something else familiar as well. So familiar to her, so recognizable, that when she saw the baby her mind switched gears. Diapers, she realized. The smell of diapers that needed to be changed.

Her mind hooked on the memory of Lisbeth's sweet smell and chubby fingers.

Was this what Odile meant by the "package"? Thrown for a loop, she looked questioningly at Margo.

"What's going on?"

Margo's face was stained with tears.

The nurse picked up the rosy-cheeked infant and checked the tag pinned to him.

"Package 195, your son," she said, handing it to Margo. "Delivered."

Margo had given birth to a baby—somehow that's what this was all about. A scrawny little thing with pink cheeks and button blue eyes. Cooing and needing love.

Kate touched her index finger to his cheek—a soft velvet. This little thing pulled at her heart.

"Why didn't you say? How old is . . . he?"

"Four months." Margo traced the pink rosebud lips with her finger. Then hugged this tiny bundle. "His birth was difficult. I hemorrhaged and couldn't nurse. Couldn't take care of him. At the maternity home my cover was blown. I had to leave him. Disaster from start to finish."

"I'm so sorry." It made sense now—Dieter, the baby's uncle, had wanted his nephew and Margo to escape. Right?

Not exactly high-level secrecy here. The baby squirmed and Margo transferred him to her other arm. Kate's first impulse was to rush forward and support his wobbling head.

The nurse unpinned the baby's tag and tossed both paper slips into the incinerator.

"Wait here," she said. "Your guide is arriving."

The baby mewled. Hungry? All Kate's mothering instincts returned.

"Dieter hid your baby," said Kate. "Did he risk his life for you and his . . . ?"

"Nephew." Margo stiffened, cradling the child. "My son is his brother's child. But he's dead. Shot down."

Kate blinked.

"*Au contraire,* Margo. He's very much alive and eating well at the officer POW country house."

Disbelief shone in Margo's eyes.

Kate continued. "Lisps, full of attitude and a mole on his wrist, enveloped in a hideous pine cologne."

"He's not dead?" The baby squirmed in Margo's arms. She looked awkward holding him.

"Captured in '40."

It was just a guess. But from the look in Margo's eyes, Kate knew she'd hit the bullseye.

"You're serious . . . He's alive?"

"So Dieter can't be the child's uncle, right?"

Margo's thin lips pursed. She looked around the warm

room, at the swaddled infants in wooden and cardboard boxes, at the nurses tending them. Leaned close to Kate.

"Father," she whispered. "But no one must know. Do you understand, Kate?"

Struck speechless, all Kate could do was nod.

No time to think about it now. They had to get on the plane with this baby. Margo felt around in the baby's blanket, fingered an object and pressed a small hard thing into Kate's hand.

A ring. A man's thick gold pinkie signet ring with a coat of arms and something in Latin. She remembered seeing one like it on Dieter's finger.

The inside was worn smooth.

"This goes with the baby," she said. "Now I really can't go back to London."

"No, you can't *not* go back. Your husband's held in a high security facility but no threat to you. Whoever held your baby's life over you doesn't anymore."

Catacombs Entrance

———

The guide wore mud-caked boots and overalls fitted with a flashlight looped to his belt. The beam illuminated the clay limestone tunnel, leaving his hands free. Without a word he gestured for Margo to put the bundled baby in the small metal wagon. Kate struggled to keep up with him as he took off pulling the wagon down the tunnel. The air was a surprisingly moderate temperature. At least there weren't bones sticking out of the dirt, as she'd feared.

Margo faltered and stumbled. Her chest heaved. But she shook off Kate's arm, stopping to lean against the flaking limestone.

"Wait!" Kate called after the guide.

She heard a *merde*. But he paused, struck a match and lit a cigarette.

She stuck her flashlight in her belt like he had and handed Margo the last half of her pink pill. Margo, however, had already tied off her arm and pulled a hypodermic needle from her bag.

Good God, Kate thought. Margo was an addict. How

dumb could she be? Her mind went to Margo's shaking, her thinness, mood swing and those pinprick pupils. Maybe she hadn't wanted to see. Repulsion filled her.

"Is this really why you left your son? Or did your son get taken away?"

Margo tapped a vein. A thin blue line snaking under her translucent white skin. Kate saw the ropy muscles in her hands.

"I almost died from blood loss when he was born," said Margo, pricking the needle's ampoule with her forefinger. Kate heard a ting off the glass. "I couldn't even nurse him. That's why they gave me morphine. Still do."

"The nurse gave this to you, Margo? That doctor?"

A nod. "I help them. They help me." After a moment, Margo untied her arm strap and rolled down her sleeve. Closed her eyes.

She'd made all this effort for a junkie? Angered, Kate looked at the little bundle, another victim.

Margo's head slumped back. Out of it. Not now. She couldn't let Margo's addiction strand them.

Kate shook her. "Margo, for God's sake, think of your baby."

"Don't lecture me." Margo blinked, bleary-eyed.

Kate slapped her.

"Show me you care, Margo. You're lucky to have that baby. I'm fighting the bastards that killed mine. What I wouldn't give for my Lisbeth to . . ." A sob caught in her throat. She made herself go on. "Be alive and in my arms."

"I know." Margo's eyes teared, her blasé bravado gone. "I'm sorry."

Within a short time Margo had turned into a druggie Commie double agent who didn't really want her baby. But that didn't change Kate's mission.

"Hurry." Kate shoved Margo ahead, popping the pill half

herself. The man ground out his cigarette, waiting where the tunnel forked, soothing the baby with his knuckle. The baby sucked hungrily, broke away to cry as no milk came. Tried again.

"Give him this." He handed Margo a bottle and a bag with diapers. Kate realized he wore a stethoscope around his neck—a doctor. "The milk's laced with a mild sedative. Only give him half. Don't let him drink it all at once."

Watchful, he stared at Margo's eyes, felt her pulse. Everyone, it seemed, had known Margo's condition except Kate.

"Can she make it, doctor?"

"*Ça dépend*," he said, "on what you mean by make it."

Kate thought. Tough decisions were what she and Margo had been taught to make.

"For the next six hours."

He passed Margo a metal tin of throat lozenges. "Inside there's something to help with withdrawal. Our morphine's gone."

Margo's eyes shuttered. "Now you tell me."

He handed Kate a diagram. Different from the map the nurse had given her. A warren of underground tunnels designated by lines, arrows, circles and tiny, tiny writing in French.

But the devil to decipher.

"Any words of wisdom to get us where we need to go?"

"Follow the chalked symbols." His flashlight beam spread over limestone grooved by pick-axe marks. Every so often she saw a circle, a square and a broken arrow.

"Circles take us out?"

A nod, then a big sigh. "Broken arrows mean cave-ins or rubble barring your path. Stay alert, follow the circles and don't backtrack."

Already Kate felt the walls closing in.

"How long will this take?"

"Keep moving and you'll make the exit in fifteen, twenty minutes. You'll be met at Montrouge and taken to the plane."

She stared at the map, trying to see if she understood their route.

"And if we don't make it in twenty minutes?"

"You're on your own."

In the Catacombs

———

Kate re-settled the baby in the wagon and pulled it with her left hand. Margo followed behind. The wagon wheels thrummed in Kate's ears and Margo's labored breaths echoed off the walls. The limestone tunnel narrowed in the feeble flashlight beam. Her feet slowed on the crumbling gravel-like stone dust. The air felt dry and temperate—not too cold or warm.

Would they ever get out of here? Kate's claustrophobia hummed at the edges of her brain. Gnawing, inching her closer to full-blown panic. She had to keep going, keep Margo on point, keep the baby quiet, and follow the chalked circles.

She wanted to scream.

Instead she put one foot in front of the other, made herself take slow, even breaths. Trying to curb the tightening in her chest.

Dammit, she was a country girl. At home in the mountains, on the land. Not God knows how many miles underground in ancient caverns that could cave in and bury them any minute.

It wasn't natural.

What if she misunderstood the directions? Her tiny amount of confidence faltered. Had he really said follow the circles? Or had she made a mistake?

Part of her feared they'd wander down here until forever and no one would ever find their bones. What if the little one cried and brought the Germans? What if he overdosed on the dangerous sedative?

You're on your own.

Anger filled her.

"Margo . . . Margo?"

She turned to see Margo trudging in the tunnel. But it took her too long. Her stamina seemed almost gone.

"Keep up."

An answering sigh.

Kate's nerves frayed ready to split. What if she just ran?

They only had one shot of getting out of here alive.

Focus on basics. Nothing else.

"Let me borrow your scarf, Margo."

She tied and double knotted one end of Margo's scarf to the Nazi's mistress's, then to the rope. Slipped this around her shoulders. Now she could pull the wagon like the pack mules did on their ranch.

"Hop in and hold the baby."

"You're kidding," she said.

Margo weighed nothing.

"We'll go faster if you get in and I pull."

"Don't be silly," Margo said.

Kate forced herself to concentrate, breathe slowly and not give in to panic. Or anger at Margo—why was she so difficult?

"Whoever's meeting us won't wait," she said. "Get in the wagon; it'll be quicker if I pull you both."

Kate felt like a ranch work horse. She pumped her legs, ignored the scarf cutting into her shoulders. Sweat beaded her upper lip and her back protested but she kept going. Luckily, the limestone tunnel's ground was worn semismooth from carts removing stone since time immemorial.

The pain and sweat kept her mind off the idea of the walls suddenly collapsing in on them. Of being stuck down here forever.

The circle showed left at the fork. Her pace quickened. She kept her eyes on the walls.

Another circle at another fork. This time right. Now she was almost running.

Her skin burned where the rope cut into her. She stopped to pull her sleeve over her fingers and wedged her hand in between her shoulders and the rope. She glanced back to make sure Margo and her baby were secure.

When she turned forward again, she didn't see the circle anymore. She looked around.

No circles on the walls.

She'd taken a wrong turn. Lost. She was lost.

Panicked, her breathing came in heaves. She couldn't get enough air. Stop, stop, she told herself.

Tons of earth above her. The chalky limestone walls crumbling around her. They'd never get out of here.

Her breath was so jumpy, she felt like she was choking.

Too many pink pills.

"Kate . . . Kate, you missed a turn . . . Can you hear me?"

Margo's voice brought her back from fear.

"Go back over there, Kate," Margo said. "Where the tunnel branches."

Concentrate. Slow it down. Breathe.

The sweet baby smell wafted through the tunnel and hit her like collapsing limestone. So familiar and she felt a stirring in her breast. Lisbeth was hungry.

But her milk had dried up. Pain sliced through her.

"Kate? Can you hear me, Kate? You all right?"

She shook herself back to reality, as she had a thousand times before. Lisbeth was gone. But this baby, Margo's boy, was hungry. An innocent. He deserved to live.

She couldn't save her daughter but she could save him. Or die trying.

"Okay, let me back up. Hold on."

Kate maneuvered the wagon to the widest point of the tunnel and somehow turned it back around. Her flashlight illuminated a circle. Another circle at the fork going right.

"When will we get there, Kate?"

Not soon enough.

Focus on this. Almost there.

"We're close. Any minute now."

Near Porte d'Orléans

Kate climbed metal rungs that would take them to street level. At least she hoped they would. At the top, she caught her breath and inhaled air that had never tasted so sweet. A metal doorway was wedged open with a sputtering kerosene lantern.

She stuck her head out and whispered, "*Allo?*"

"You're late," hissed a voice in the shadows.

A middle-aged woman wearing a cloak and a dark scarf over her head appeared.

"There's an ill woman and baby below. I pulled them through the tunnel." Out of breath, she panted. "Is there another way to get them out?"

Her breath frosted in the evening air.

"Let me see. Meanwhile put this on."

The woman handed her a Red Cross armband and a beanie-type hat with a Red Cross logo stitched on the side.

Kate realized she'd emerged in a semi-wooded field that provided a vantage point of southern Paris, all of it smothered in darkness now with lights out at curfew. So they were on the old fortifications by Montrouge. Beyond, she figured, lay Meudon, site of the observatory and the forest with the runway. She oriented herself. Meudon must lie to the west, she believed. If only she had that compass that fitted in a button.

An old ambulance powered by *gasogéne* on its roof was parked by the bushes. She heard voices, footsteps. She stayed alert, but let this group handle Margo. Expecting trouble, she was surprised that within five minutes she and Margo, holding a sleeping infant, were on the road into Meudon. Thankful, Kate leaned back and thought for the first time that they might make it.

Margo had entrusted Lange's documents to Jaro, a woman who could be a double agent. If Margo was passing war secrets to the Russians—weren't they Allies now? Still, it didn't sit right, as her pa would say.

Or was this a technique? What training called never putting all your eggs in one basket? Either way she had half of Lange's documents from Schlüssel's bag following Margo's second instructions. Damn instructions changed all the time—but one had to stay fluid, as Stepney said.

The woman drove with her headlights all but out with the regulation dimmers. Huddled in the back with them were two men who spoke, what Kate took for Polish, to each other. The woman drove on small roads, skirting houses. Kate kept a look out for checkpoints. Even an ambulance would be subject to search.

Then they were in the woods. The ambulance stopped. Kate heard a dense hush of a world blanketed by pine needles.

Fog curled, like beckoning fingers, in a gauzy mist blanketing the dark night. Great. Just when the plane would need clear visibility to land.

The sound of a propeller and sputtering engine destroyed the peace. Beyond the trees in a clearing a plane had roared to life. She inhaled a deep breath.

Then another.

But she couldn't relax yet.

"Ready?" asked the driver.

Several lit kerosene lanterns spread light along the clearing, piercing the misty blackness. Kate's eyes adjusted. She helped Margo and the baby from the ambulance toward the plane. Damn nettles caught in her support stockings. Stinging and biting her skin.

Jaro, the woman Kate recognized from Square Boucicaut, strode forward to meet them. Jaro was wearing overalls and goggles over a pilot's leather head gear.

Kate didn't know what to make of it. "You've got Lange's documents, correct?"

Jaro pulled out a sealed envelope.

"Here."

Kate reached for it.

"But this goes to Margo. Not you."

After all this. Kate's anger and frustration boiled. The two Polish men from the ambulance were boarding the plane. Kate didn't like any of it.

"What the hell?"

But Jaro had handed the documents to Margo. "You're taking these, Margo," said Jaro. Margo slipped them in her bag and, holding the baby, headed under the plane's wing.

"Fine. We're all getting on that plane."

Kate leaned down to take out the stinging nettle. Plucked it out between her fingers.

Jaro flicked her flashlight three times. Turned to Kate. "New orders. You are catching the next plane."

"C'mon, Margo, tell your comrade to quit playing games."

But she didn't see Margo and the baby anymore. The fog spread like a film over the woods. The plane door slammed shut.

"Wait. I'm supposed to be on this plane."

The plane's engine revved. Panic hit her.

"The plane's too full. The documents must go first. We'll get the next one."

The woman was serious. This was all happening too fast.

"No way."

"The pilot can't take any more weight."

She blamed those two men. Unfair. Who were they anyway?

The plane was taking off down the runway. Without Kate.

"Hurry, we've been spotted." Jaro pulled her to the other side of the makeshift runway. "We have to leave before the German patrols get here."

And then all of a sudden the gusts of wind and roar of propellers signaled Margo's plane lifting off in the dark. Meanwhile another plane had landed and was taxiing toward them.

"I thought you were the double agent," said Kate. "A Polish Mata Hari."

"To some people I am." Jaro grinned. "But not to you. Not now. You, me, we work together. Orders from the Polish government in exile in London in conjunction with your SIS section. Your mission's code red, Cowgirl."

Cowgirl. She knew Kate's code name. SIS section was Stepney's turf, wasn't it?

"That's it? No other information? Why me?"

"You were in the neighborhood, so to speak."

Neighborhood? How cheap could the Brits get?

"It's a quick job, in and out," said Jaro. "More materials and instructions will be provided. Hurry." Then she and Kate were running toward the Lysander that had just landed.

As the door opened, Jaro said, "Good luck."

"Wait, aren't you on this plane, too?"

"Next time."

"What? Where am I going?" Kate yelled into the sound.

"Need to know."

All this unnecessary secrecy taxed her patience.

"Good. I need to know."

Jaro grinned again. The wind blew leaves into the plane door. "Cairo."

Part II

Over Cairo

—⁓—

Kate jerked awake as the plane sputtered and lost altitude. Maybe it was a forced landing. Had the Luftwaffe spotted them?

They'd stopped and refueled somewhere—an island?

Out the window three blots of honey appeared in a vast beige expanse. The blots became triangles, growing bigger and dimensional until Kate recognized this was the desert and those were the pyramids she'd seen in her history book.

They were descending in bumpy fits and starts. Her stomach went to her mouth. Any minute she'd be sick.

Why give her a mission in Cairo? She didn't speak a lick of Egyptian, or whatever Arabic dialect they spoke here. Why not send her back to London with the documents?

In her pocket she felt the signet ring Margo had given her. This should have gone with the baby.

"We're landing at Heliopolis. Put on the harness and brace your legs against . . ."

The rest was lost as the plane hit an air pocket. Bile rose in her throat.

Thank God she'd found the harness. Already strapped herself in as they'd been taking off.

By the time the plane rumbled to a halt, Kate had opened the Red Cross canvas bag Jaro had given her. Inside was her own bag with her disassembled Lee-Enfield rifle, as well as a pair of binoculars and a red-ribboned Chanel lipstick tagged *bonne chance, Cowgirl*. She took deep breaths. Jaro's gift touched her.

"Who do I take out?"

The pilot had pulled a whiskey bottle from under his seat. He took a gulp.

"I'm just the pilot. You'll be escorted to HQ."

Great.

The pilot wiped off the bottle with his sleeve and passed it to her.

"You're going to need it."

"Another time," she said.

He grinned. "Oh, and welcome to Cairo."

THE CARGO DOOR OPENED TO a blast of heat. Airplane fuel fumes hit her nose and a spray of fine grit whipped her face.

Sand lodged in her eyes, nose and in her ears. She blinked the granules out. Found small sunglasses to wear against the glaring light.

A man wearing a khaki jumpsuit and goggles with a scarf wrapped around his neck and head checked a small clipboard. Shouted over the propeller noise.

"You the item I'm to escort to HQ from this Paris night flight?" Without waiting for her answer he said. "Of course you are. Hop in."

He jerked his thumb to his Triumph motorcycle's side car—an open rusty tin can bucket.

"Welcome to Cairo."

British Command HQ, Cairo

⌒

Kate was shown into the sweltering HQ main office, where ceiling fans whirred lazily and dead flies stuck to a dangling sticky yellow spiral tape like squished chocolate M&M's. The clicking of typewriters, low conversations and familiar pungent tang of strong tea filled the sprawling room. Groupings of rattan furniture dotted the space bordered by adjoining offices and colonial shutters.

The motorcyclist, who'd introduced himself as Richards, was rusty haired, with a matching mustache. He'd removed his jumpsuit and cleaned up well. He now stood in crisp khaki shorts. Kate's papers in his tanned right hand and a riding crop in his left. He guided her toward the doorway, where a man stood eyeing the typists.

She wished she'd had time to clean off the grit from the motorcycle ride through the desert. Shake the sand out of her hair. Wipe off the camel dung stuck to her shoes courtesy of the Cairo street.

Richards introduced the man as the Commander, and they stepped into his cramped office.

"Commander . . . ?"

"Full stop. That's all you need to know." He took a lit

cigarette from an overflowing ashtray and puffed. "Close the door on your way out, Richards."

Richards executed a sharp salute, threw Kate a side-wink and left. Tired and hungry, she faced the Commander, a middle-aged man who'd plastered thin strands of hair over his scalp. He reeked of old sweat and stale cigarette smoke. He sat at a scuffed olive-green metal desk, sweat circles showing under his arms. Not exactly top command material.

Was he the resident spy chief?

"I'll get to the point. You're the backup," said the Commander, in a no-nonsense tone. "A team was dropped here two weeks ago and there's been no communication from them. We need you to take out their target."

Kate nodded. In other words the first team was dead in the desert and she was up to bat.

"The target's about to be transferred to France. A double agent for the Gestapo in Paris. You're going to make sure he doesn't get there."

He checked a file, rustled some pages.

"May I remind you that you signed the Official Secrets Act? No careless talk of the mission. Understood?"

As if that were a question.

"Yes."

"And you'll address me as sir."

"Yes, sir."

She was thirsty. So damn thirsty and he hadn't even offered her water. Wasn't that some kind of protocol in a place surrounded by the desert?

He took a sheet from the desk. "You're billeted here. Await orders."

She couldn't get a read on him apart from his stiffness and by-the-book manner.

"Top secret mission, I get it, sir. But how long will this take?"

His forehead crinkled in annoyance. "You need to be ready at a moment's notice."

Not an answer. Kate looked at the paper he'd handed her. A sheet with squiggles all over it.

She shook her head, incredulous. "I don't read or speak Arabic. You've ordered the wrong sniper."

No wonder she felt out of her depth. Was this all a big mistake?

"That's to show the rickshaw walla or if you get lost." He gestured her to the door. "That'll be all, Madame X," he said, his voice acid. "Oh, and welcome to Cairo."

If anyone else welcomed her to Cairo she'd scream.

Cairo

—

Kate didn't mind her assigned lodging in a large white bungalow on a pasha's palm tree lined grounds. She didn't even mind sharing a room.

"Everyone here's involved in war work," said Sasha, her roommate. "Troops, pilots, logistics—it's a revolving door."

"How many are spies?"

Sasha grinned. She had a chipped front tooth, fiery red curly hair and a full figure. "Real or pretend ones?"

"Is there a difference?"

Kate had jumped into what passed for a shower in the shared tiled bathroom. Pulled the rope cord. Lukewarm water tumbled all over. She soaped up with a bar of local milky coconut soap and scrubbed her face and hair and between her toes. Dried off with a thick Turkish towel and felt clean for the first time in days.

Sasha had greeted her with a small steaming cup of coffee.

"This packs a wallop."

"Wallop?"

"I mean it's lethal. Don't drink the grounds. I got it from the stall outside."

Kate sipped the dense, hot sweet drink. Felt a jolt. "It's not the kind of coffee we have in Oregon."

"Just be warned. It's Sodom and Gomorrah here," said Sasha. "No one thinks about tomorrow. The Germans will invade any minute."

Just what she'd been hoping to hear. Apparently her mission still might be a suicide mission.

"You're serious? Look, Sasha, catch me up here, okay? What's the score?"

"Score? Sounds like what they'd say in a film." Sasha looked around for listeners. Only a gardener in the courtyard, where low tables and cushions grouped around a pool with a gurgling fountain. "Listen, you're a Yank and I don't care why you're here. Just know security's lax; the soldiers throw money around and become targets. Mousy English farmers from the countryside, Manchester bus drivers and Liverpool dockworkers who can't believe what their wages buy here. There's sun, heat, cheap liquor and women who act fascinated by them."

Kate tried to guess what Sasha was warning her about.

"Soldiers find it exotic," Sasha said. "No curfew enforced. No black out here, either. They can't get over it."

Neither could Kate. Not that she'd seen much.

"I mean the Germans—"

"Everyone's paranoid the German's will invade. But it's . . ." Sasha looked down. "Sorry, I've said too much."

Kate figured Sasha and the other women in the FANY digs worked in coding, signals intelligence work. They used the term FANY but it was an umbrella for most women's war work. Why else in God's name would they be stuck in Cairo doing four-hour shifts, then eight hours off? Probably part of the same Y signals corps who worked at that fancy manor house where the German Jews translated the Nazi big mouths' war secrets.

If the women wondered about Kate, they kept it to themselves.

But that didn't stop them from going out drinking that night. Sasha, it turned out, was of Russian descent. She didn't seem like the other girls—she and Kate were the only two not knocking them back. They found a back table away from the loud Brits under a lazy spinning ceiling fan that still didn't keep away the flies.

"How did you get into this?"

Sasha's eyebrow arched.

"Into what?"

"War work in Cairo?"

"I imagine it's like you. You go where you're sent."

But there's always a story, thought Kate.

"Don't mind me then," said Kate, miffed. She felt on edge and could only clean her rifle so many times. She'd prefer target practice shooting bottles in the desert to trying to make conversation.

"Don't take it personal," said Sasha. "I know you feel like an outsider. So do I. I grew up doing crosswords with my mother at the kitchen table. On weekends I watched Grandfather play chess in Holland Park with all the other old White Russians. Grandfather always plotted several moves ahead. I applied for war work at eighteen like everyone at school. We all became members of the FANYs. Who knows where the war took them?"

Kate nodded, surprised Sasha opened up. "What did your family think?"

"Not much. A relief, really. I was told to pack a bag and tell them goodbye."

Kate understood. It would have been the same for her if she'd had any family to tell. If her pa had lived and her brothers weren't scattered to the winds.

"My mum said to write when I could and didn't even ask

where I'd get posted. Not that I had any idea. But they'd lived in Czarist Russia and escaped during the Revolution. A daughter going off to war was not a huge surprise."

Kate had never met anyone whose family lived under a czar and escaped a revolution. "So you're Communists?"

Sasha snorted. "No, my family's émigrés who fled Lenin and the new Communist regime. But let me ask you, did your family run the Indians off the land?"

Kate felt herself redden to the roots of her hair. Touché, Sasha.

"My ancestors probably did."

One of the FANYs beckoned them to the bar, where a soldier mimicked the Egyptian waiter, then brayed like a donkey to the applause of the drunken crowd.

Sasha buried her nose in a crossword.

Cairo

———

Cairo was full of flies and heat and sand when the wind they called scirocco blew. It was dirty streets, calls to prayer from the mosques, an incredible sweet called halvah, more flies, pastel and terracotta buildings, the drifting khaki Nile, oils with intriguing scents, swaggering British soldiers with colonial airs, sewage in the streets. All pulsing energy. She'd never been anywhere like it, anywhere so alive. She loved it.

Her swollen blistered feet wouldn't fit into the *Blitzmäd-chen* shoes anymore. Despite orders to lay low, she asked Sasha where to buy sandals. Sasha brightened at the request.

Lonely, like her.

Sasha took her to a small leather shop for handmade sandals in the Khan el-Khalili bazaar, ablaze with spices, colors, beaten copper pots, alabaster, silver, carpets and everything under the sun. While the cobbler hammered out the leather and fitted the sandals to her feet, she and Sasha sipped mint tea from little glasses. From here the Sphinx at Giza didn't look like it had in her high school history book.

Cairo, to her amazement, was the top party town.

According to Sasha, it was considered a plum posting. She advised Kate to avoid the fleshpots in the red-light Birket area. As if Kate wouldn't. But that was Sasha's attempt at humor—the Army had already shut the seedy district down.

Sasha showed her where to get a kebab, then left for work.

The heat glared, the kebab was mostly gristle, and Kate's eyes ached, from strain or sand or she didn't know what. Her accuracy depended on good vision. Any moment she could be called to take a shot. She went back to their bungalow, sliced a cold cucumber from the icebox and lay down with her feet up and the slices on her eyes.

One of the other roommates sprawled asleep on the veranda. Kate tried to sleep. So sticky and clammy. She got up several times. Drank water and wished the wooden shutters blocked out the sounds: the braying of a donkey, shouts of a water seller, the tapping hammer of the jeweler in his shop across the street.

If only her room were on the quiet courtyard side, she could sleep. Refresh.

At least her feet didn't hurt.

Finally, she lapsed into a fitful sleep wracked by dreams of newsreels she'd seen at the cinema. The nightly scrambled Spitfire dog fights against the Luftwaffe in the desert sky. The fanning loops of their exhaust and smoke trailing over the pyramids. Rommel's tanks careening down the sand dunes. This turned into Margo injecting herself, Lange laughing, Dieter lying crumpled on the cobblestones. Kate was running after the baby's mewling cry amid red-yellow flames and strings of a newspaper headline looped like a ribbon.

She woke up. Sat bolt upright. The newspaper headline.

Could that be it? A code. Code in the photo of Margo holding the *Paris-soir* newspaper with the grinning Nazi at Café de Paris.

But a code for what?

She wrote herself a note before she forgot it. Thought. Wiped the perspiration from her neck.

Sasha worked in Signals. That meant she handled code, right? Not that she really understood what Sasha did. Quiet as Sasha had kept it, wouldn't she have some way to . . . What? Get this to Stepney? Or whoever sent her here.

Now somehow she had to figure out how to reach Sasha.

Late Afternoon, Cairo

Before she could grab her things, insistent knocking erupted from the courtyard door. Alert, Kate hurried over the worn blue and white mosaic tiles, smooth and cool under her bare feet. Despite the sweltering heat, a coolness clung to the inner courtyard. Mist from the fountain sent a welcome spray.

Richards stood on her doorstep. "I was afraid you'd disobeyed orders. Strayed and accepted the drink invitations to the officers' bar at Shepheard's Hotel."

If that was an attempt to compliment her in some backhand British manner, it didn't work. Green eyes, a cut-glass upper-class accent—he was handsome and he knew it. She wondered why all the posh men had the same accent.

She wasn't his type. Nor he hers. She could spot the ones who'd bed everyone and brag afterward. It was a contest with them.

Like Gregory.

No kiss and tell for her.

"I need to go to—"

He lifted a palm. "The mission's on. We leave now. Bring your equipment."

She had her rifle packed under her bed. Yet it gave her pause.

"On whose authority?"

"Orders, missus."

At least he'd got the missus right.

From the kitchen, one of the roommates peeked through the green beaded curtain. The beads swished and clacked.

"Will you be back in time for my birthday party at the Mocambo club?"

Kate didn't have to look at Richards to know that answer. She'd been brought in as a sniper and the job would take as long as it would take.

"Tell Sasha I'll join up with you later. Don't wait for me."

With the custom Lee-Enfield in a specially equipped canvas tennis racket bag with a thin sporty canvas shoulder strap, she hopped in the sidecar of the Triumph. This time she tied a scarf around her head and accepted a pair of goggles.

Off they rode through the teeming streets and narrow alleys toward the Nile. The slow-moving river of life to Egypt. The irrigated strip of green land next to it made her sit up in wonder. Date palms swayed on the bank while white-robed men rigged the sails on the graceful feluccas gliding down the river.

Timeless. A world unchanged for centuries. The rhythm immemorial.

Peaceful apart from the motorcycle engine's roar. And the looming tanks in the distance with clouds of sand billowing behind them.

Were they taking her to an advance column of German troops ready to invade from the desert? Would she be put in position behind a sand dune?

Her mind filled with visions of Marlene Dietrich flitting through the Casbah—or was it Hedy Lamarr?—in that movie she'd seen with Dafydd.

But the Cairo casbah lacked Hollywood's lens of glamor and romanticism. Kate liked it even more. Thought of Dafydd. He'd have loved Cairo's baking heat, the dusky sunlight stretching a pool of orange toward her across the Nile.

Burros, goats and horses grazed along the bank close to a riverside village.

The motorcycle downshifted. Fifteen, twenty miles later he'd parked. There were tall green reeds bordering the shore and brown, weedy bushes that made a crackling noise.

Richards pointed to a moored houseboat with two sails. Strange. No other boats were here. The last village was perhaps a quarter of a mile away.

"Your target's inside that *dahabiya*," said Richards. He gave her a knowing glance. "It's just a tarted-up sailboat. When he appears, you've got two minutes." Richards's green eyes narrowed as he scanned the horizon. "You'll be picked up by the clean-up team. They'll carry buckets. Understood?"

Kate bit her lip. "Clean-up team?"

"Don't worry," he said, putting his hand on her shoulder to reassure her.

As if that helped.

"Concentrate on what you're skilled at. Focus on your target."

He was right. Focus on the target. Kill the Kraut.

Payback time.

"When's the target coming out?"

"It could be minutes or hours." Richards set a bag on the wet, sandy loam. "Water, biscuits. Your provisions."

"What if there's someone with him, or—"

"Handle it as you handle him."

Richards handed her a photo. She didn't know what she

was expecting but it wasn't this. The man's pale yellow robe contrasted with his weathered, brown face.

"A sheikh?"

"He's Lange's contact."

Was, she thought.

"This sheikh works with the Nazis. He's a threat and hates us with a passion."

Now she got it. After taking out Lange in Paris, she was here to take care of all the loose ends. Yet she wanted Richards's take on this.

"Why me?"

"You're deniable, Madame X. And we never had this conversation. Or took this trip."

A small ripple of hurt crossed her. But what else did she expect? Why else had they given her a cyanide pill?

At least for once someone was being honest.

She unzipped her tennis racket bag.

"You forgot," she said. "I'm the best."

He grabbed her. His hot breath on her cheek. Pressed himself into her and kissed her hard. Surprised, she tried to pull back. Then didn't.

"That, too."

And then he revved the motorcycle and was gone.

She didn't understand him. But maybe she didn't need to—wartime made feelings less complicated. Here today, probably dead tomorrow.

Not that she hadn't liked his kiss of death. Its neediness had been the most real thing about him. It had been a while since she'd been in a man's arms.

A pang of regret hit her, but she couldn't afford that now.

Focus. Blot out everything from her brain except the job at hand. This sheikh, Lange's contact, who aided Rommel and his Afrika Korps, was no pal of hers.

It would never be over for her. Her Dafydd and baby

Lisbeth were gone and nothing would bring them back. Still, while she breathed, she'd make the Germans pay.

She assembled the Lee-Enfield and attached the telescopic lens. She'd cleaned and oiled the rifle this morning, as she'd done several times since she'd gotten to Cairo.

She slotted in the bullets. Checked and then rechecked. Then got on her hands and knees and crawled forward.

The reeds swished and tickled her arms. No wind. A stillness and heat in a dense band.

With twilight hovering, now would be an ideal time. But no counting on that. She surveyed the short ramp from the boat deck and wondered where it led.

A waiting vehicle? Camels?

He'd probably need illumination to go down the ramp. Without light, it would be a problematic shot. Still, nothing she hadn't done before in worse conditions.

She kept edging forward on all fours to within a hundred feet of the boat ramp. Then seventy-five feet. Behind the rushes she waited. Picked her target point—noted the kerosene lantern approximately four hundred yards away on the opposite shore. She tabulated that a man between five foot six and six feet would be within range for an accurate head shot using the lantern as a guide.

Across the sky came a low roaring of propellers. Tiny blue lights dotted what must be the wing. A bomber or . . . ?

The landing wheels dropped with a distinctive thump.

Somewhere on the Nile

⌣

Kate readied her aim, keeping her eye on the houseboat's door. Her neck felt clammy and her knees were damp from crawling through the marshy loam. Her elbows, however, braced in the knee pads she'd brought, kept her arms dry and steady.

Just like shooting at that dummy in the country home's garden, the low-visibility category in the spy school's curriculum. Easy once you got the hang of it, she'd told the students.

A simple technique her pa had taught her hunting in the Blue Mountains in northeastern Oregon. If you're hunting a wolf, think like the wolf. Be the wolf.

Be the sheikh.

The houseboat's door opened. She saw a man holding a lantern making his way down the ramp. His features were indistinguishable. Following him was the sheikh, evidenced by his long robes and a brief glimpse of his face in the light. A sharp nose, a hawk-like gaze that reminded her of Lange. His gait was slow, careful.

Kate calibrated, gauged the distance, breathed in and shot on the exhale. Re-loaded and without assessing the impact or where her first shot went, she aimed at the chest. Two cracks in rapid succession. She adjusted her aim and shot two more at the lantern bearer.

Always double tap, her pa said.

A woman's screams came from the houseboat's door.

Kate felt her stomach tighten. She didn't want to shoot a woman. Especially one in the glittering outfit of a belly dancer, gold belt resting on her bare hips.

Voices and then running footsteps as two figures rushed from the plane toward the boat. The lantern had fallen on the ramp and in the light she saw men with drawn pistols. No buckets. This wasn't the clean-up crew. Who the hell were they?

One man checked the bodies for life. Shook his head.

The other aimed toward the belly dancer.

"Not me!" More screams. Garbled English. "No, the shooter's over there."

She was pointing toward Kate. The man pivoted and pointed in Kate's direction.

Kate reloaded. She shot. Double tapped the first man. By then the other had sprinted off, dodging through the reeds.

The plane's engine revved nearby. Dust whipped through the reeds. Shouts and then the plane's engine smoothed like it was ready to take off. Seconds later the plane taxied off down the road. Just like that, the belly and wings lifted. The plane's updraft hit her, roiling over her along with a wave of unease.

These dead men made her a sitting duck. The woman had slammed shut the houseboat's door. What could Kate do about her? If the clean-up crew came they wouldn't let this witness survive.

From her perch, the village lay dark. No vehicles traveled on the road. The shafts of moonlight fell on a quiet desert.

Where was the promised clean-up crew?

Why was she so stupid?

It finally had sunk in. The two-man crew from the plane had come to make sure she didn't get away. She'd done the job—shot the sheikh and his accomplice—and would be left holding the gun. Literally.

No clean-up crew was coming. If she sat here waiting for them, she would rot her life away in a Cairo prison.

No way in hell if she could help it.

She wrapped the scarf around her head and covered her face.

She had to get rid of the bodies. Get the woman to safety. And get out of there.

A sickening feeling in her stomach overtook her. No way could she bury these bodies by herself. She couldn't speak Arabic. Would the woman speak enough English to understand?

Kate got to her knees. Trod over the wet marsh ground toward the boat. Her sandals made a sucking noise each time she lifted her foot.

"Hello? Do you speak English?"

She saw the door open and the woman came out.

"Look, I won't shoot you," she called out. "Please believe me."

Behind the moored boat, moonlight glinted on the Nile, whose soft ripples lapped at the bank. The woman retreated behind the houseboat door. Scared? Unable to understand?

All Kate could do was continue speaking. Try to enlist her help somehow. "But if anyone knows you've witnessed this you're next."

"Liar. They already know," said the woman in thick accented English. Her guttural voice sounded like a smoker's.

So she spoke English. Knew more than Kate, it seemed.

"The men from the plane? They've gone."

Kate stepped onto the ramp. She had to find out who the other body was. Take the ID. Training rule number six: *leave no evidence.*

A sob came from deep in the woman's throat. "You're going to shoot me."

"That's too much trouble," said Kate. "Help me dig."

She needed the woman's cooperation.

"You're crazy."

Kate sighed. "If you don't help me I'll have to shoot you."

"You'll shoot me anyway." Kate heard her choke back another sob. "We can't bury them," said the woman.

"Why?"

"The Nile floods." Her tone was one she might use to explain something to a child. "They'll surface and be found immediately."

Kate should have paid attention in geography when they studied Egypt. What to do?

"We weigh them down," said Kate, "and tie them to the boat like anchors."

"Why do you care?" said the woman. "Why don't you leave?"

"Look," Kate said. "I've been set up here. Lied to. I will take the fall—the responsibility—if I don't hide them." What could she say to stir the woman to help? "If there are no bodies here, no trace or proof, I can turn the table on who set me up. Get us both out," said Kate.

"Don't understand," the woman said.

Kate didn't need her to understand. Just to act. The Nile's soft lapping on the bank filled the air.

"Fine. Ten thousand piastres after they sink in the river."

After a long thirty seconds the woman said, "Show me."

Kate reached for the money in her bag. Didn't even know if she had enough. "Tell me who they are. Then help me weigh them down. I'll give you five now." Kate got to her feet. "The rest when we get to Cairo."

The woman nodded, took a rope and started rigging it up.

After much resistance, the woman had come around too easily. Kate didn't trust her. But she'd deal with that later.

Then Kate heard the woman's deep laugh. "You shoot them and don't know who they are?"

"Should I? It's a job. One's a sheikh . . ."

"Not just any sheikh," said the woman. "Leader of the Shali tribe, powerful Bedouins."

Not good.

"Who's the other one? German?"

The woman's golden belly bangles caught the moonlight. She tied a chiffon scarf embroidered with small mirrors around her shoulders and knotted down the rigging of each sail. She clearly knew her way around a boat.

Was this hers?

"Him?" She spit. "English."

This got worse.

"Likes threesomes," said the woman. "Likes to watch."

Had she come upon an orgy? She should have ascertained whether others were on the boat. Never assume.

"Tell me who else is here," said Kate.

She shook her head. "They had a meeting. Talking. I served drinks. No one was supposed to know."

"Did you see any papers? Documents?"

"Maybe. And maybe you pay me now."

She didn't trust the woman—a belly dancer who had orgies on a houseboat for money—yet how could she judge her? Weren't they both in deep trouble? Trying to survive?

"Like I said, five thousand when we get them in the water."

A shrug and she was uncoiling a chain with weights for

fishing nets. Kate righted the lantern and went through the sheikh's robes. Gingerly, she checked the deep pockets, avoiding the blood and his musty old man scent. She found documents, a map, what looked like a list in English. All with the heading of British Command HQ and stamped in red with TOP SECRET.

Her gut fluttered. Why did a sheikh have a map of British troop movements in Libya?

She had been roped into something criminal.

The other man's blood spattered the ramp. She noted his khaki shirt, skinny legs and shorts. She turned him over.

Gasped.

She'd stood in his office in the Cairo HQ. He'd given her orders and told her to address him as Sir. The Commander.

A traitor.

She remembered the sweat-stained shirt, his hungover eyes and hair plastered over his bald spot. The looks he'd thrown at the clerks when she'd arrived with Richards. What was his name? She'd never known it.

But she did know two things. With the wad of cash and a gold ingot in his pockets, the Brit was a traitor. And she'd for sure been set up.

No one wanted to be seen killing their own who'd betrayed their country. Perfect job for an outsider. Get the Yank.

Bad to worse.

She'd heard the Egyptians hated the British but worked with those who sold out to the Germans.

Still, she'd never wanted to shoot a Brit, no matter what he'd done. Didn't they court-martial for that? Yet nabbing him would stop the flow of information to the Germans.

The cynic in her said, *until the next time.*

But the Commander couldn't have been the one behind

this mission—he wouldn't have stumbled into his own assassination. So who had arranged it? What mission had the Commander thought she'd been brought to Cairo for?

Right now that was the least of her worries.

"Hurry up," Kate said to the belly dancer.

Together, they each pulled a leg until the three bodies were on the narrow deck. While the woman released the ramp's clamp, unmoored the boat and cast off with a pole, Kate searched the deck for a covering, some kind of canvas, to wrap the bodies. It took a lot of work to wrap and fasten the bodies of three men on deck.

Destroy the evidence.

Leave no trace.

If that wasn't possible, leave nothing that led to you.

One of her earliest memories as a child was when a small wooden barge in the Willamette River caught on fire. Blew up. A few charred bits of timber were the only traces that floated onto the riverbank.

Whoever was involved had a plane at their disposal and would come back. Soon.

"We need to destroy the boat. Torch it, leave no trace and escape."

"It's my home." She straightened, wiped her hands on a sail. "*Dahabiyas* are expensive. This is a classic."

Really? Kate doubted that, but then again, who knew.

"You can buy another," she said. "Bigger. Newer." Kate gestured to the gas canisters on the deck by the engine. Three of them, hopefully full. "Let's—"

"You want to blow up where I live?" said the woman, her voice quivering. "This is your mess to clean up; leave me out of it. You shot them. You're the assassin. Killer."

"And I've got a solution to get us out of here," said Kate, improvising. She didn't deny the woman's accusations—couldn't. "If you prefer to take the blame . . ."

"Why would the blame be on me?"

"Did anyone else know you'd be here?"

"Does it matter?"

"Don't you think they'll track and blackmail you?" said Kate. "You'll get locked up in a British prison. Or a cell in Cairo. And that's just for starters."

"But I had nothing to do with this."

"Tell that to whoever returns on the plane. You're in too deep."

Pause. Moonlight glimmered on the river's surface. Insects chirped.

A breeze had broken the still air.

"What's your solution?"

"We destroy the boat with the bodies," said Kate. "You insist your houseboat was stolen, you didn't know by who or why . . . Doesn't that make more sense? What's your name?"

"Nadira." Her voice was haughty. "Everyone in Cairo knows me."

"Not the circles I'm in, Nadira," said Kate. "Sorry, but that's even more reason to burn your boat. Now. Before the plane returns."

A motor throbbed in the distance. White lights. Sweat prickled her brow.

Kate put two wads of piastres from the Brit Commander's pocket on the deck rigging.

Nadira swiped it and pointed to the middle of the river. A sandbar loomed in the warm mist. Trees, some bushes.

"I'll start the engine. Takes five minutes to get there. But we'll have to get off the boat quickly. There's a reed raft. We go downstream, go to a farming village. My cousin's there."

Nadira outlined the rest of the plan.

Kate uncapped the gasoline canisters.

They just might make it.

Outskirts of Cairo on the Nile

⌐

Kate led her burro to the well as dawn streaked pale orange over the distant pyramids. These wonders of the world stood silent, brushed by the sun's glow. Even more distant sat the colossal Sphinx oriented toward the rising sun, barely visible with its worn-away nose and sand-burnished paws, looking sad and tired. As tired as she felt riding all night.

Her thighs ached and her shoulders were stiff after hours in the saddle. The sand flies had feasted on her ankles, leaving her itchy and uncomfortable. What a softie she'd become. Pathetic.

Back in Oregon she'd gone hunting all night in the snow with her pa. But now the humidity and dense heat had caught up to her. Or maybe it was the shooting of three men, the disposal of the bodies, the rigging a boat to burn and explode, the paddling the raft downriver to Nadira's cousin's. All of it found her out of shape.

Nadira's cousin's burros pulled the cart loaded with things Nadira had managed to salvage from her houseboat. They'd trudged all the way to Cairo through the dark along the riverside path—the road was too dangerous; they'd be spotted right away.

If the pursuers recognized two hijab-clad farm women.

A long-legged white bird winged a spray of water in the dawn glow on the Nile.

Kate followed Nadira, feeling as if she were in the sandalled footsteps of time. Her seventh-grade history book with its skinny chapter on Egypt came back to her—those drawings of slaves pulling the stone blocks from feluccas in the Nile to build the pyramids, the tombs of the pharaohs. In the bible, baby Moses had been hidden here in a basket in the reeds.

Nadira stopped. Kate almost plowed into her.

"It's a sign," Nadira said. She was pointing to the bird.

Superstitious? Kate couldn't let this unnerve her. She felt for the knife on her thigh, the miniature Fairbairn killing knife.

"A sign of what?"

"The pharaohs mummified egrets as sacrificial offerings. A good omen."

Kate marveled at the sight. In Oregon the cattle egrets had short dumpy legs. This thin, graceful bird reminded her of a prima ballerina.

"We must reach Cairo before dawn," said Nadira. "Hurry."

Cairo

———

"What are you doing here? Miss your plane?"

Kate stared at the surprise in Sasha's face.

"What do you mean?"

"Richards just brought a new girl who moved into your room."

Just like that.

"He's here right now—"

Kate put her finger to Sasha's lips. Pulled her outside the door. There was sand between her toes, grit in the back of her throat.

"Where's my stuff?"

"Someone took it to the airport. What's wrong?"

"What's right? I'm in trouble."

Kate led Sasha through the tiled courtyard and out to the street. They stepped into the café next door, full of men smoking hookahs. The sweet odor of tobacco and something else . . . kef?

"Look, Sasha. I was set up. Can you listen and not ask questions?"

"You're scaring me, Kate." Her fingers fiddled with the clip holding back her hair.

"If you end up helping me, this has to stay between us. Understood?"

Sasha nodded. "Did the *bawab* see you?"

"Who?"

"The building doorkeeper—bald and nosey."

Kate shook her head.

"They hope I'm dead," she said. "But they're still searching for me in case I got away. I need a place to stay, to get a message to London, to meet an officer you trust. Then I'm out of here."

"You don't want much, do you?" Sasha thought for a moment. "Planes aren't a good idea. It's all military transport. Best to get the boat from Alexandria."

Kate peeked out the door, hoping she wouldn't see Richards striding out. "Don't trust Richards."

"You want me to approach intelligence at SOE? It's not at HQ," said Sasha.

SOE, Special Operations Executive, had absorbed Section D, where Stepney had been her handler. But something made her hold back.

"Not yet. Tell me about SIS here. Aren't they your bosses? Who has the office next to Richards? A commander, going bald, sweaty, hangover eyes, skinny legs?"

"He was my boss."

"*Was* is the right word. He's ashes now."

Startled, Sasha looked at Kate. Shrugged. "A lush. His unit covered for him. But what happened?"

"He sold secrets. He was a traitor and I've got proof. Do you think Richards was in on it?"

"I don't know." She wrote down an address. "Go here."

Richards emerged from the wood door.

Panic flooded Kate. She ducked out of sight.

"Meet you at this location," Sasha said. "After my shift."

Gezira Island

———

Sasha had written *Tara, Gezira Island.* Kate showed the taxi driver but he couldn't read. But when she read it out he nodded and hit the meter. "On Sharia Abou el Feda, in the Zamalek district. Spy house."

He grinned.

Then he craned his neck around to see her response.

"How do you know that?" she asked.

Stupid thing to say. It was admitting it.

"It's near the Kit Kat club. All taxi drivers know. Who else take taxis there?" He honked the horn at a donkey. "But maybe you're a girlfriend. Not a spy."

And maybe you're an informer. Taxi drivers were notorious for it. An informer in pay of the police. Or the Brits or German Abwehr. Or all three.

But she had no time to think of another plan and she was so tired.

They had sped off down a long avenue lined by pepper trees.

Kate had to put him off track.

She pretended to stifle a sob. "It's my fiancé. He's . . . I'm breaking it off."

By the time she reached the address, he'd given her relationship advice and claimed he had discounted her fare.

Inside, a gardener wearing a *kaffiyeh* swept a palm frond across the garden courtyard of a spacious faded pink villa. Moorish arches, intricate *mashrabiya* lattice screens and purple bougainvillea climbed lush terracotta brick—an oasis.

The gardener inclined his head.

"*Salaam alaikum*," she said, as Sasha had told her to.

He touched his hand to his heart. "*Alaikum salaam.*"

Had she said it wrong?

He gestured her toward the tall open doors that let a breeze through and into what appeared to be a grand ballroom with mirrors and parquet floors. She looked like a dusty mess with a canvas racket bag holding her disassembled rifle.

A pale-faced man reclined on a pearl-studded divan, next to a collection of empty bottles and a phonograph machine of inlaid wood. He wore a white wrinkled linen suit and snored.

She walked around, wondering who she could approach. A couple of Westerners were passed out on lawn chairs in the adjoining courtyard with a spraying fountain. The lush drizzle felt welcome. About to give up, she smelled the tang of strong coffee and followed it to a kitchen where, on a balcony with a metal filigreed railing, an older woman fanned a small charcoal fire in a brazier and a copper curlicue coffee pot bubbled.

"Thank God someone's awake and alive."

The languid British clipped accent belonged to a bearded man in white shorts and tennis shirt sipping coffee on the balcony under cascading red hibiscus.

"Coffee?" he asked.

"Thank you," she said, accepting the small cup.

Took a sip. It was that lethal Turkish stuff.

"Don't meet many Yanks here," he said.

"Sasha sent me," she said. "But you're not very discreet."

"Why?"

"The taxi driver called this the spy house."

"Of course, but we call it the hangover house."

No stretch there.

"You mean it's full of loose lips and double agents?"

"Well, I know for sure that we've got two mongooses. The countess's pets, really."

What was she doing here in a villa with decadent foreigners who bragged about spying?

"Look, I've got to lay low until . . ."

He leaned forward. Put his fingers to his lips. Then used it to beckon her down the balcony stairs to another fountain.

"Identify yourself," he said in a low voice.

Trust no one. Yet she was hunted, on the run, and stood out as a female foreigner. If Sasha hadn't betrayed her, she stood a shot here—she would take a chance. If things looked grim, she'd slip out and use Nadira's connections— if she'd share any—to get to Alexandria to find a boat.

Did she have any other choice?

"Cowgirl."

A brief nod.

"I'm Brian. I've heard about you."

"You have?"

"Been to Groppi?"

Kate shook her head. "Look, this isn't a social call."

"Groppi's a café with the best pastry and coffee in Cairo."

Like that interested her?

"I didn't come here for small talk."

He gestured and she followed him again, this time to a small library. He closed the door, picked a book from the shelf seemingly at random.

A leather-spined book with an embossed gilded design.

Brian opened the book, ruffled through the pages, then sucked in his breath.

"Cowgirl was supposed to check in at Groppi's two days ago."

She could still hear her pa's voice.

Never admit to anything if you don't have to.

"News to me."

"Funny no one told you," he said.

More than funny.

"Don't play ignorant," she said, on the attack. "No one tells us anything. Orders come, a mission's assigned . . ."

"Us?" Brian interrupted.

She didn't like where this was going.

"Who do you think?"

Was this place a sham? A party villa set up to lure agents?

He grinned. "That Stepney was right. You're a prickly pear all right, just without the cowgirl boots."

Surprised, she stepped back. Could she believe him?

He handed her a sheet of paper with code at the top and the deciphered message at the bottom. This didn't look very official or the way she'd seen it done. Granted that was one time. And yet, the message made sense.

Target Sheikh Aliyah + partner or accomplice.

"You killed the rat?" he asked.

"Three of them. But you know what they say, you find one and there's an infestation behind the wall. The Commander, for starters. What about Richards?"

"How do you know?"

She pulled from her racket case the documents she'd recovered from the Sheikh's deep pockets.

"That's it?"

"There was money and a gold ingot, but I used it to bribe my way to get to Cairo."

Most of it, anyway. She'd leave Nadira out of it.

"Look, this Sheikh Aliyah who sold these documents to the Commander, a traitor at HQ and a hitman from the plane—unknown to me—are all gone. No trace. Remember, these documents as far as anyone's concerned, are gone, too," she said. "Now it's your problem. Inform London. I need to leave. Now."

He was pulling over a wood cabinet with a record player. Its wheels rolled smoothly on the parquet. He dropped the needle and Glenn Miller and his band filled the room.

Then he opened a drawer in the cabinet. Behind fake shelving rolled out a radio transmitter.

"Sit down and finish your coffee."

She did. For ten minutes he was busy consulting the book he'd pulled from the shelf and coding. After a burst of Morse he'd taken off his headphones.

"My scheduled transmission's later but I put this priority."

"Quite ingenious," she said, admiration filling her.

"I transmit and receive and it doesn't affect the records playing. Despite what you think, we are effective. We foster a reputation as eccentrics. No stretch since we are."

"Eccentric spies?"

Brian half-grinned.

"We throw parties around the clock. Inept and decadent as we appear, the comings and goings mask meetings and our real work."

"A front?"

"More or less. We're successful in moving people in and out, running a network, transmitting and receiving messages."

He switched off the radio transmitter.

"So I'm confused as to why I don't know about the Commander."

She finished the small cup of strong coffee. The grounds on her tongue.

"All I know is we found Lange in Paris. Now we've taken out the sheikh who fed him info."

A dark-haired woman, striking in a green satin robe, walked into the room with two striped, long-nosed animals on leashes. She threw each of the ferret-like creatures a scrap of meat from her pocket.

"Meet the countess—"

"Sophie Kowalska," the woman interrupted. "Pietr and Gus, the mongooses. They fight cobras, very useful here."

Here? Kate couldn't help but look around the room, wary.

"And you are?"

"Cowgirl."

"You're late."

"That's what he said. But no one informed me."

"Tell her the rules, Brian."

What rules?

Brian finished his coffee. Winked. "Done already."

What kind of game were these two playing?

"Can you get me out of Cairo tonight?"

"As soon as we get the orders to."

Noon at the Villa Tara

⌒

In the dense midday heat, Kate battled to keep her eyes open. To stay awake for London's radio response. From the terrace the chocolate pistachio Nile spread below and an egret perched on the wall.

Kate leaned forward as Brian turned knobs on the radio set. "Any word?" He'd sent a second message.

"Be patient."

It was murder sitting on these stiff rattan chairs trying to keep alert and focused.

"Easy for you to say," she said.

Brian laid down his headphones, unperturbed.

"If they don't respond immediately then it will be the next scheduled transmission."

God. The heat. The beady look from the rat-like mongooses.

"Which is . . . ?"

"Tonight. Twenty hundred hours."

So much could go wrong before 8 P.M. She should be getting on a plane now. Irritable, grimy and pinching herself to stay awake, she wanted to scream.

"I know what you're thinking."

Kate doubted that.

"Let's get you a bath and some clothes. You can rest up until I hear how to spirit you away."

What else could she do in the heat's zenith? She couldn't even think straight, never mind function well enough to escape if she needed to.

She needed help.

Too bad she didn't trust these types.

The marble-slabbed bathroom, built for the pasha's harem, held hot baths, a cold dip and a steam chamber. A grinning, toothless Bedouin woman with tattoos covering her chin gestured for Kate to strip and handed her a muslin towel.

A bath attendant? What kind of spy post was this?

She pointed Kate to a marble slab. Naked, wary, Kate lay down on the hot marble. Gritty black soap was spread over her body. Pungent, charcoal lather, flecked with straw and root bits, raked her skin. She felt layers of dead skin coming off as the woman rubbed her raw. Every bit of her vibrated. All of this was followed by a hot rinse. Steam clogged her vision.

Then a pummeling massage by the Bedouin woman. Her skilled, strong fingers found every tight muscle and worked them without mercy. Kate cried out in pain as her back cracked; then, she cried out in relief. The magic fingers kneaded out every kink in her back and neck.

Another hot rinse and the Bedouin woman took her to the steaming marble tub. Kate lay back until she couldn't stand the scalding water.

The woman helped her down the steps to plunge her into the ice-cold bath.

Shivers ran up her spine. She was awake, alive, every pore of her body tingling. Then into the steam room, foggy with condensation. A whiff of eucalyptus oil reached her nose.

Every bit of dirt had been scrubbed off. Now came the sweating out of whatever she was holding on to inside.

Another rinse and her cheeks and body were baby pink. Kate was reminded of Lisbeth, how she'd soap and bathe her in the old copper tub. For once, the memory was a sweet one—laced by pain, but a beautiful moment.

On the divan she lay with a scented sheet around her. Wrung out and relaxed for the first time since Scotland, her mind returned to the previous night on the riverbank; how she and Nadira had pulled the bodies onto the houseboat. How Nadira adorned the burros with blue beads as protection against the evil eye and rode them to Cairo, all the way looking out for the dead sheikh's minions to wreak revenge.

She could still smell the kerosene fumes, the boat's timber and the stink of the burning bodies. Thank God for her rudimentary lesson on explosives.

Nadira, however well-compensated, owed Kate no allegiance. But Kate felt a grudging admiration for the belly dancer, who'd quickly smelled the future, as she said, and pitched in and used her contacts to get them downriver to Cairo. After Kate had paid her the balance, Nadira had disappeared on her burro. Saved her own skin. Why not?

But if Nadira was caught and interrogated, she'd spill the story. She could even be on her way to sell the information on what happened to the sheikh and the Brit. Kate would be easy to find. She had to leave.

The heat overtook her, the blazing fire, the crackling timbers, the engulfing smoke. She was running, running to find the vehicle in flames. To find Lisbeth and Dafydd. But she only found ashes. And then the boat was exploding on the Nile, the cinders and ash floating in the sky like fireworks. Screaming, she was screaming for help.

A hard shake woke her. She was wrapped up in a eucalyptus-scented sheet in a dark, green-glassed atrium surrounded by orchids. Richards was staring in her face, his breath warm on her chin.

A spasm of panic convulsed her. Richards had set her up to be killed.

He wiped a strand of hair from her cheek. Almost a caress.

"Sorry, Madame X."

His snake-green eyes studied her.

"You were dreaming. Nightmares, I think."

The nightmare that never went away.

"What are you doing here?"

"Drinking champagne," he said.

A chilled magnum sat in a silver ice bucket, next to two glasses of fizzing topaz.

"It's Bollinger. Excellent. And, of course, it's French."

She tried to keep her sheet wrapped around her naked body as she struggled to sit up.

"You set me up to be killed, Richards," she said. "I'm sure you've poisoned the drink."

"About that . . ." He trailed off as he sipped from each glass. "No poison, honest." Grinned with a sparkle of fizz on his lip.

Damned handsome and he knew it.

"Forgive and forget?" he said.

"I can't believe you just said that."

He handed her a glass. She couldn't believe for a moment that they were having this conversation. Yet she accepted his champagne.

She sipped. A velvet tickle in her throat.

"Is there a point to this?" she said, thinking, *besides softening me up to stab me in the back.* "You're here to put me out of business for good. Right?" She reached for the heavy bottle to club him.

He tsked, caught her arm.

"Actually, we're offering you full-time employment. You've done such an excellent job. Consider this a celebration. The local HQ sent me here to tell you."

Here? They knew already she'd taken out the sheikh and the Commander?

"Me? Not interested. My orders come from London."

He clinked his glass against hers. "So do mine."

"Where's the proof? Or is it like the clean-up crew you said would arrive? It's all fiction with you."

"My part was done. I had no idea the crew arrived too late," he said. "The boat was gone by then."

"No thanks to you or them," she said.

He had the grace to look sheepish.

"There was an airplane, Richards. An airplane landed right when I needed to take action."

Interested now, he leaned forward. "Airplane? Who did you see?"

"That's just it. They came after me but I couldn't see them."

"What do you mean they came after you?"

She told him. He rubbed his forehead.

"How many men did you see?"

"Two, three, I don't know. I had no idea the man with the sheikh was a Brit, the Commander."

He took her hand. Her hand warm in his. Concern pooled in his big eyes. Those movie star looks of his battered her defenses.

"Can you forgive me? Understand why I did what I did?" he said. "My orders were to take you to the boat. Give you the instructions, then leave. Today when I heard what happened it made me sick. It's not the way I would have handled it. But it's war, it's all for the cause."

A good-looking, charming upper-class man had shafted her and wanted her to be a good sport over it.

Did he really think she'd go along with "HQ," whoever that was these days?

No doubt it was between the warring military factions within the ministry at Whitehall. For a moment she wanted her handler Stepney to somehow come through. Just this once.

She hated thinking he'd thrown her to the wolves. That she'd fallen for it.

Again.

"What's wrong?" said Richards. His green eyes bored into hers.

She didn't know who to believe anymore. Knew she couldn't trust anyone.

She didn't mean to tell him; perhaps it was the champagne. "The Germans killed my husband and child. I volunteered to fight the Nazis, stop them any way I could. But what's the point of lies, the endless politics, and risking my life for this when I don't even know if I'm taking out good guys or bad guys?"

He touched her bare shoulder, ran his fingertips down her arm. "You're beautiful, you know." A shrug and his mood changed. "And you're right. You should be given the truth. Treated as a soldier. That's what they want you for, so why not say it."

None of this was her job. She longed to go back to training. In the highlands.

She assessed her chances of leaving Cairo. Getting back to London wasn't like finding a fishing boat in the Channel, with only U-boats to worry about. There was the Mediterranean to cross, the straits of Gibraltar, the Atlantic with its minefield of shipping lanes. Crossing occupied Europe was no easier.

If she went along with him, what would that get her?

Twilight
Cairo

Twilight brought the call of night birds along the Nile. A symphony from egrets, seagulls, and the chirp of crickets. After staying near Command HQ in the center digs with Sasha, the riverside villa felt soothing, secrets flowing discreetly around her. God, she hoped she was safe.

Richards had left with a promise to furnish more information later.

Her fear that Nadira would betray her hadn't diminished. Stop it, she told herself. She could worry all night and still change nothing.

London's radio transmission wouldn't be until later. Brian had roped her into taking his place at some event with the countess. Better she go than him, he'd said in that persuading way he had; he'd be on hand in case a message came in early.

"Let's look in my armoire," said the countess, "and find you something to wear. The green chiffon? Or a slinky blue satin with tulle? What's your poison?"

Talk about clichés.

Trained never to stand out, she pointed to the only dress that caught her eye. Simple yet elegant. "That one."

"A little black dress with a bit of cleavage. Good choice." If it would go over her hips.

"Agents should blend in," Kate said. "Not call attention to themselves."

Kate realized she sounded like a schoolmarm—stiff, prim, and disapproving.

"Oh, this is how I do that, too," said the countess, joining the clasp on her double loop pearl choker. "As Westerners and Occupiers, we're highly visible. Stand out. You're either an officer's wife, a nurse or a FANY. I say play it to the hilt. Act the dumb, vacuous party girl. You'd be surprised what I overhear or how men confide in me."

Pivot and use a new opportunity, Stepney would have said. Kate could do that, couldn't she?

Kate took the black dress off the hanger. Stepped into the soft silk. Elegant, and with a Parisian label. A pre-war Schiaparelli.

"What's with Richards?" she asked abruptly.

"Pretty boy?" A sigh. "Fancied him once. Playboy."

"You don't trust him?"

"He's at the beck and call of his masters."

He'd told her that himself.

"Not many original ideas in his head."

Kate doubted that. Something simmered under the surface.

The countess threw her a long scarf. "We'll go to the club. Party happening here later."

The last thing Kate wanted to do. Besides, she needed to be back in time for London's transmission.

"I want to let Sasha know."

But Sasha didn't answer at the old digs. She must be at work.

After they left Gezira Island and crossed the Tahrir Bridge, the countess decided to keep walking.

Kate heard a motorcycle along the riverbank. A distinctive roar. It sounded like Richards's Triumph.

Cairo

⌣

"Hurry." The countess took her hand. "We'll need to make a grand entrance."

"What do you mean? I thought Brian was your escort and I'm pinch-hitting for him."

"Don't get coy," said the countess, reapplying lipstick.

Nervous, Kate wanted to ask more, but a trio of officers in khaki appeared on the bridge and insisted on escorting them into the "pulse" of Cairo. Not what Kate wanted to do.

She'd go along with it for now, figuring Brian knew the haunts and would join them.

Half an hour later, "going native," as one of the sunburnt officers declared it, they were standing at a kebab stand in the night souk. After which the countess dragged them to the Kit Kat club.

So far no sign of Brian. Across the river Kate saw the outlines of Villa Tara.

The heat and dense perfume mingled with the sweat of waiters. The dim interior was all black and white lacquer, gilded mirrors, and red velvet booths resembling an art nouveau brothel. The ten-piece orchestra of Western musicians played in the background while a magician performed on a small stage. A rabbit was produced out of a top hat.

Ridiculous. This wasted time.

Kate pulled the countess aside. "I'm going back."

"Not now, the best belly dancer in Cairo's coming on."

Kate hesitated. Could it possibly be Nadira?

If so, she had no desire to relive the memories of the night they'd spent together. Or reacquaint herself. Nadira could turn her in.

"Must get ready for the . . ." She mouthed the words *radio transmission.*

The countess put her hand to her mouth. Whispered.

"It came through before we left. Brian meant for me to tell you. I'm so sorry."

Sorry? She'd been killing time.

Sure, she was sorry. Had the countess been under orders to get her out of the way?

"What's the message?"

"He'll tell you."

"Tell me now."

"I've got no idea."

Kill time and get her out of radio range.

"I need some air," she said and smiled.

Kate beat her way out of the club and ran across the bridge to Gezira Island, then up the winding street. There was enough of a moon to silhouette the tops of the date palm branches by the villa's lit bay windows. Humidity bloomed around her.

Perspiring, she hurried, wiping her lip. Jogged to the courtyard's gate. Locked.

Of all times. Strange for this free and easy party hub.

She called out, "Hello?"

About to ring the bell, she saw the pull had been cut.

Everything told her to leave. But she had to get inside. Find Brian for her escape orders.

She trailed down the wall among the bushes. Why were the insects and birds in the courtyard quiet? In the back of her mind she felt danger spiking.

She followed the wall until she could find a foothold. Took off her heeled sandals, hiked up her dress and stuck them in her panties' waist band. She pulled herself up by the odd root and branch. The only sound she heard came from the gurgling fountain.

Kate crested the wall, gripped the edge, and let herself down onto a built-in bench. Crouching, she kept to the shadows and slipped through a courtyard door. Took a breath. Looked around. No one.

Inside, she padded to the ballroom, hardly navigable in the charcoal gauze veil. Music drifted from the library. The Glenn Miller Band.

A crack of light showed from the door which lay ajar. She rolled down her dress, slipped into the sandals.

"Brian?"

No answer. The radio played to an empty room—bookshelves a silent witness—illuminated by the warm yellow glow of a single Anglepoise lamp. Kind of useless for a library, she thought.

The mezzotint pictures showing scenes of the Grand Bazar in Istanbul seemed out of place.

Stepping closer to the radio set, her sandalled feet hit something hard. Damn, she'd stubbed her toe. Looking down, she saw it was covered in blood. For a stupid second she thought she'd cut her toe.

Then she saw him.

"Brian!"

But Brian wouldn't answer, now or ever. His tennis whites were soaked red in his own blood.

She backed up in horror. Caught herself, knelt down. She didn't need to feel for his pulse.

She turned him slightly and saw the gaping slit of what had been his throat. Nausea welled up. She pushed it aside.

Read, Assess, Decide, Act.

Murder. She saw no knife. Quickly she scanned the area for a decoded message. Under his body, the sofa, in the machine. Nothing.

Think.

She'd been here only a few hours ago.

Assess.

She remembered. Searched the shelf for the leather-bound book he'd consulted and kept the message in.

Annie Oakley, Cowgirl and Circus Rider.

The book, with gold embossed letters on the spine, was on the shelf exactly where he'd taken it from before. Her hand jittered as she shook the pages.

A paper came loose. Fluttered to the floor. But it was the same decoded message he'd shown her.

Now she understood. Brian's killer had taken the latest response from London.

The killer had to be near. Brian's blood hadn't even coagulated on the floor. A deep burgundy pool spread soaking into the carpet.

Hating to, she wiped her bloody feet on the Turkish carpet.

Noises came from somewhere deep in the villa. Or was that upstairs?

Quickly, she searched for a weapon on the desk, rifled through the drawer and found a blunt letter opener. Forget that.

She thought of the old Shanghai policeman who killed with his bare hands. On second thought, a letter opener was better than her fingers. But what she really needed were tools from Churchill's toyshop—Stepney's phrase for where he'd had her fitted with a disguise and the Welrod sleeve gun. Damn, she left it on the plane.

But this book was the key to the coded messages—she'd seen Brian using it to compose his response. She stuck the paper back in the book, fit the book in the scarf, then twisted and tied it cross-body style. She took a breath. Tried to control her shaking. Show this to Sasha in Signals and find a train to Alexandria. Right?

This whole thing was a damn nightmare.

Now her goal was the bath wing, where she'd left her clothes and her rifle. Wherever that was—she'd been so tired when Brian had led her there. But wait, the old Bedouin woman had taken Kate's things to the countess's room.

After only one minute wandering the hallways she'd gotten lost. Concentrate.

What was happening?

She should be sharper, quicker, but after that drink in the club . . . she'd only taken a sip. Someone had slipped her a mickey—this she suddenly knew. She felt the effects—the slowing up, the extreme exhaustion, the swirling rooms.

She found the kitchen. Stuck her finger down her throat. Retched until she couldn't retch any more. She rinsed her mouth out, slapped water on her face. Better already. She stood on the balcony, set a chair on the table, climbed up and reached the iron railing of the countess's balcony.

Dafydd had once called her a little monkey. They'd been locked out of a hotel. Instead of waking up the small Welsh village, Kate insisted she could climb from Dafydd's shoulders, reach the railing, and get in.

She'd done it. Earned a kiss and her nickname "my little monkey." Lisbeth's version had been *mamamokee.*

Focus.

The inside of her arms tingled. All she knew was she had to get inside.

Cairo

⌒

Kate found her clothes—Nadira's hijab and her own khaki summer uniform—freshly washed, ironed, and folded by her tennis racket bag. She held her breath. Felt for the familiar bulge of her rifle.

It was just as she'd left it.

Good. If there was a killer still in the house, she'd be armed.

She was about to take out her rifle and stick her clothes in the bag when she heard something. A noise that felt off. She padded to where she heard a faint scuffle. Water gurgling.

A cone of yellow light beamed on the landing. The light came from a high-ceilinged, arched Moorish gallery. The intricate blue and white mosaic tiles with elongated Arabic writing framed a small, lit fountain surrounded by wicker furniture. Was this the old harem?

Not that it mattered. There was Sasha, hunched over the water, her arms bound behind her and tied to a metal spigot feeding the fountain. Her red hair hung, dripping. Her chest heaved. Choking sounds echoed.

A male voice she knew said, "Ready now?"

Richards emerged from the shadows. He wore an officer's white uniform. His shoulder insignia glinted and his medals rattled as he grabbed Sasha by the neck.

Kate silently began to assemble the rifle.

Richards kept looking at his watch, then up at the door that Kate had slipped behind.

Kate attached the rifle shank and fitted the buttstock.

"I didn't hear your answer."

Sasha spit. The gob landed on his white shoe.

Kate covered the rifle with her scarf and gently loaded the cartridge. No matter how she muffled it the metal snick of loading it sounded like thunder. Her nerves jangled.

"You're going to lick that off when I'm finished with you. Hurry, I'm late to an officer dinner."

Thank God he hadn't heard.

He'd picked up a black phone trailed by a long cord to the wall.

Kate fitted the scope. Aligned it, feeling the cold metal, and slid it into place. She could do this in the dark.

"Ask your partner at Signals division for the code key. Simple."

Sasha shook her head.

He rolled up his sleeves. Grabbed her neck with one hand and pushed her face toward the water. "You don't want me to do this again, do you, Sasha?"

Sasha struggled. Water splashed as he put half her face in, all the way up to her nose.

Crouched on her knee, Kate aimed and kept her hand steady.

"No, she doesn't, Richards," Kate said.

A grin on his face as his head swiveled. His other hand held a small pistol. "Just who I was waiting for, too."

Kate put her finger on the trigger. Breathed in.

"Speaking of waiting, hope the countess isn't waiting for you, because you're going to be late to dinner."

Kate shot on the exhale. A temple shot. Blood sprayed over the tiles. Her next shot to his heart meant to say she didn't think he had one.

He let go of Sasha's face and collapsed on top of her body, dead weight.

Sasha was thrashing, and Kate saw that her head was trapped underwater. Her arms tied behind her, flapping. Good God.

Kate dropped the rifle, ran across the tiles and shoved the dead man off her friend. Spluttering and choking, Sasha coughed water. "I . . . almost . . . didn't make . . . it."

"But you did," said Kate, cutting her wrist and ankle ties.

Kate looked for a towel to dry off Sasha's shaking body. Nothing. "Shh, I need to check if anyone else is here."

"Everyone left." Sasha shook her head. "But the countess or a servant could return."

"So we've got to hurry."

Kate steered her back into the building and found her a towel. In the countess's wardrobe she grabbed the first thing—a long dress—and gave it to Sasha.

"Good job, Sasha. I meant to come sooner. But we're not done yet. There's the countess to expose, and I need the message from London HQ."

"In Richards's pocket." Sasha zipped up the dress then looked at her. "Forget about her for now. She's a small fry."

Small fry? But she'd deal with that later. Hating to, she grabbed her bag and led Sasha back to the fountain.

Kate's fingertips probed Richards's lapel pocket. No. Too easy. She tried the inside of his jacket.

"Found it."

But Brian hadn't decoded it.

"Richards kept saying if I didn't furnish him the Signals

code sheet, he'd prove I betrayed the Signals branch. That I gave the Germans certain maps." A little sob escaped Sasha. Her words caught. She took a deep breath. "Liar. But it's everything that the Commander has been doing. The Commander's been intercepting operation orders. Selling them."

Wasn't that why she was brought in—to take care of the leak? Richards had admitted she was deniable. Expendable.

Snipers had a job to hit their target. Accomplish it or not. But she didn't get Richards's role.

Kate kept her voice low. "Do you mean the Commander was a traitor betraying secret orders in league with Richards?"

She still didn't get why Richards would have her shoot him. Unless after GQ or London had cottoned on to the Commander, he'd jumped on the orders.

"It follows but I don't know." Sasha raked her shaking wet fingers through her damp jumble of hair as they crossed the courtyard. The chirping buzz of insects filled the night air.

She'd been told by Jaro that the SIS ordered her on a new mission. It turned out to be Cairo. All she had were questions.

"Maybe they had a falling out, or Richards got greedy."

Kate nodded. "So Richards knew and had me do his dirty work?"

Sasha gulped. "He was loyal to no one. He would have sold to the highest bidder."

Kate showed Sasha the book with the previous message. "Think you can decode it with this? Use Brian's machine and transmit to London?"

Sasha braided her damp hair in a few quick twists. "Let me try. I'm gonna need to see that book."

Villa Tara

—

Sasha shook her head. Lifted a shattered, milky glass tube.

"The cathode tube's worthless now. It's impossible to transmit."

Brian had destroyed the radio to prevent Richards from forcing him to send a false message. His fingers had been sliced by the glass shards.

Kate saw Sasha's pallor. The metallic tang of Brian's blood stifled the room.

"We can't stay here," Kate said.

"But we can't leave Brian like that."

"Too late, Sasha. Nothing we can do for him now."

She hustled Sasha through the strangely quiet villa. Disconcerted, she sensed the eyes of ghosts past and present. Soon all of the bodies would be discovered. Add the British military on her tail now.

Kate found Richards's motorcycle parked behind bushes in the courtyard. The conniving coward. Someone should have discovered his betrayal. Or was he in league with others? Cairo seemed a nest of double agents.

"Where are we going?" Sasha asked.

"You've got to help me get word to London," said Kate. "Show me the quickest way to HQ from here."

After Sasha managed to unlock the gate, Kate tied her tennis racket bag across her body, draped the hijab over her, and put on Richards's helmet. Kate had taken the keys and ID from Richards's corpse. Now she keyed the motor-cycle's ignition and it roared to life. The instrument dials were covered in mud, impossible to read. Kate shook the bike back and forth to hear the slosh of gas. Half a tank, she figured.

Sasha, in the countess's long dress, tied a scarf over her face and stowed herself low in the sidecar.

Sasha directed her. The night held a shimmering rib-bon of stars and a half moon hung over the Sphinx. The humid-dense air cooled in the darkness and the sewer smells mingled with the spices of the night market. Here and there, soldiers drank at outdoor bar terraces or hob-bled drunkenly on the cracked pavement.

A party town with betrayal at its core.

"Richards, give me a lift," someone yelled. Loud wolf whistles. "Look at her."

Kate hadn't counted on everyone recognizing his motor-bike. It seemed they all knew each other in this small world.

"Turn left."

Kate recognized the bougainvillea-covered walls and the acacia trees overhanging the street leading to HQ.

"Your ID, miss?" The sentry extended his hand.

"Forgot it in the office. We had to come back or they won't let us into Shepheard's for a drink."

Sasha had come alive.

"Too right, miss."

She waved at him from the sidecar. Burped.

"That bar's restricted to officers," he said.

"So?" Sasha smirked. "You know me, Benny Stanton."

He looked down at his feet.

"It's not allowed, Sasha."

"You mean I'm not allowed to be a little tipsy and grab my things from the office? You've let me in before, Benny . . ."

He stepped up.

"Shhh, you go. Your friend stays here."

Not good. Kate wanted to scream with impatience. Every second mattered.

As Sasha left, Kate walked the bike along the wall. Assessed her options: ride the motorbike to the airfield and try to talk her way onto a troop plane. Or to the port and sneak aboard a ship.

Neither scenario was optimal.

London needed to know.

She stood in the shadows and removed the hijab while listening to the guard greeting people who left the compound. It looked like a shift change. While Benny was occupied, she looked both ways.

Clear.

She hopped onto the bike's seat, balanced on the handlebars and gripped the metal fence. She pushed herself off, swung a leg over the fence and heard a rip. The lush silk black dress slit up the side. No matter. She swung the other leg over, then hung before a quick drop to the gravel.

"Psst, over here."

Sasha held open the side door of HQ leading to the Signals wing. Kate remembered reporting here to the Commander. Her mind churned. No, he'd given her no clue. And Richards had seemed an indefatigable ladies' man, not the sadistic brute she'd seen tonight.

It reminded her of what Stepney had said. The best agent is one you don't suspect. One who puts on a front and lives a double life. Who helps or betrays, whichever his handler demands.

It didn't matter why Richards and his circle sold out. Why the Commander betrayed British troop movements, equipment numbers, maps and plans to the Germans via the sheikh. Motive mattered to the police detective. Not to her. She wanted revenge. Give him what was coming to him.

Kate followed Sasha to her desk, where she studied Brian's decoded message. Shook her head.

"It's like apples and pears—they're both fruit but taste completely different. This SOE code would take too long to decipher."

Kate sat down on the stool next to her.

"Better idea. Via the official channel, send a coded message: Attention Stepney, from Cowgirl."

Kate wrote:

Commander and Richards at SIGINT = mole. Need extraction tonight from Cairo—airfield or port. Advise immediately.

Sasha's mouth set in a hard line. She nodded. Got to work encoding.

Kate opened the book titled *Annie Oakley, Cowgirl and Circus Rider.*

She blinked. Hadn't she seen that book on the shelf in that odd room in Trent Park? This time she studied the book. Inside she found the tissue paper-thin transparent sheet with small cutouts. About as big as a letter or two.

She spread the transparency over the title page. No, that didn't work. It jumbled up the letters.

Concentrate. Think. But her brain felt scrambled.

"I can't figure this out, Sasha."

Sasha stood and looked over Kate's shoulder.

"Go to page ten, the number of the month, then look at each thirteenth word, for today's date."

Kate turned the pages and then aligned the transparency cut outs. It was a code and must have been the message Brian sent.

"Where'd you learn this . . ."

"That's what we call Finnegans Wake—it can go on forever but it doesn't. Every day even with the same book, the
key changes according to the date."

"If you can figure that out, so can—"

Sasha interrupted her. "You'd have to have this edition
in English and there's under twenty in existence."

"How do you know that?"

"It's a requirement for a key code book."

"Can you decode this, Sasha?"

Sasha decoded the return message in two minutes.

"It's from Command HQ, ordering you to continue here
and assist the operation. Signed by a Wessex."

"Operation?" she asked, dumbfounded. "That's an old
message. I'm done. Carrying on here is local business."

Why didn't Stepney answer? This felt wrong.

"Any luck hearing back from Stepney at the London HQ?"

The blood-smeared message sat next to Sasha's decod-
ing machine.

"The latest decryption concerns the countess."

"Wait . . . you mean this isn't a reply to my message about
extrication?"

"From London—a package in Paris needs pickup. Destination London."

Margo, the baby . . . She'd taken care of all that. They'd
gotten on the plane.

Hadn't they?

In her gut she knew somehow the operation had gone
sideways.

"Who's the sender?"

"I speak Polish, so I translated. It's for the countess."

"Wait, how is she involved in this? She kept me away
from the villa and probably covered for Brian's murder."

Sasha looked up. "The countess is shifty, but I think

Richards played her. Lied to her. However, this latest decrypt from SIS came from someone working with a Jaro, asking the courier to come and pick up a package."

Jaro. The Polish Mata Hari who put her on the night flight to Cairo. The woman who worked with the Polish government in exile and SIS.

Or so she said.

Another package?

A thought hit her—if she'd been sent here to assassinate the traitor and get whacked in the process—had Richards communicated she'd been taken care of? Had he lied about everything? Was that why no messages were replied to? Or . . .

"Wait a minute. I was with the countess when Brian sent a message requesting my extraction."

"This ranks top priority. The transmission came ten minutes ago."

What about her? Was Stepney leaving her stranded?

"But there aren't any flights out except military. How can I get out of here?"

"You got here," said Sasha, "didn't you?"

True.

"There's military flights out every day—supply, aerial recon, or secret drops we're not supposed to know about."

"So who's meant to handle the package? The countess?"

"Brian. He is . . ." A stricken look painted Sasha's face. "Was . . . a courier."

Brian had saved her. He'd broken the cathode tube and died before revealing the code. Kate decided—she'd go in his place. But it wasn't even a decision. She owed him like she'd owed Margo.

"I'm going. Find out which flight Brian was scheduled on. Meanwhile I've got to reach Stepney."

"Who?"

"My handler. He's with SOE." She hesitated. "Or SIS." A thought struck Kate: that suspicion that Stepney might have been Secret Intelligence all along.

"But he didn't answer, did he?"

"It's different branches," she said. "That's why you have to keep trying for me."

Sasha pulled back in her chair.

"I'm not supposed to do this," Sasha said.

Kate grabbed her hand. "We're not supposed to do a lot of things. And the things we're supposed to do, like listen to Richards, would have gotten us killed. So what do you say?"

Sasha broke into a grin.

"The war's raging and I could be killed tomorrow. Why worry about it?" said Sasha. "I'll request a transfer. Deny everything."

"You're learning, Sasha."

"I'll put the countess in some hot water. So I've got some work to do." She winked and reached for a sheaf of messages.

Kate stood. "Atta girl. But first, show me Brian's decrypted courier instructions."

She did. Now Kate had to get to the aerodrome and somehow talk her way onto the plane as Brian's replacement.

"Nice knowing you, Sasha," she said, heading for the door.

"Likewise, Yank."

KATE EMERGED FROM HEADQUARTERS TO hear someone saying, "That's Richards's bike. What's it doing here? He's supposed to be at the staff dinner at Shepheard's Hotel."

"Canceled, old boy."

"Officers, give this a looky-loo, will you?"

A cluster of Egyptian policemen congregated at the insistence of the soldier.

Not now. She had to get away. Just her luck Richards's pals had noticed.

"What's the fuss? He's working, isn't he?" one of them was saying. "No law's been broken."

True. The police had more to worry about than Richards's bike parked in front of HQ—his bloody body, for a start, across the river.

Her pulse raced. It seemed like forever before these men tired of discussing the bike and moved off.

In the shadows she waited. Let three minutes pass. More.

The Cairo policemen had moved into the souk to catch pickpockets—their favorite pastime, according to Sasha, since the thieves gave them *baksheesh*, payoff.

Kate put on the helmet. Slid the racket bag under her hijab. Wrapped a scarf over her mouth.

She pulled the bike off the kickstand. Walked it a foot, swung her leg over, keyed the ignition, and took off. Damn noisy thing sounded like a German buzz bomb.

She rounded the corner onto the busy street.

"Oi . . . hold on!" Shouts. "That's Richards's bike."

Dumb. Her heart pounded. Had she really thought she could get away with this?

But she'd studied Sasha's map. She had to go this way to the outer road that led to the RAF at Heliopolis Airport. Glancing in the side view mirror, she saw them running. She gunned the engine, losing them in the crowds.

Noisy but fast. She only had half a tank and prayed to make it in no time if traffic stayed light out of the city. Only half an hour by tram, the little white one, she remembered from arriving in Cairo. The road stretched northeast, past the donkeys, the carts, and the dwindling crowds of people walking. The stream of a plane arced white in the dark sky. In the right direction, thank God.

She downshifted. Pulled off the road into a gravel shoulder. Despite the bike's loud engine and her helmet, she'd sensed a high-pitched noise. Her imagination or not, she wheeled the bike behind scraggly bushes, some rocks.

A siren's whine gained. It traveled over this rough and unattractive section of wasteland. A police car. Any moment she'd be discovered.

Near Heliopolis

⁓

The Cairo police car blared past.

What if they'd found Richards's body? She didn't know for sure but couldn't risk being caught for riding a murdered man's motorbike.

Think. Concentrate.

She'd come this far, she had to do this.

The RAF section at Heliopolis Airport lay a mile or so away. Sand piled in drifts by small houses. She noticed planes, what must be camouflage netting over plane hangars and fencing.

She kept the headlight off, said a prayer she wouldn't hit a rock that would bounce her off the seat and drove slowly, weaving across the sand to what she hoped were the two departure runways. The bike was running on fumes.

On second thought, as she drove over brambles, stones and uneven ground, maybe runways were used both for takeoffs and landings. She needed a plan. Needed a story on why she'd replaced Brian. Nothing credible had come to her so far.

Kate drove toward the RAF section. A Spitfire and a Halifax idled on the runway. She turned off the motorbike's ignition and coasted down a small hill to a hillock. This would shield the bike from view until light.

She took off the hijab and helmet. Good thing she'd lost weight, she thought as she slid on her FANY uniform jacket and skirt over the torn black silk dress.

With the hijab, she wiped down the motorcycle's handlebars, as well as the controls and keys and helmet. Slung the tennis racket bag holding her disassembled rifle, wrapped in her khaki summer jacket, over her body. After she strapped on her Cairo street sandals, she inhaled the desert air, with its mix of aviation oil and fuel, and made for the Halifax.

According to tonight's routine flight schedule via Sasha, the four-engine Halifax was bound for the Paris region with a supply stop in Malta. Brian was meant to be on this plane and she would be the last-minute replacement. If the police were in the small terminal and the military was looking for her, boarding here was her best option.

But she had no orders to show and her name wasn't on a flight list. She'd killed a man. Three, no, four, here in Egypt. And she had to go back to Paris, crawling with Nazis, to pick up another *package*.

A cold sweat went up her back.

Concentrate. She buttoned up her FANY jacket.

Believe.

From the shadows, she walked onto the runway with an upright posture and her best attempt at authority. A young officer stood by the airstairs.

"My name better be on the flight list," she said, clipping her consonants and trying to sound vaguely British. Smiled. She kept her eyes wide and flirtatious as she focused on the young flight lieutenant. "But of course, it's not. I'm the last-minute replacement for Brian . . ."—dammit, what was his last name?

He consulted what looked like a flight manifest.

"Cox, Brian," he said. "That him?"

She nodded.

A low-lit beam from the small terminal illuminated only part of the runway with a fine dusting of sand. Blue lights fringed the plane's wing.

He turned to the cockpit, waved, turned back to her. "You are?"

"Kate Rees. Drop zone Paris region."

"No one told us."

"I just found out myself, less than an hour ago. Courier replacement."

The plane's engine revved. Propellers whirred. A stinging blast of sand whipped her legs.

She had to get on this plane.

A shout from the ground crew. "We don't have all day. Flight path's cleared. That all you have?" He pointed at her belongings.

She nodded. Go. Don't let him think.

"I travel light."

"Where's your chute?"

She put her hands on her hips. "My instructions were to suit up on the plane."

"Good thing I asked because we don't have your size."

Like she cared.

"A small men's fits me. I'm big-boned."

TEN MINUTES LATER SHE SAT in the bare-bones belly of the Halifax, a work horse bomber, beside five Greeks and a Maltese priest. She'd put on the flight suit, taken care with the parachute and hoped to God she wouldn't throw up at takeoff.

Wishful thinking.

Night Flight to Paris

———

The plane flew low over Libya. Two benches lined either side of the aluminum and steel-ribbed uninsulated interior. Below in the dark expanses of desert, flashes of battle fire and flames showed from the window in the floor.

What if the plane got hit, what if it crashed?

No more missions, she told herself. Thoughts of Dafydd passed over her. How he kissed her neck soft and slow, the way he tickled behind her knees, rendering her helpless with laughter, how his eyes crinkled when he was angry. She woke up to someone shaking her.

"Malta's the last stop, darlin'," said a Cockney voice.

"Malta?" She rubbed her eyes and stared out the smudged oval window. "But I'm scheduled for Paris."

"You'll want to hurry then. That Paris night flight's about to take off."

Kate slung her tennis bag over the flight suit and parachute pack. Quickstepped down the plane's stairs onto a dark runway.

Wind whipped her hair as the propellers spun. She yelled up to the RAF man who was pulling the door closed.

"Wait! I'm the Paris drop. Are you the night flight to Paris?"

"What's it to you?"

"Replacement for Brian Cox."

"Then hurry up."

He shouted something to the pilot and extended his hand. She landed inside feeling like a beached whale.

She had vowed not to get on another RAF plane after last time.

Yet here she was. Again.

THE PLANE HELD STACKED SUPPLY boxes and a handful of soldiers in camo.

"You're not on any list," said a man coming out of the cockpit.

"I'm like that," she said, without the energy to try a British accent. Winked.

"And a Yank to boot." He grinned. "So what kind of trouble you been up to, luv?"

"You name it." She grinned back. "And you probably don't want to know."

"A girl with spirit, eh?"

"Spirit? Where I come from we call it hellfire."

"Given the delayed takeoff on your account," he said, "the pilot's doing a swoop and grab."

"Which means?"

"I'm Rafe, by the way." He shook her hand. That done, he got down to business. "It'll be almost dawn when we approach. You'll jump out. Pick up the waiting package as we turn around and jump back in as we taxi out."

She unbuckled and shrugged out of her parachute pack.

"You do understand," said Rafe, "we're literally not stopping. Slowing, yes, but the Germans will be wise to us. Got to catch the tailwind over to Bordeaux and head out over the Atlantic. Once we reach Bordeaux we've got air power and Spitfires that will cover our tail from there."

"So are we landing at Meudon?"

"You know it?"

"Sort of, that's if it's the same area as last time."

"We've used it for a week," said Rafe. "We won't much longer."

Had it only been a week ago?

"What's the package?"

"Not my remit."

Meaning he was keeping this from her so if she got captured she couldn't reveal it.

It could be scientific files, a fugitive POW, an SOE agent, a stranded RAF pilot, stolen German documents. Her role would be to protect and load whatever or whoever it was.

Do Brian's job right.

Don't think too much.

But she couldn't help it.

She recalled those dense, dark pines, the choppy runway. Margo's gaunt face.

Prepare.

She couldn't run in the bulky flight suit and took it off, along with her FANY jacket and skirt, leaving only her Egyptian street sandals, the slit silk black dress, and her bag across her body.

"Sexy," he said. "But cold, right?"

The temperature had dropped and there was no heat. He spread a khaki wool blanket over her shivering lap.

The soldiers ignored her. This was strict protocol on these flights.

What you didn't know couldn't hurt you. Nor anyone else.

She hoped they'd land soon and she'd get this over with.

On the blanket on her lap, she laid out her rifle pieces,

cleaned and oiled them one by one. As the plane dipped and dropped altitude she reassembled her rifle. This she could do in the dark. She timed herself.

Five seconds over her record. Not bad.

"You think you're going to need that?" Rafe asked.

"Probably. Or maybe not." She smiled. "It's a surprise, right?"

She attached the telescopic sight and clicked the canvas shoulder straps to the small rings on the rifle's buttstock to sling it over her shoulder. As the plane descended she took deep breaths, filled her lungs and exhaled. Oxygenated and feeling steady, she felt the pressure lower. Her ears popped. The plane's door scraped open and wind rushed in.

A thin line of gold enameled the horizon above the tree line. She got to the door, sat down, and watched the ground whizz by as she let her legs hang out. The smell of forest, earth and damp air. France.

She held on to the door as the wheels touched down; felt the bump and pull of the brakes and scanned the trees.

"There." A small white light, flashlight sized, blinked behind the trees ahead. Somehow in the dawn she recognized this place, this part of the forest, this same spot with the felled trees to mark it. It was where she'd put Margo on the plane.

It made her nervous to think they were still using it.

"Ready?" asked Rafe. He gripped her bare shoulders as the plane slowed, bumping on the dirt.

She nodded. "This gives new meaning to hitting the ground running."

"We'll taxi to the end by the wood piles, turn around, and come back to pick you up here. Got that? Right here by the felled trees."

He let go of her shoulders. She launched into the air

and her right foot caught, then her left, and then she was running. Wobbled forward; somehow gained her balance. She headed to where she'd seen the blinking light. Almost there when she slowed enough to whip out her rifle from under the bag. Pointed it.

"Where's the package?" she said, stepping forward.

No answer. Rustling came from nearby branches. Was someone hurt?

"*Le paquet,*" she said, louder. "*C'est où ça?*"

A curious noise, like a hurt animal—she edged closer. The plane was turning at the end of the makeshift runway. What if this was a setup?

But the mission was to get the package.

Her finger moved to the trigger.

She parted the branches, saw a bundle in the leaves and knelt down. Caught that smell and gasped. Hadn't the baby gone to London with Margo?

What in God's name had happened?

Margo's baby had a note pinned to his blanket:

Take him and keep him safe.

It wasn't Margo's writing.

The plane was taxiing back.

"Hallo?"

No answer. The baby looked fine. Pink cheeked.

A car's motor came from the woods. Kate picked up the baby, who'd started to whimper, placed him in her tennis bag, and ran through the woods. A black Citroën, the Gestapo car, with Jaro gagged in the back seat, blurred by.

Kate aimed and shot out the back tires to get it to stop. Drilled the side view mirror away from Jaro's head. The Citroën plowed into a tree. Glass tinkled.

Kate was running and ducking from behind trees as bullets came her way. The baby was jouncing, a warm whimpering bundle. So she slid the bag to her side, protecting him with her arm and using the rifle shank to support his back.

The shooter had gotten out of the car. With no time to waste, Kate positioned herself behind a tree, knelt. She lifted the rifle, slung the bag behind her so the baby was against her spine, out of range and away from the rifle's kickback. The baby shifted as he molded to her back, and Kate focused while she shouldered the rifle. Aimed using the scope. Picked out her target in a long dark coat moving among the trees.

She took a deep breath.

Caught him in her crosshairs. Exhaled. Took a head shot.

He was down. Kate saw another man from the passenger side. He took shot after shot in her direction. Tree bark dust blinded her.

She had to get Jaro out and the baby on the plane. She heard the Halifax's propellers coming closer.

Her next shot nailed the man in a long black leather coat. It got his knee and he screamed. Her next shot got him in his chest.

Kate yelled out, "It's okay now." But no Jaro.

God, had she been shot? Wounded?

Had Kate shot her?

Kate couldn't leave without her.

She found Jaro slumped back on the headrest, a dark bullet hole in her shoulder that oozed blood. What looked like a bloody gash in her neck, matted blood in her hair. A dark red wound in her thigh. No time to check her pulse.

"Jaro, Jaro?"

She was breathing. Alive.

"Goddammit, answer me."

Her eyes fluttered open . . . a faint whisper of "Cowgirl."

"That's right, Jaro, and we need to run to get the plane."

Kate pulled her up and supported her as well as she could.

"Help me and use every bit you've got left. Okay?"

Jaro nodded weakly.

"Now!"

Running, pulling her on her shoulder, slinging the gun behind her and trying to gently cradle the baby in her other arm, somehow Kate made it through the thicket of trees. Panting, she saw the plane on the makeshift runway. Took Jaro's flashlight and flashed it as dawn washed a light apricot. The plane kept going. Now it was almost past them and Kate's breath was coming in heaves. Her legs hurt as she dragged Jaro, who weighed her down. Kate's thin dress was wet and heavy from Jaro's blood, but she kept her grasp tight and with her other arm held the baby against her in the bag. Kate stumbled on the upturned dirt, caught herself.

"Go on . . . without me," said Jaro in a feeble gasp.

"Not a quitter, are you, Jaro?" Kate managed. "Try, just try."

Some reply in Polish was drowned out by the propeller's whipping leaves and dirt in the air, and the engine drowning out the baby's mewling.

She put her last bit of strength into running, pulling Jaro's immobile body along. Her useless leg trailing. All of a sudden, shots rang out from the forest. Dirt spit from the damp earth as bullets peppered the ground. Any minute they'd be gun fodder.

She screamed at the open door, "Slow down, goddammit."

Arms were reaching out. Sweating, she swung the bag with the baby inside, and, catching a grip on the rim of the plane's open door, shoved Jaro up with her other hand. So heavy, she was so damn heavy. Kate kept running, gripping the door, exhausted trying to catch her breath. Her lungs burned and she saw Jaro pulled inside.

Even in the propeller's roar the gunshots sounded closer.

The dawn light broke. The outline of Paris glimmered in the distance; the wind rushed past. Kate reached out but all she felt was air. Her other hand was slipping off the door. She couldn't hold on anymore.

And then Kate felt hands and arms pulling her in.

Guy's Hospital, London

⁓

Kate set down a small vase of pathetic daisies, all she could find in bomb-ravaged London, on Jaro's hospital window-sill. She unbuttoned her FANY uniform jacket. Boiling in here. The place felt like an orchid hot house.

"How's the Polish Mata Hari?" said Kate. "Not giving you trouble I hope, nurse."

The ward nurse looked up, arching her brows, disapproval tightening her mouth in an O. Her wispy gray hair was cut short, and her eyes, dark and round, matched her round spectacles.

"I won't have you bothering this patient, miss," she said. "She's recovering from surgery."

As if Kate didn't know. Extensive reconstructive facial and thoracic surgery, from what she'd learned. Kate's attempts at lightheartedness seemed doomed from the start.

"I realize that. And it's missus."

"I'm fine." Jaro yawned and tried to sit up in the hospital bed as the nurse left. She was in a body cast and part of her face wrapped in bandages. Her one visible lidded eye, hooded with sleep, blinked before she pulled the pillow over her face. Her good shoulder heaved.

"My God, what's wrong? Jaro, does something hurt?"

About to call the nurse back, Kate felt her arm pulled. Jaro had dragged her close. "Is she . . . she gone?"

"The nurse? Yes."

Jaro exploded in laughter. "Did you . . . did you see . . . see how she looked . . . when you called me Mata Hari?"

Kate erupted laughing. "Like . . . a surprised owl! I expected her to start hooting."

Jaro clutched her arm, howling with laughter.

"Ow, that hurts. Stop it. Or you'll make my stitches burst."

Kate's stomach hurt by the time they stopped laughing. She couldn't remember when last she'd laughed so hard.

She poured Jaro a glass of water. Propped her pillows and helped her sip. Sat down on the hard-back visitor's chair beside her bed.

Time to get serious. "Why didn't Margo bring her baby?"

"I knew you'd ask," said Jaro. "Crazy as it sounds, Margo thought he'd be safer in France. Dieter had hidden him with nuns in a convent. No one knew. Or so Dieter thought. But Margo . . . I don't know, she didn't make a lot of sense at the end . . ." Jaro's words trailed in the air.

Dim sunlight cast a faint glow over the metal bed frame. Tree shadows from outside the window mottled the linoleum floor.

Why couldn't Jaro finish that thought? "At the end of what, Jaro?"

Jaro took another sip. Her bandages crinkled.

"You know Margo and the baby never got on the plane."

Kate recoiled inside. She set down the water. Wanted to leave. She'd been set up. But she wanted to know why. To know who was behind this.

"You knew all the time. Used me."

"You've got it wrong, Kate."

"So help me get it right before I'm out of here."

"You're hurt. But don't take it personally."

Forget the piercing shaft of how everyone betrayed each other? She wasn't a spy. Didn't like this world.

"I don't work like this."

"But Margo does. She ran two networks. One under Russian orders, I'm pretty sure. I know she loathes the Nazis and loves the Commies."

"What did Margo have to do with Cairo?"

"Nothing. Who said she did?"

"No one's told me anything. All I know is I failed my mission."

The room felt so hot. She fanned herself with her hand.

"My orders were to assist a sniper, you, to assassinate Lange. My further orders were to send a sniper, you, to assassinate Lange's Cairo connections. Success. You get a pat on the back and anonymity, but you deserve more. The North African invasion is proceeding, thanks to you."

A half-smile showed on Jaro's bandaged face.

"You did it, Kate."

Why did Kate feel hollow?

She couldn't help the feeling of failure washing over her.

"But my mission was to extract Margo and the baby."

"Margo's a loose cannon. Unpredictable. London should have warned you."

"Warned me? That's the only reason I went. I owed her my life."

Dust motes danced in the shafts of sunlight over the starched white covers. Everything smelled of antiseptic.

"Oh, she played that one on you?"

"What? But it's true. And—I slept with her boyfriend."

"She's a seducer and tells you what you need to hear so you'll do what she wants. Plays on your guilt. Classic."

Kate felt stupid. Out of her depth. Again.

"I don't understand."

"Undercover agents learn techniques to manipulate. Some, like Margo, are naturals."

Jaro leaned back. Coughed. Took a few breaths. Tubes fed into her arm from a clear drip on a trolley.

"Their first technique is to make someone in their 'debt' so despite any ideals, moral code, loyalty or whatever, you're in their pocket," said Jaro. "It's manipulative rule one. To do this they stage an almost accident or supposed attack and save you."

Kate's mind went back to that afternoon Margo saved her from a knife attack near Marble Arch. Could that have been staged? Try as she might, she couldn't force herself to abandon the feeling of loyalty that had brought her to Paris in the first place.

"What happened to Margo?"

"Admitted to a private Parisian clinic, where she stole their morphine and discharged herself. No one's seen her since."

"And the baby?"

"Leverage. We had her baby and I couldn't hide him anymore."

Some piece was missing in all this.

Kate shook her head. "I don't get it."

"More water, please." Kate lifted the glass and helped Jaro sip. She talked a lot for someone recovering from major surgery; she looked exhausted, yet it was as if she burned with something to tell her.

"Kate, it's about holding the baby over her and her husband." Jaro had lowered her voice. "Margo hid the pregnancy but her POW husband had found out and threatened to out her as a double agent," said Jaro. "He knew the baby wasn't his—couldn't be."

"Her husband, the engineer. He's Dieter's brother, right?"

"It was an open secret. But somehow Schlüssel in the Abwehr discovered the baby. He was pressuring Margo to blackmail Dieter—the baby's actual father—to uncover Canaris's plot to overthrow Hitler. That's why she'd asked for extraction. She couldn't keep playing both sides under those circumstances."

Kate tried to piece it together. She thought about the pinkie ring. A horrible thought hit her. "Did Margo inform on Dieter, get him run over?"

"We Poles say, 'When among the crows, caw as the crows do.'" Jaro gave Kate a sharp look. "But no. Whatever else Margo did, she didn't betray Dieter. I heard Schlüssel was attempting to kidnap Dieter to interrogate him; Schlüssel's minion botched it and Schlüsell ran him over instead."

She'd seen him. Still, it didn't add up.

"With Schlüssel gone, who still cares about Dieter and Margo's baby? Who were those men in the car with you? Gestapo?"

"The ones you killed?" Jaro yawned again. "Good riddance. Parisian gangsters who got greedy."

"You were using them to save the baby?" said Kate, fitting the pieces. "Why, Jaro?"

"I delivered him, you know. Margo had to give birth in secret." Jaro closed her eyes. "And, well, I can't have my own."

"Then why didn't you accompany him to London? Why stay in Paris?"

Jaro shook her head. "Ow." She winced adjusting her bandage. "If I left, who'd run my Polish agents or facilitate my network?"

"A network of gangsters, double and triple agents and Commies who get the job done?" said Kate. "A real Mata Hari, eh?"

But the laughter had gone from her voice.

"Kate, you must help that baby."

"Margo's his mother."

"Margo's gone. She could be in Trieste or Russia. Or Rome."

"Typical. She got me into this. I still don't understand why."

"Margo needed you. She needed someone to take care of Lange and Schlüssel, and she knew you could and you owed her. That's all—she discards people when they're inconvenient."

"Jaro, she saved my life."

Perspiration pooled in the cleft of her neck. How could she reconcile Jaro's vision of Margo with her own? More and more she kept feeling let down.

"And you more than paid that debt, if you had one in the first place." Her voice ragged, Jaro pulled Kate close. Whispered. "Despite what Stepney or anyone says, this baby's the Special Branch bargaining chip. The supposed POW father's the genius engineer of the V rocket program. The baby's his nephew or his son for their purposes—he will carry on the name. The top British command want this POW to work for them. To run the rocket research laboratory."

Kate remembered a spoiled, arrogant Nazi officer. A genius? But maybe that was why she'd been sent to Trent Park. The setup had to be authentic. She had to know details to make it real and convince Dieter and Margo.

Stepney's words came back to her: *We need his cooperation and he's a top engineer.*

"By the way, who sent me to Cairo? Was that the plan all along?"

"SIS. But I don't have a name." Jaro's eyelids drooped. "I'm tired, Kate. So tired."

The nurse appeared pushing a cart with Jaro's meal covered by white cloth napkins. Medicines in brown glass bottles.

"Visiting hours ended. You need to leave."

The nurse was shooing her out. Kate reached for her carryall. Stood, about to leave as the nurse fiddled with the drip bag that fed into Jaro's arm. "Bye, Jaro."

No answering goodbye.

She walked out the door. Paused in the hallway. Felt guilty at the abrupt goodbye and despite her comments on Margo she understood her concern over the baby.

Kate turned around and entered the hospital room. Everything was quiet. No machines humming.

Kate stopped in her tracks. She saw the nurse removing a needle from the tube in Jaro's arm. The blood pressure monitors beeping had stopped.

"Jaro . . ."

"Visit's over," said the nurse, blocking her view.

Kate stepped around her. Jaro's shoulders slumped, her mouth half-open. Horror-stricken, Kate saw Jaro's half opened eye staring straight at her. Unblinking.

"Good God, what the hell did you do to her?"

Out of the corner of her eye Kate saw the dull metal snub nose of a pistol under a napkin on the tray.

Before she could react, the nurse raised the pistol and pointed it at Kate. "You weren't supposed to be here. But I'm late. So you never heard anything. You know nothing."

Jaro's dead gaze chilled her.

"Who are you?"

"You really don't want to know." The nurse's flat gaze was unreadable.

"Like I said, get out, and you never saw or heard anything in this room. All the players are off the board. Except you, and you're expendable."

And the old crone was going to shoot her in a hospital.

Her mind shot into sniper mode; calculated the pistol's distance. Not even three feet. If she shoved the cart would it be enough to surprise and throw her aim off balance? Those little pistols had 72 percent accuracy. Kate had a fighting chance.

The nurse's eyes hardened.

"You wouldn't shoot me in a hospital," said Kate.

"Not now." She pulled an envelope from her smock pocket and handed it to Kate.

"Your orders. Remember, loose lips sink ships. In your case never forget you're expendable."

"Like Jaro?"

"They were supposed to take care of her in Paris until you got in the way. You prolonged her misery."

"Misery? She just had surgery. How could you kill her in cold blood?"

Kate felt everything she knew was upended. Churning and out of her control.

"Look, the surgeon gave her twelve hours, if that. Her spleen's gone."

Yet she'd just said she was supposed to be taken care of had Kate not gotten in the way. Pain flayed her. In her pocket she still had the tube of Chanel lipstick, Jaro's gift to her. The nurse checked the time on the timepiece pinned to her apron. Such a silly place to put it. Kate wanted to pin it to her heart, if she had one.

"You'll be late for your train if don't hurry." The nurse hadn't put down the pistol. "Jaro was a triple agent, too. And I never said that."

Was that true?

Was anyone telling the truth? Who were the bad guys, and were the good guys still good?

SHE STUMBLED INTO THE HALLWAY. Checked the envelope and saw her train ticket. Back to Scotland. Poor Jaro. Even if she'd been lying she didn't deserve to die like that. Treated like a traitor when her use was up.

But Kate was still useful. Until . . . she wasn't. What if Margo had been right?

They were all the same.

"Kate . . . Kate?"

A voice jolted her from her thoughts. Familiar. She turned in the long hospital corridor that led to the canteen.

Philippe.

Her shoulders tightened. She'd last seen him in another hospital. Wasn't this for women and children? Then she saw the ward sign: REHABILITATION.

He was standing with the aid of crutches. He wore a robe over his hospital gown with a slit sleeve for the cast on his arm. And a hopeful smile.

Those incredible eyes.

"Why haven't you answered my letters, *chérie?*"

Answered his letters? First she'd heard of them. But it didn't matter.

The weak sun cast rectangles of pale light on the old tiles. Conversations drifted from the canteen's open windows.

If he put his arm around her she'd go Jell-o legs. Melt.

Time to be strong. Face the truth, for once.

She liked him too much for a casual wartime affair. She was old-fashioned and not as sophisticated as this French man expected. War was hard enough—no way she'd be number two.

Expectant, Philippe reached out and she backed away.

"*Quoi?*" Hurt shone in his eyes. "What is it? What's happened?"

"It's best we don't . . . you know, see each other," she said. "I hope you're okay."

"*Moi?* Fine. Doing well in *réhabilitation*, they say. But weren't you coming to see me now?"

Kate shook her head. Looked away. Surprised, he searched her face.

"*Je ne comprends pas* . . . why?"

"I think you know why, Philippe."

No, maybe he didn't. As a Frenchman it wouldn't enter his mind that having something on the side wasn't normal. *De rigueur* in wartime. Anytime.

Perplexed, he shook his head. Then his lip tightened. "You've met someone."

"Eh, what if I . . . but no, that's not the point."

"Point? How can you say that? You've met someone and didn't have the *tendresse* to tell me. I must find you at the hospital visiting, what . . . a new amour?"

"You're married, Philippe. Your wife and child are here. Get another mistress. I'm not French and it's not my style."

"*Quoi?*" His face paled. "Reducing me to a cliché? Where is this wife and child of mine?"

"That's your business, not mine."

Suddenly a smile flickered across his face. "You mean this woman?"

He'd pulled out a creased small photo from his pocket.

A chateau in the background, family members in front and the blonde woman and child.

Kate nodded.

"She's my cousin Mireille. We grew up together. That's her daughter. Her husband's an RAF pilot now."

Stunned, Kate averted her eyes. Talk about a dumb mistake.

"True, I had a fiancée, but we grew apart. We'd known each other since childhood. The war changed everything."

"I'm sorry, Philippe."

She wanted to make it right. Fix it. She reached for him. For those arms to enfold her. But she had to be careful of his cast.

This time he maneuvered his crutches and stepped back. "You didn't trust me, Kate."

"I came to visit you last week, right after you'd been injured. The nurse said you were with your wife and child and I had to wait. At that point . . ."

"The point being you should have come in, talked and you'd have understood."

She shrugged.

"You didn't trust me. Assumed the worst."

Hurt shone in his eyes.

"Trust is hard for me," she said. "Can't you understand?"

"*Et alors*, I must accept you this way?"

She took a breath. Glanced at her watch. In a few hours she'd catch the train to Scotland.

"If you can, Philippe, let me know."

AT THE HOSPITAL GATE SHE paused. Thought until the warring emotions subsided and she knew what she had to do. Follow her heart.

She turned back into the hospital. Ran.

Kate found the pediatric wing across the hospital courtyard, the makeshift nursery with four cribs smelling of disinfectant and freshly laundered baby blankets. Kate stood at the first crib and tucked the blanket around the baby. Then picked him up, inhaling the sweet baby scent. Glancing around and seeing no one, she cuddled him.

Big button eyes, wispy blond fuzz on his head and a mushroom nose. Perfect.

She whispered in his ear, "You can't help it. No one picks their parents."

A gurgle answered her. But there was something of Dieter in his eyes. He whimpered and she gave him the bottle from one of several prepared by the crib. The little thing drank and drank. On her shoulder he gave a good healthy burp.

"Atta boy."

She stroked his fuzzball head. So soft. He gripped her finger but he'd already taken her heart. She cradled him, savoring his warmth. His smell.

Time to say goodbye.

He yawned, his pink tongue and toothless gums on display. Such innocence. Just like her little Lisbeth.

She'd fallen in love with this little thing on the plane. Had held, soothed and rocked him all the way over the Channel on the bumpy flight. Now he was Baby X, according to the card plastered to his crib.

"Of course, doctor." A nurse was speaking into a wall phone in the corridor. "The file's complete now. We received the baby's birth certificate from Special Branch."

Special Branch meant SIS, Secret Intelligence Services, the ones who'd sent her to Cairo. The secret puppet masters who pulled the strings. Hell, she'd danced to their tune and even now, was none the wiser as to who'd orchestrated all this.

"Of course, sir, he'll be transferred when transport's available. I'll check on this now."

The nurse's footsteps clattered away over the linoleum.

Baby X. Branded with Nazi parentage and a triple-agent traitor for a mother. Raffled by Stepney, or the SIS if Jaro was right, and used as leverage to recruit his supposed father, the elite Nazi POW engineer. An innocent pawn in a war of spies.

But in the long run, would this impact the war effort? Would a selfish elite Nazi POW engineer really give up secrets for a child whose paternity he doubted? Ten to one he'd end up working for the Brits with or without the baby as a bargaining chip. Types like him always landed on their feet. He'd get issued a get out of jail card at war's end, citizenship and a full bank account.

The damn Nazi would get away clean.

Her mind went to poor Dieter, who'd sacrificed his life to oppose the Nazi regime from within. Run down before her eyes. He'd done his best to save his child. Her insides curdled.

Maybe she could do something about that. For Dieter.

Kate set him in the crib and peered out of the nursery. No one sat at the pediatric station desk. She eyed the medical charts slid into wall slots above the desk—there were only two—and looked around. No one. She had to hurry. With a deft reach, she thumbed through the two files, found a birth certificate. The birth certificate was filled out for a baby male, four months old, birthplace London, named Pieter von Holz, father Rolf von Holz and mother Margo von Holz. She slid this inside her uniform skirt waistband and tried not to take a deep breath.

Footsteps sounded down the long corridor.

She just might make it if she hurried.

Back in the nursery, she stuck a bottle, blanket and some nappies into her khaki regulation carryall. Tucked the baby on top, removed and draped her jacket over the carryall she slung over her shoulder. Keeping her pace unhurried, she strolled out of the ward and left from the back exit.

Twenty minutes later, as the train left the station, she was headed back to her Scottish assignment. She'd torn up the birth certificate, flushed the scraps down the gutter along with the von Holz pinkie ring and studied her orders. Back to the training site in the highlands. What a relief.

She spent the first leg of the journey in the WC where

she'd put an out of order sign outside. Baby X was already a seasoned traveller and with a few diaper changes, replenishing milk when they changed trains, and naps, they travelled the long hours to their goal. A sympathetic RAF pilot even gave up his seat on the last leg and a generous mother shared extra milk.

Finally she and the baby reached the highlands and the small station. Woody, mossy scents permeated the air. Her view took in windswept hills of heather and mist curling to the mountain crags.

As usual, Alana, the gamekeeper's wife, met her and looked taken aback.

"Had a wee bairn since I last saw you?"

"He's special." Kate grinned. "And he's yours if you can keep him safe."

Alana blinked.

"What about his parents?"

Kate hesitated. But she knew she was doing the right thing by him.

"Gone. He's an oprhan."

"Kate, you're serious?" Alana's lip quivered.

"Dead serious."

"Kate, I mean even if I could . . ."

"You can, Alana. Decide now."

Torn, Alana stared at the baby. "Hasn't the wee one got a name? Or a birth certificate?"

"I'm sure you can handle those details, Alana. He'll grow up at the lodge, you'll be a wonderful mother and I'll see him every day."

Alana's brow creased.

"Yes to everything but the last thing, Madame X."

What did that mean?

Alana handed her a packet. "You've got new orders. They came last night, but you'd already left London."

Kate's heart clenched.

"Your train's on the next platform," said Alana. "It's waiting for you. I'm so sorry that . . ." Alana's throat caught.

"Raise him as your own. Tell no one. Promise?"

Alana nodded.

"Promise."

Kate kissed Baby X, inhaling his smell for the last time. No, she'd see him again. Wouldn't she?

After handing him to Alana, she crossed the footbridge to the next track and boarded the train. She found her seat and read her new orders.

As if she'd follow them. She wouldn't be made a fool the third time.

Closed her eyes. Made herself breathe. No time to look back.

ACKNOWLEDGMENTS

Operation Torch, the Allied invasion of Vichy-occupied North Africa, happened in 1942. Fact. It almost didn't. Declassified files report a diplomatic plane crash in the North African desert in 1942. Fact. Further files remain classified as of today. In Paris in 1942, Drs. René Suttel and Jean Talairach, of le Centre hospitalier Sainte-Anne, mapped the quarry system under the hospital and southern Paris creating a "free" underground map and offered it to the Résistance. Fact. In 1942, a young nurse in le Centre hospitalier Sainte-Anne, her name lost to history, hid ill Jews about to be deported. Betrayed, she was executed. Fact. Questions grabbed me, and the *what ifs?* wouldn't let go. My research led to many stories of courage during this time that remain to be told.

I owe much gratitude to Jean Satzer, cat *maman,* JT Morrow, Susanna Soloman, the gang at *We Have Ways of Making You Talk* podcast, James N. Frey, Dr. Helen Fry, the SOE *Manual,* and Dr. Terri Haddix, for her patience in advising on all things medical. Huge thanks to Katherine Fausset, agent extraordinaire, and especially my wonderful editor Juliet Grames, the indefatigable Taz Urnov—*merci* for all your hard work, Bronwen who helms Soho, Paul, Janine, Rudy, Rachel for her patience, Alexa, Sheri, Steven, *et toutes!*

I'm so grateful for a life-changing long-ago motorcycle trip across Tunisia, Algeria, and Morocco. In Cairo, many thanks to Salah Shehata Hassan. In Paris: Institute Pasteur, who hid people—and while penicillin wasn't widely available until 1943, Kate's mission there has taken a fictional license; Gilles Thomas; Naftali Skrobek—*ancien Resistant*; les Archives Nationales Pierrefitte-sur-Seine; Musée d'Art et d'Histoire de l'Hôpital Sainte-Anne; Anne-Françoise Delbegue; Cathy Etile; Blandine de Brier Manoncourt; and Dr. Christian de Brier. Huge thanks to Hannah Lammers-Ishimuro, Jun, and Tate without whom nothing would happen.